THE HOUR
OF THE OUTLAW

ALSO BY MAIYA WILLIAMS

The Golden Hour
The Hour of the Cobra

THE HOUR OF THE OUTLAW

Maiya Williams

AMULET BOOKS

NEW YORK

Cataloging-in-Publication Data may be obtained from the Library of Congress.
ISBN 13: 978-0-8109-9355-6
ISBN 10: 0-8109-9355-4

Published in 2007 by Amulet Books, an imprint of Harry N. Abrams, Inc. All rights reserved. No portion of this book may be reproduced, stored in a retrieval system, or transmitted in any form or by any means, mechanical, electronic, photocopying, recording, or otherwise, without written permission from the publisher.

Printed and bound in U.S.A.
10 9 8 7 6 5 4 3 2 1

HNA
harry n. abrams, inc.
a subsidiary of La Martinière Groupe
115 West 18th Street
New York, NY 10011
www.hnabooks.com

For Mom and Dad,
who gave me what counts most,
with love

CONTENTS

THE HOUR
OF THE OUTLAW

PROLOGUE

THERE IS A MEADOW ON THE COAST OF MAINE WITH grass so green that it hurts the eyes. This meadow leads up to a dark wood thick with birch, aspens, maples, and pines. Few people venture into this wood, but if they did, they would see that just beyond it, shrouded by mist, lies a craggy, rocky shore, carved over hundreds of thousands of years by forces of nature. During most of the day these rocks look dry and barren, but when the tide comes in and the deep crevices transform into sloshing pools, life appears.

So it is with the resort hotel that sits above this rocky shore. Most of the time it appears quiet, abandoned. But at certain hours, right before sunset and again before sunrise, the resort transforms, and its hidden life is revealed. At these golden and silver hours, the entire hotel property comes alive; the decor regains its newness, guests appear, fantastic gadgetry abounds, and townspeople arrive, eager to use the Owatannauk Resort Hotel's most popular feature, the amazing elevators that are in fact time machines.

Don't look for the hotel in the guidebooks. The only people who know about it are the residents of the small town of Owatannauk (population 104), and they're not talking. Built by toy-maker-turned-inventor Archibald Weber, the time machines are a secret attraction that all the local people employ. As a result, there are time-travel souvenirs scattered throughout the town. Hilda Bingham, owner of the gas station coffee shop, gets recipes for her scrumptious pies from revolutionary France. Captain Morgan, chief of police, has collected cars from all different eras. Nana Alexander, also known as "the crazy bird lady," learned how to make birdhouses from the famous ornithologist John James Audubon himself. Best friends Gertrude Pembroke and Agatha Drake have culled the corners of time for the knickknacks that crowd their enormous curio shop.

Of course, such an incredible invention requires vigilant protection. A governing board strictly monitors the use of the hotel elevators (called "alleviators" because they alleviate curiosity through their capacity to transport passengers to other eras). It also shields the resort from prying outsiders.

But even with these safeguards, there are problems. People get stuck in time or inadvertently alter history, and that is when Gertrude Pembroke, the Time Detective, is called in to help make things right.

Recently, Agatha and Gertrude recruited a group of young people—Rowan and Nina Popplewell, and Xanthe and Xavier

Alexander—to help Gertrude on her missions. This is the third book of their adventures.

The Popplewells and the Alexanders were not the first children to be granted permission to use the alleviators. There was one who went before them, a young man who traveled through time with disastrous results . . .

OWATANNAUK RESORT
HOTEL, 1919

THERE WAS A NEW CLOCK IN THE ROOM. THIS ONE was huge, something you might see in a train station. It had a big, round face framed in black lacquered wood, with roman numerals for numbers and long elegant hands. It took up a third of the wall, leaving little room for any other decoration; however, there was no other decoration, only clocks.

Agatha Drake drew her shawl around her shoulders. When the first clock had appeared in Archie's den, its cheerful ticking promised constancy and continuation. Time goes on, it seemed to say. Soon it was joined by a second clock, and a third. Now, ten years later, the collection had grown to over a hundred timepieces, and the sound had grown ominous. The whirring and grinding of gears, of minutes tick tick ticking away sounded more like a warning, that time was fleeting, that time was running out.

The room was chilly, or perhaps it was the conversation

she was anticipating that caused her to shudder. Agatha had known Archibald Weber since he was a teenager, a student at a parochial boarding school for boys where she taught when she was a novice nun. She'd always been fond of his brilliant mind, his quick wit, his exuberant personality, his twinkling eyes. She'd followed his career after he left school as he made his name as a toy-maker tycoon, then as a benefactor of various charitable institutions, and finally as the owner of the wildly popular Owatannauk Resort Hotel in Owatannauk, Maine. She herself had left St. Ambrose's School and gone on to other jobs, but when one of those jobs brought her to the hotel and reacquainted her with her star student, she knew that fate must have had a hand in this reunion.

Archibald hired Agatha to teach his son, Balthazar. Agatha could see right away that the boy was rambunctious and in desperate need of reining in. But she fell in love with his charming, prankish personality. As she got to know him better, Agatha suspected that Balt's wildness was a cover for loneliness. There were no other children who lived at the hotel, and the ones who came on vacation provided some diversion, but only too soon they returned to their lives elsewhere. She felt sorry for him, but there wasn't much she could do. She would take him on outings, but he always returned to the hotel a little sadder, as though seeing how ordinary children lived was somehow a cruel tease, waving a life in front of him that he could never understand or join.

Then things took a turn for the worse.

After a prolonged illness, Balthazar's mother passed away. Archie, who already spent an extraordinary amount of time on his inventions, immersed himself in his work even further. What little social interaction he had with Agatha, the Owatannauk Board of Directors, and even Balthazar, ended. When Balthazar wasn't with Agatha studying, he wandered through the hotel halls like a lost puppy. It nearly broke Agatha's heart.

She had finally mustered up the courage to speak to Archie, to scold him really. But before she'd been able to contact him, he had summoned her himself. From the tone of his voice she knew she would only hear bad news. Now here she was, sitting amid the ticking clocks, waiting. She felt like a prisoner on death row.

"Miss Drake?" Otto, the only person Archie allowed around him, stood at the door. Of course, Otto hardly counted, being a robot. He smiled pleasantly, as was his manner—or his programming, to be more precise—and Agatha followed him into Archie's workshop.

When she saw Archie, hunched over his drafting table, writing in one of his many notebooks, a feeling of sadness swept over her. What had happened to him? Here he was, at the zenith of his career, having invented possibly the most amazing contraption ever devised, a vehicle for time travel, and yet he looked utterly miserable.

"I've decided that I no longer need your services as Balt's tutor," Archie said without looking up. "What he needs is my guidance. I'll be teaching him myself."

"I hope I haven't disappointed you in some way . . ." Agatha stuttered, disturbed by the alarms going off in her head.

"Not at all. You have done a splendid job with him. However, he is becoming a man, and he must be prepared as such."

"I'd be happy to give you the lesson plan I've devised for him. It includes some very fine poetry books, as well as music appreciation, and . . ."

"That won't be necessary," Archie said, finishing what he was writing and shutting the notebook. He turned to face Agatha, his eyes brooding and troubled. "I have my own ideas about Balt's instruction. He'll be learning from the masters themselves."

"Masters . . . ? Surely you don't mean to take him . . ."

"Yes."

"But he's so young!"

"My dear Agatha, I am not asking for your opinion. I know what my son needs. Believe me when I say that I deeply appreciate all you've done for Balt up to this point; you have been indispensable. However, I will take it from here."

"But . . ."

"Thank you, that will be all."

Otto led Agatha back out to the hallway. Immediately Agatha sought out her best friend and housemate, Gertrude, who at this time of day would be gardening in back of their Cape Cod—style home. Agatha had converted much of the house into a curio shop, to unload some of the thousands of knickknacks she had collected from her time-machine travels, but now the house was bursting at the seams with souvenirs. If she wasn't careful, she and Gertrude would have to move into the garage.

Agatha had to admit she'd become addicted to time travel. She couldn't get enough of it. Visiting exotic places, meeting fascinating people, sampling the variety of foods, fashions, and festivals . . . it was all so thrilling. Agatha the thrill seeker. Who knew she had it in her?

Agatha found Gertrude checking her tomato plants for snails. Gertrude spent a lot of time in the garden; it was one of the only things she claimed she understood. She was constantly confused by the Victorian Age, herself being a product of another time. In a way, she was one of Agatha's time souvenirs. Agatha had rescued her from the Spanish Inquisition. Gertrude, too, started to time travel, but it wasn't the thrill that drew her, it was a moral imperative. She was searching for something in the past that she never seemed to find.

"Did you speak with Archie?" Gertrude asked, sitting next to her friend on the steps.

"Yes . . . and no," Agatha admitted. "It was not the conversation I'd hoped. I'm afraid that I've been relieved of my duties. Archie will be taking over Balt's instruction."

Gertrude pursed her lips, tapping her clog with the spade. After a prolonged silence she exhaled heavily.

"I don't like the sound of that."

"Neither do I, Sister," Agatha sighed. "Neither do I."

Gertrude and Agatha had good reason to worry. Within five months Balthazar disappeared. Archibald Weber went into seclusion. And by the end of the year the Owatannauk Resort Hotel closed forever.

+ CHAPTER ONE +
THE ZONE

Xavier stared out the car window as it cruised along the highway. Fence posts, mile markers, and the occasional cow flashed by, but Xavier saw none of these. He was completely focused on the scene being played out in his head. He was lost in The Zone.

(Music)

(Applause)

HOST: Hi, and welcome to *Great Guys*. We're here talking with Xavier Alexander, a young man with incredible talent, who is going to tell us about some of his fantastic discoveries. But first, Xave, I've gotta ask you, how did you manage to accomplish so much in your life so soon? I mean, you're a pretty young fella!

XAVIER: People do great things whether they're five or ninety-five. It helps that I was raised to think for myself. I was one of those kids who questioned everything. My teachers hated me!

(HOST laughs)

XAVIER: No, seriously, they really hated me. It got so bad I had to be homeschooled.

HOST: Wow, that must have been tough.

XAVIER: No, it was good for me. I could learn the material at my own pace, and had lots of time left over for my own interests. Karate, for instance. I earned my black belt when I was twelve.

HOST: Whoa! I wondered how you got in such remarkable shape.

XAVIER: You're lucky you're on my good side! (Laughs) Anyway, learning at home also taught me self-reliance and independence. It made me the maverick I am today, you know?

HOST: Fascinating. But you're not telling us anything we don't know. Your discoveries of the flammerjammer and the dingleflingle are nothing short of brilliant! They revolutionized modern society! How does it feel to be the first person to—

XANTHE: Xavier, we're here! Snap out of it! Yoo-hoo? Anyone
home?

Xavier blinked. His parents and his sister had already gotten out of the car, but Xanthe had leaned back through the
open door and was snapping her fingers two inches in front of
Xavier's nose. He slapped her hand away.

"OK, OK! You don't have to be annoying."

"You're like a zombie. What were you thinking about
anyway?"

"Nothing."

He couldn't tell her; it was too silly. Besides, he doubted
Xanthe would understand what it was like to fall into The
Zone. The Zone was a sort of self-induced trance, an extreme
form of concentration where he closed his mind off to the
outside world and focused on what was flying around in his
head. It helped him visualize things and was useful when
attacking a complex problem. But more and more often he'd
fall into The Zone just to daydream about his future. A future
he was certain would hold fame, fortune, and lots of television interviews.

Really, it was embarrassing the amount of time he spent
crafting his answers to these future interviews. He also spent a
lot of time crafting acceptance speeches for the Nobel Prize, the
Pulitzer Prize, and an Academy Award. Recently he started
mentally shooting the documentary film of his life.

The only thing missing from these daydreams was the thing

he would actually accomplish to deserve the accolades and attention. What was it going to be? He knew he was destined for greatness; he had to be. He'd been grooming himself for it as long as he could remember. But what form would it take? How would it happen? That part remained a mystery.

Now he had something else to think about. His parents had driven him and Xanthe to their grandmother's house for the first month of their summer vacation. Nana had requested they come up a little early, so now, in late May, they stood in her front garden, still in the bloom of spring. The air was damp and cool as it had rained earlier that morning. Coastal Maine didn't get very warm until late July and August, but it didn't really matter what the weather was; they wouldn't be in Maine for long.

As they walked up the path to her cottage, songbirds rustled overhead, flitting back and forth between the trees and the forest of birdhouses Nana had built herself. Xavier recognized a few of the birds: chickadees, thrushes, warblers, sparrows. Higher up he saw an osprey circling, no doubt interested in the activity below. It's not that he had any real interest in ornithology, but it was his goal to know as much about everything as he could—part of his grooming for greatness.

Nana always took her time answering the door, and today was no exception. After their father knocked several times and their mother floated several hypotheses about where the old woman might be—buying birdseed, in the bathroom, flat on her back after falling off a ladder—the little window in the door opened and Nana's nut-brown face appeared.

"Oh. It's you," she said.

The little window closed. When the door swung open, Nana stood with one hand on her hip wearing a slightly irritated expression, as though she'd been interrupted during some important business. Xavier glanced at Xanthe and saw that she, too, was suppressing a smile. They knew from experience that Nana's grouchiness was really a put-on for their parents. The twins weren't sure why, but Nana took great pleasure in giving their parents a hard time.

"I expected you earlier," the old woman said in her smooth Jamaican accent as she ushered them in. "Thought maybe you changed your mind. I know you all have better things to do in your busy lives than to be visiting an old woman, but thanks for making the time. Now what can I get you? Helen, do you want some cake?"

"We really can't stay too long," their mother said hastily. "We're really just dropping off the kids."

"If you don't like my coconut cake, Helen, just say so," Nana said, hurt.

"I love your coconut cake, Nana, I just . . . we . . . Andrew has a thing he has to do today." Helen nudged her husband.

"I think we can stay for an hour or so, honey. We don't get to see Mom that often," Andrew said, settling into a chair. Helen sighed and sat next to him.

"OK, I suppose I will have a slice of that cake, Nana. And coffee, if you have it," Helen said.

"Well, all right. If you insist," Nana said wearily.

Xavier snorted, trying to keep from laughing. Nana narrowed her eyes at him.

"I'll be in the guest room," Xavier said, grabbing his bag and heading down the hallway. Xanthe followed with her bag, shutting the door behind her and collapsing in a fit of giggles. The twins stuffed their clothes into the dresser, arranged their toiletries in the bathroom, fought over who got the bed next to the window, and had just started to examine the glass bird figurines on the shelves when their parents stuck their heads in the room.

"We're taking off," Andrew said. "Have fun. And help out your grandmother."

"Yes, and don't fight," Helen said, adding under her breath, "we could hear you two squabbling all the way in the living room."

Xavier and Xanthe kissed their parents good-bye, then listened to their footsteps as they walked back through the living room, out the door, and onto the gravel driveway. Finally they heard the sound of the car starting and pulling out. Xavier looked at his watch and gave a low whistle.

"She got them out in an hour and fifteen minutes."

"That's got to be some kind of record," Xanthe said.

"It would've been an hour and five minutes," Nana said from the doorway, "but your father noticed I had some new prints by John James Audubon on the wall, and he was amazed that they had been autographed to me personally, since Mr. Audubon died in eighteen fifty-one. I had to come up with a fancy story to explain that one."

She opened her arms and gave them a broad smile, showing off the gap between her teeth. "Now come on over here and give me a proper hug."

They did. Then they went into the kitchen for the coconut cake.

"Nana," Xavier said between mouthfuls, "don't you like when Mom and Dad come to visit?"

"Of course I do, child. I'm just playing. Besides, I've got more important things to be talking about with my grandchildren. Private things. You know why you're up here, don't you?"

"We've got an assignment from Aunt Gertrude and Aunt Agatha, don't we?" Xavier blurted. Gertrude Pembroke and Agatha Drake were the great-godmothers of Rowan and Nina Popplewell, Xanthe and Xavier's good friends and fellow time travelers. After their adventures with the Popplewells, the twins had adopted the term *aunt* for the old women; indeed, at times they felt like they were all family.

"That's why you wanted us to start our summer vacation early!" Xanthe chimed in. "Something happened in history at the end of May, and we're going to go there!"

"What is it?" Xavier asked. "Where are we going?"

"I'm going to let the Sisters fill you in on that," Nana said, pulling a leather case out of the pocket of her sweater. "I don't pretend to know what they're doing or what they need. We'll all be meeting at their house for dinner, and we'll find out about it then."

"Then what was it you wanted to talk about?" Xanthe asked.

Nana opened the case and removed her long, thin pipe, which she proceeded to stuff with a pinch of tobacco from a rolled-up plastic bag. After she rolled the bag back up and tucked it into the case, she slipped a match out of its box, flicked it with her thumbnail, then lit the pipe, sucking on the end to get it started. Finally the old woman settled back in her chair, staring at them through the wispy clouds of aromatic smoke.

"All right, I'll get to the point," she said. "I don't know exactly what it is that Agatha and Gertrude want you to do, but whatever it is, you don't have to do it if you don't want to. You still have free choice, understand? Nobody is forcing you to do anything. This is not a game, remember. It's serious business, with real consequences. I know you're excited to go, but there are dangers, not all of them obvious."

Xavier expected this, the warning speech. Nana felt responsible for them, and if anything happened while they were in her custody she'd have a lot of explaining to do. During his last trip, a gladiator had ripped his back open, requiring a row of stitches. His parents believed the fib, that he'd fallen while climbing a fence, but they weren't stupid. Too many injuries and everybody would be in big trouble. But Xavier wasn't about to stop before they'd even started.

"Don't worry about us, Nana. We're ready. The Board of Directors wouldn't have chosen us to be Time Detectives if they didn't think we could do it."

"Maybe," Nana said. "And maybe not. Sometimes when

folks are desperate, they make decisions that they wouldn't otherwise make."

"What do they have to be desperate about?" Xanthe asked.

Nana chewed on the end of her pipe thoughtfully. "Just keep your eyes open, and use your heads. And remember that time travel is hard. Every trip changes you in some way."

Xavier nodded but shot Xanthe a look, which she answered with a shrug. She clearly didn't know what Nana was talking about either.

"Well, now that we got that talk out of the way, Rowan and Nina are in town," the old woman continued. "They arrived from New York this morning by train . . ."

Before Nana could finish her sentence the twins were out the door, on the bicycles that Nana kept on the porch, and streaking down the driveway, scattering gravel in their wake.

+ CHAPTER TWO +
HIDDEN ROOMS

The twins found Rowan and Nina leaving Hilda's coffee shop. The scene they made in the street, whooping, squealing, and tackling one another, drew the curious looks of shopkeepers and passersby. After this celebration, the four of them headed down Main Street, chatting about their activities over the past few months, things they had left out of their e-mails.

Xanthe described her jazz dance recital, her volunteer job at an animal shelter, and how her new cat, Spice, a souvenir from their trip to ancient Egypt, had eaten half of her jazz slipper. Nina talked about her trip to Japan to perform in a Chopin festival where she got to meet the prime minister. Rowan dropped chess club to take an after-school job at a comic book shop to help with the family's expenses. He confessed that he was worried about his father's floundering bakery business and his ability to pay the bills.

Xavier saved his story for last. It was about a rocket he'd

built in a class at the Boston Museum of Science, which caused an explosion so big it dislodged several ceiling tiles, set off fire alarms, and caused an evacuation of the entire facility.

Xavier embellished the story of course; he always did, just to make it more interesting. The part about the tiles and the alarm was true, but the full-blown evacuation was not. Out of the corner of his eye, Xavier could see his sister rolling her eyes; she hated when he juiced up a story, but he couldn't help himself. It was his nature to please his audience.

After they were all caught up, they made a short stop in the ice-cream parlor. They each purchased a frozen treat before continuing down the street.

"OK," Rowan said after taking a long slurp from his root beer float. "What do you think our first mission is going to be?"

"We were hoping you knew," Xanthe said. "The Sisters didn't give you a hint?"

"Nothing we could figure out," said Nina, kicking a rock and sending it skittering down the sidewalk. "But you know how they can be. I'm sure they've been dropping all sorts of clues that we just haven't picked up on."

"Nana mentioned something," Xavier said.

"What?" Rowan and Nina chimed in together.

"Oh, just the usual warning. You know, the 'Be careful, use your head, don't embarrass me in front of my friends' kind of thing. Hardly worth mentioning," Xanthe said.

"Actually, it was a little more than that," Xavier corrected. "She seemed to think the aunts might be rushing into something, acting out of desperation."

"Sounds exciting!" Nina squealed.

"Sounds dangerous," Rowan groaned.

"Wherever we're going, I hope it won't be freezing," Nina said, ignoring Rowan's remark.

"I hope we won't have to wear anything uncomfortable," Xanthe added.

"No lions," Rowan said with a shudder, recalling their last adventure. "I've had it with lions. And snakes."

"I don't know," Xavier said wistfully. "I could go for some-place a little wild."

By now they were far away from the business district, and were surprised to find themselves on the familiar path to the Owatannauk Resort Hotel. Xavier figured they must have been unconsciously drawn to it, like pigeons coming home to roost. Soon they could see the sprawling resort looming in the distance, a hodgepodge of architectural designs, but still stately, even in its deterioration.

"I have an idea," Nina said, eyes twinkling. "Let's explore the hotel!"

"You mean now? While it's run down?" Xanthe asked. "It'll be hours before it goes through the change."

"It's better now!" Nina laughed, darting ahead.

"She's right," Xavier said. "Once the hotel transforms we won't be able to explore. There will be too many people . . . I mean, phantoms . . . around. Not to mention Otto." Otto was the officious hotel concierge who seemed to appear out of nowhere, and sometimes in several places at once. He was the Official Time Travel Operator—OTTO—and he knew everything about the hotel, though getting the information out of him was not so easy.

"Aunt Gertrude did tell me that there were certain places that were off limits to everybody except the phantoms," Xanthe said.

"That's true. When Nina and I became phantoms we got to go anywhere we wanted," Rowan said. "There are all kinds of cool rooms . . ."

"Well, now you can show us!" Xavier grinned. "The building might be run down, but the rooms are still there, and there's no one to stop us from looking!"

Xanthe and Nina had already broken into a run. Once they reached the fence that surrounded the resort, they found the hole they had dug almost a year ago and slipped through it with ease. Then they raced to the entrance and clattered up the steps, opened the door, and walked inside.

Xavier would have thought that by now he'd be used to the faded carpeting and peeling wallpaper, the thick layer of dust on the furniture and the stale air, but in truth it still raised the hairs on the back of his neck. Even though it wasn't technically haunted—the phantoms that appeared when the hotel transformed at the golden and silver hours were not exactly dead people—it was still creepy.

"Where do you guys want to start?" Nina said, brushing a cobweb from her face. "The dining room is interesting . . ."

"Oh, let's go up the staircase!" Xanthe pleaded. "I've wanted to go up there since the first time I came to this place!"

"I bet these will come in handy," Xavier said, waving a large ring of keys he'd found behind the front desk. The sound of the jangling keys excited the group, so up they went. At the top of the stairs they found a long hallway lined with doors, each with a brass number on it. Crystal sconces, opaque with dust, lined the wall, along with paintings from different eras, some of them modern. A Ruisdael seascape hung next to a Georgia O'Keeffe desert flower. A da Vinci sketch of an angel hung next to a Cézanne still life. Xavier's eyes were drawn to a stained glass window at the end of the hallway depicting Saint Francis of Assisi, his eyes closed and his arms crossed. A dove sat in each hand. Animals lay sleeping at his feet: lion, lamb, dog, bear, rabbit, peacock.

"I guess these are the hotel rooms," Rowan said.

"Not this one," Xavier said, unlocking the door to room number one with the master key. He was surprised to find a staircase that led up to a landing, then turned to the left and disappeared behind a wall. "Come on!"

He bounded up the stairs. The others followed. At the first landing he made the turn and saw that the staircase continued upward and turned again. He scrambled up the second staircase, made the turn, then stopped. Xanthe crashed into him, followed by Rowan and Nina.

"Xave, what's the problem?" Xanthe snipped.

"The staircase ends. It just goes right up to the ceiling." He ran his hands along the walls and ceiling, searching for a trap door. "There's nothing here. Go back down."

Back in the hallway, Xanthe examined the door to room number one carefully. "It's got to be another one of Archibald Weber's puzzles. That guy spent way too much time trying to confuse people."

The door to room number two opened up to a brick wall. The door to room number three revealed another slightly smaller door of dark, burnished wood. When Nina unlocked this one, it revealed a light wood door, intricately carved with images of Hindu gods. Behind this door was a metal screen door, then a door with beveled glass, a sliding door, an upside-down door, a miniature barn door, a swinging door, a submarine hatch, and finally a painting of a door, which of course would not open.

"That was a big waste of time," Nina sighed as they made their way back to the hallway.

"There have to be bedrooms somewhere," Xanthe said. "Let's keep going."

Rowan opened the next door. The brass number four had loosened over the years so that it hung at an angle. Behind this door stretched a narrow hallway, wide enough for only one person to pass through at a time. They walked tentatively through the passageway, which twisted this way and that, leading them to yet another door. When they opened this door they found themselves back in the hallway, coming out door number six.

"This is ridiculous," Rowan said. "We're not getting any-where. Let's just go back downstairs."

They started down the hallway, but stopped. The staircase had disappeared. In its place was a wall decorated with a mural painting of the staircase. It was a very good painting, a little faded by time, but nevertheless not the real thing.

Xavier whistled, impressed. "Wow. This is a good one."

"A good what?" Nina asked.

"It's called a trompe l'oeil. That's French for 'trick the eye.' A painting that creates the optical illusion of three-dimensional space," Xavier said, recalling trivia he'd picked up from an art history book.

"Thanks, Professor," Xanthe said wryly. "But that still doesn't answer the question of what happened to the staircase."

"Xave, you were last in line, right?" asked Rowan suddenly. "Did you close the door to room four behind you when we went down the passageway?"

"No . . ."

"Well, it's closed now."

They all looked at the closed door. A smile broke out on Xavier's face.

"Brilliant! He's brilliant!"

"Who's brilliant?" Xanthe said.

"Archibald Weber is brilliant," Xavier answered smugly. "This is not the same hallway where we started."

"Except for the staircase it looks the same," Rowan said, scratching his head.

"Actually, it doesn't," Xavier retorted. "First of all, as you rightly pointed out, the door was shut, and I definitely left it open."

"Maybe somebody else shut it," Xanthe said. "We might not be the only people here."

"Maybe," Xavier said, "but take a look at the number on the door. The four is straight. The other one was crooked. I know you're not going to say that somebody fixed the number . . ."

"Hey! Look at the window!" Nina cried, pointing down the hall. "They're awake!"

It was true. St. Francis of Assisi's eyes were open and the animals were standing. Moreover, the saint's arms were outstretched and the two doves had taken flight.

"We *are* in a different hallway!" Nina laughed, clapping her hands. "This is awesome!"

"And guess what?" Xanthe said. "I think we found the bedrooms." She had taken the keys and unlocked the door to room number one. This time, instead of a staircase to the ceiling, they found a four-poster bed with a thick, purple coverlet. There was also a small desk, a sofa with a coffee table, and velvet curtains tied back with a blue and gold cord.

They explored the room, opening drawers and examining the decor. Nina discovered a closet, and Xavier found the bathroom, fitted with a claw-foot bathtub and an old-fashioned toilet, the kind with the box perched on a long pipe with a pull chain to flush, much like the one in Aunt Agatha and Aunt Gertrude's house. A third door had a brass lowercase letter *b* on it, and when opened, led to another bedroom, which was a mirror image of the first. When they went back out to the hallway from this room, Xavier noticed that the brass number on front of the door was also marked "1-b."

"I wonder why this is labeled 'one-b' instead of 'two,'" he mused aloud, but Xanthe, Rowan, and Nina had already moved on to the rooms across the hall.

The room behind the door marked with a zero was actually a janitor's closet, containing a large industrial sink, brushes, mops, brooms, and old bottles of cleaning fluid. Room number two, however, was a bedroom very much like room number one and one-b, except the coverlet and curtains were a rich, forest green.

Room number three was like the first two, but when Rowan opened the door to room number four, he found another trompe l'oeil painting, a vista of the Swiss Alps.

"Looks like they're not all rooms," Xanthe mused. "We're back to the optical illusions."

Room number five turned out to be a suite with two separate bedrooms connected by a sitting room. The door to room number six was the passageway that they had come through from the other hallway. Room number seven was another trompe l'oeil, but of a charming English country garden. Room number eight was another suite, bigger than five, with three bedrooms instead of two. Doors to rooms nine, ten, eleven, and twelve opened up to paintings of a rain forest, a Japanese tea garden, a charging African rhino, and a Mayan pyramid. Room thirteen was another huge suite, this one with five attached bedrooms and two bathrooms. The ratio of real rooms to fake rooms was getting smaller, and when Xavier quickly opened the remaining doors in the hallway, he found they were all trompe l'oeils.

"For a hotel, they don't have very many real rooms," Rowan commented after Xavier opened that last door in the hallway, door number twenty-four, revealing a trompe l'oeil of the Parthenon in Greece.

"Well, if you think about it, the suites have several bedrooms within them," Xanthe pointed out, "so the total number of usable rooms is probably the same as if each hallway door led to a real room. Right, Xave? Xave?"

Xavier was lost in The Zone. He stared at the doors. There was a pattern here, he just knew it. Out of the corner of his eye he saw that Nina was standing quietly next to him, concentrating on the doors as well.

"It's so weird . . ." she murmured, twisting a strand of hair in her fingers. "One and one-b. And there's a door with a zero on it . . . I've never seen that before. This is definitely a puzzle . . . a number pattern . . ."

"You noticed it, too?" Xavier said, somewhat surprised.

"Studying music gives you a head for numbers and patterns," Nina said matter-of-factly. "Does anybody have a pen?"

Xanthe whipped a ballpoint pen from her pocket and handed it to Nina, who started scribbling something on the palm of her hand.

"These are the numbers on the rooms that are actually

rooms," Nina said as she wrote. Xavier leaned over her shoulder and saw she was writing a number series: 0, 1, 1-b, 2, 3, 5, 8, 13. With the numbers written out it was as plain as day; he was surprised he hadn't seen it sooner.

"The Fibonacci sequence," he announced.

"Oh yeah! You're right!" Xanthe squealed.

"It has a name?" Nina said.

"You add the last number to the number that came before it to get the next number in the sequence," Xavier explained. "It's really cool, because it mathematically describes a spiral pattern that you find in nature: in flower petals, the shape of shells, animal breeding . . ."

"Archibald Weber loves spirals," Xanthe added gleefully. "They're built right into the architecture of the hotel . . . like that spiral staircase to the ceiling!"

"Yeah, except it doesn't work," Rowan said. They all turned to him. "I mean, the pattern breaks down after door thirteen. If you're right, the next door that should have a real room or a suite behind it should be door twenty-one. But it doesn't. It's one of those trompe l'oeils."

Rowan opened door twenty-one, revealing a painting of prison bars. They all fell silent, wondering what it could mean. Xanthe drummed her fingers on the sill below the stained glass window. Suddenly she gasped.

"You figured it out?" Nina said.

"No, we're in trouble!" Xanthe cried. "Aunt Gertrude's here! Her truck's parked outside!"

"Look at the sun!" Rowan added. "It's almost the golden hour! C'mon, we gotta get back through the passageway!"

They dashed through door number six, raced through the twisted hallway, scrambled into the first hallway, then flew down the flight of stairs. As Xavier bounded down, taking three or four stairs at a time, he felt the familiar tingle of the onset of the golden hour. Every molecule in his body seemed to vibrate with increasing intensity until he was entirely numb. Then an explosion of color rushed upon them like a tidal wave.

The next thing he knew he was sprawled at the bottom of the staircase, his face in the thick, maroon carpeting. As the high-buttoned boots and wide crinoline skirts of the hotel phantoms brushed by, he noticed a pair of black penny loafers slowly approaching and then stopping right in front of his face. They were huge, like two leather canoes, size twelves at least. Xavier's eyes scanned up the tall, dark-trousered legs to the wool poncho, finally lighting on the stern glare of Gertrude Pembroke.

"It's time for dinner," she said.

+ CHAPTER THREE +
CLUES

Dinner consisted of meat loaf and gravy with mashed potatoes and fresh string beans. Xavier had been afraid that Gertrude would be furious with them for exploring the hotel, but she seemed uninterested in their apologies. In fact, she seemed so completely unresponsive, Xavier imagined she had turned into a trompe l'oeil herself, but every once in a while the creases at the corners of her mouth would sharpen in response to one of Agatha's wandering stories, and he knew she was very much aware of everything going on around her.

They were all eager to help clean up the dishes, for they knew it would hasten the next part of the evening, when they would find out about their first assignment. Sure enough, after the last plate was wiped and put back in the cabinet, Agatha erected her easel and set a large stack of cards on its narrow shelf while Gertrude passed out manila envelopes.

"Well. Now to the business at hand," Agatha began. "This is certainly an exciting time. The four of you are about to embark on your first mission alone. We wanted to start you out with something simple, a way for you to dip your toes in the water of time detection, so to speak." She paused. "Unfortunately, that won't be the case."

The children exchanged glances. The tone of the presentation had taken a turn toward the deadly serious. Xavier recalled what Nana had said about desperation and realized her fears might be valid.

"Please open your envelopes," Agatha continued.

Xavier pulled out a dark blue binder with the words BLOOMINGTON, ILLINOIS, UNITED STATES OF AMERICA, 1856 stenciled in gold, along with his name, "Xavier Alexander."

"I know that this may not seem like an exotic locale," Agatha continued, clearly reading the minds of all four of the young detectives. "But this is a mission of the utmost importance. You'll be looking for this young man."

Agatha placed a card on the easel with an enlarged sepia-toned photograph of a teenage boy. He had dark hair and eyes, and he wore a dark suit with a light shirt. The expression on his face was hostile.

"There's somebody who didn't want his picture taken," Rowan murmured.

"Yeah, what a sourpuss," Nina whispered.

"Are you sure you want to find him? Maybe he's better off lost," Xavier joked. Gertrude gave him such a sharp look that he sank down into the sofa, trying to disappear.

"This 'sourpuss,' as you call him, is Balthazar Weber," Agatha said, but she was immediately interrupted.

"Weber! Is he related to Archibald Weber?"

"I didn't know Archibald Weber had a kid!"

"Why is he so angry?"

"What did he do?"

Agatha held up her hand for silence. "Balthazar is Archibald Weber's son, his only child. Please, hold your questions until I finish; I may answer them as I go along.

"Balthazar is fifteen years old in this picture," Agatha began again. "Not long after it was taken, Archie took him on a trip to Bloomington, Illinois, to this place . . ."

She removed the first card, revealing the second, a grainy photograph of a boxy, three-story brick building.

"This is Major's Hall," she said, "the site of the first state Republican Convention in Illinois."

Xanthe and Xavier both gasped.

"So you two understand the significance of this?"

"Archibald Weber took him to see Abraham Lincoln!" they said in unison.

The twins both knew quite a lot about this time period; their father taught American history at Boston University and specialized in Western expansion, much of which happened during the eighteen hundreds. The Illinois convention was a turning point in Lincoln's political career. Up until then he was thought of as an outstanding circuit lawyer, but nothing more. After the convention, many foresaw his destiny as president of the United States.

"It was the 'lost speech' that did it," Agatha explained, reading Xavier's thoughts.

"What's the 'lost speech'?" Rowan asked, trying to catch up.

"First things first," Agatha said, revealing the third card, a photograph of Abraham Lincoln, without the iconic beard and stovepipe hat. "Here's a familiar face. This is Mr. Lincoln in eighteen fifty-six. He hardly looks presidential. Tall, gangly, big country hands, big nose, big ears, ill-fitting clothes . . . kind of funny looking, if you ask me.

"I don't think I need to remind you of the rift developing at this time between the Northern states and the Southern states over the issue of slavery. As the West became settled and states continued to enter the Union, the Northerners were determined to keep them free of slavery. In their view, slavery degraded the very pillars of belief on which the nation had been founded. Meanwhile, the Southerners depended heavily on slaves for farming the plantations, and they were not about to give up their way of life.

"The convention was held to address this issue. It attracted all types of people, from wildly different political groups, but they were united in their dedication to keep slavery from extending to the new states."

"Wait a minute," Rowan interrupted. "Why just the new states? What about getting rid of slavery everywhere?"

"This was less about slavery and more about just trying to keep the Union together," said Gertrude, removing a bag of her favorite bitter horehound drop candy from her pocket. "The Northerners were afraid that if they pushed for the complete eradication of slavery the Southerners would secede from the Union and create their own country."

She took a candy from the bag and popped it in her mouth, then offered the bag around to the others, who all politely shook their heads no. Xavier didn't know how she could stand the things; they tasted like bug spray with a hint of honey.

"Back to the story," Agatha said. "It's May twenty-ninth, close to five-thirty in the evening, and the convention is drawing to a close. Abolitionist James Emery had just finished his speech. Lincoln was not listed as a speaker on the program, but as the day was winding down, people in the audience called upon him to say a few last words. No doubt they were expecting a couple of jokes to send them on their way. What they got was completely different.

"According to eyewitness accounts, in the next ninety minutes, Lincoln delivered a speech so powerful, so electrifying, that it left his audience hysterical. It solidified all those disparate groups and catapulted Lincoln into the public consciousness as a contender for the presidency. Strangely enough, there is no record of what he actually said. Every single person there, including members of the press, was so gripped by his words that nobody wrote them down. It is only remembered as 'Lincoln's lost speech.' Many claim it was the greatest speech of his life."

Gertrude stood up. "At some point after the speech, Balthazar got separated from Archie. Every year, on May twenty-ninth, I go to Bloomington to look for him. I search the hall, I search outside the hall, I look in every closet and under every bush. There's no trace of him.

"After these many years I have come to the conclusion that Balt is not lost; he's hiding. He doesn't want to be found, at least not by me. And he knows what I look like, so he can spot me a mile away, even when I'm disguised."

"Why don't you just go earlier in time?" Nina suggested. "You could stop Archibald Weber and Balthazar from even going in the first place."

"Though that is tempting, it's extremely dangerous. It's hard to explain, but going back in time and telling people what's going to happen in the future can create some very knotty problems—morally, I mean. You should understand that this is going to be a very delicate operation."

"If you can't find him, what makes you think we can?" Xavier asked.

"Balthazar doesn't know the four of you," Agatha added. "He may be able to evade Gertrude, but he won't see you coming."

"And it's important we find the boy," Gertrude said grimly. "He accidentally changed something in history that kept his father from being born. All these years, Archibald Weber has been a hotel phantom, in perpetual limbo. And time, I'm afraid, is running out."

A silence fell over the room again. Nobody, except perhaps Agatha, knew what Gertrude was alluding to, and something in her manner kept them from asking.

Finally Rowan cleared his throat. "Excuse me, but what's Balthazar so mad about?"

"I'm not sure," Gertrude answered. "If I knew, it might

make my job a little easier. The only person who might know is . . . well, let's say Archibald Weber is a private individual and leave it at that. All you have to do is find his son. I'll take care of the rest."

Gertrude produced a compact disc from her pocket and placed it into a portable CD player. "This is an interview of Archie, conducted right after he returned from Bloomington. Initially I used one of Thomas Edison's early tape-recording machines, so the quality isn't perfect, but I've since transferred that recording to this disc."

She pressed a button, then leaned back, pressing her finger-tips together. The foursome crowded closer to the machine. After the initial hissing and crackling sounds, there came a man's voice. It was slightly muffled from the early recording equipment.

ARCHIE: *Balthazar and I were in Bloomington to see the man whom I consider my greatest influence, and to hear Lincoln's "lost speech," an event which I had been eagerly awaiting for months. You see, President Lincoln was a personal hero of my father's. My father joined the fight for freedom because of his deep respect for Lincoln, serving in the Union army under General George Meade before dying in the Battle of Gettysburg. I was five years old at the time, but I still remember how proud he was to wear the Union blue . . .*

(Long pause and shifting sounds)

GERTRUDE: Why don't you start from your arrival in Bloomington.

ARCHIE: We arrived on May twenty-fourth. From the out-set, Balthazar was unhappy. I had procured a part-time job for him as an errand boy for Judge David Davis, a good friend of Abraham Lincoln's. For much of the time, Balt and I were sepa-rated; in fact, several nights he slept at the judge's house. I believe it was during this time that he plotted his disappearance.

(Long pause and sounds of fumbling)

GERTRUDE: When did you notice Balthazar was missing?

ARCHIE: The morning of the twenty-ninth, a young Negro, whom I recognized as Judge Davis's stable boy, delivered a note from Balt instructing me to meet him at my hotel, and not to go to the convention without him. I knew Mr. Lincoln would not speak until five-thirty or so, but by three o'clock Balt had not yet arrived and I began to worry. I rushed to Judge Davis's chambers at the courthouse and inquired as to the whereabouts of Walter Ebb, but most of the employees were at the convention and the errand boy, the young Negro who had given me the letter, was a mute and was not forthcoming with any useful information. At Judge Davis's home my inquiries also went unsatisfied.

At this point I must admit my anger got the better of me. I suspected that Balt was intentionally trying to make me miss

Lincoln's speech. I refused to fall victim to his childish prank. I went straight to Major's Hall in time to hear one of the most moving speeches in human history.

How can I describe it? How indeed. Abraham Lincoln is a master of the spoken word. His voice strikes you like lightning, igniting the soul. He began with a few jokes, but right away he turned to his main point: the protection of the Union at all costs. Several times he was interrupted by enthusiastic applause. He would wait until it died down before he fired us up again. He would withdraw from the platform, then slowly pace forward, his frame appearing to grow even taller and more gigantic. Then, without warning, he'd thrust both hands forward, as if hurling his comments, causing people in the front row to flinch. He kept us enraptured for ninety minutes. Nobody moved to light the oil lamps. The hall had become dark, but it didn't matter, for Mr. Lincoln blazed brightly, his eyes lit up with the divining light of a seer. I shall remember it the rest of my life. And it was particularly distressing to me that Balt had missed it, for he could've learned much.

After the speech I returned to the courthouse, where there had been no word from him. At the Stratton Hotel the story was the same, no word at all. I spent the entire night searching for my son, but to no avail. His trail was cold.

Gertrude shut off the machine. Everyone sat quietly for a moment.

"Who is 'Walter Ebb'?" Rowan asked, breaking the silence.

"It's Balthazar," Xavier answered. "Walter Ebb is an anagram for Balt Weber. Just mix the letters around in Balt's name."

"Very good, Xavier!" Gertrude said, her eyes wide with genuine surprise. "That's exactly right. Archie thought it wise to use assumed names rather than their own. Of course, with their love of puzzles, they each chose anagrams. I believe Archibald traveled under the name Charlie Brawbed. Anyway, as soon as Archie returned to the Owatannauk he immediately sought my counsel. I went to my tracking station to listen to what had transpired during the trip. As you know, the alleviator keys act as a sort of transmitter. They allow me to hear conversations, surrounding noises, and so forth, but only during the golden hour and the silver hour. These noises help me pinpoint the location of the lost person."

Xavier and the others nodded. During their last trip Xanthe had been given the opportunity to try out the tracking station herself. She described it to Xavier and the Popplewells as a long console with twelve knobs that corresponded to the twelve time-traveling alleviators. Each knob could be tuned in to the different keys of the travelers.

Gertrude rubbed her chin. "I keep a recording of these transmissions. The recording of Balthazar's key during Lincoln's speech has an echo. You can tell he's not in the main hall exactly, but perhaps in the hallway. Yet when I've gone back I haven't been able to find him there. There is no closet big enough to hide in, no blankets to hide under, no corner to hide behind. And he couldn't have jumped out the window, it's too high."

Xavier and Xanthe exchanged uncomfortable looks. They were thinking the same thing.

"Er, Aunt Gertrude, can I say something?" Xanthe finally said.

"Of course. That's why you're here. If you have suggestions, I want to hear them."

"You keep talking about Balt hiding. I'm sorry, but I don't think that's what's going on at all. I'm guessing you haven't spent much time around kids, right?"

"I'll say!" Agatha giggled. "If you hand Gertrude a baby, she'll try to hold it by the scruff of its neck, like a kitten!"

"Oh, that's not true," Gertrude sniffed, "but sometimes young people do baffle me, I admit."

"What I'm trying to say is, I don't think any kid over the age of seven would try to hide by ducking into a closet or under some blankets. We're all fourteen, except for Nina, but I don't think even Nina would . . ."

"I stopped playing hide-and-seek in second grade," Nina growled.

"Xanthe's right," Rowan said. "Mr. Weber says he thinks Balt was 'plotting his disappearance.' *Plotting.* That suggests something a lot more clever than just hiding. A teenager can come up with some pretty good plots."

"That's for sure," Nina said. "I mean, look at us. We've all managed to keep time travel a secret from our parents. And from the look of Balt in that photograph, he may have even been plotting *before* they left!"

"And why did they use pseudonyms, anyway?" Xavier broke in. "They didn't just do it for the fun of it. It makes things much more difficult to have a fake name you have to remember; there had to be a good reason for it."

"Well, it looks like we've definitely found the right team," Gertrude said with a rare smile. "Why don't I play the recording of Balt's key? You may be able to make more of it than I could."

"But first let's take a short break," Agatha said, pushing back her hair and repinning it with a teaspoon. "Who wants dessert?"

After poached pears and vanilla ice cream, they listened to the recordings of Balthazar's key. There were fourteen in all, marking the golden and silver hours of each day that Archibald Weber and Balt were in Bloomington. The first two times the foursome listened to these recordings, they listened all the way through, taking notes on what they heard. Then they played them again, stopping the machine every few seconds to analyze the background noises and float theories about what was happening. After hearing the recordings about twelve times, they all knew them by heart. Gertrude and Agatha encouraged them to pursue their own line of reasoning, without their interference.

"I don't want to influence you," Gertrude explained. "I want you to tackle this from a fresh perspective."

There were several transmissions during which the four junior detectives heard nothing but light snoring. These were the ones that happened during the silver hour, when Balt was asleep. The golden hour transmissions they divided into four categories: conversations between Balthazar and Archibald Weber, conversations between Balthazar and Judge Davis, random conversations between Balthazar and unknown persons in the law office where he worked, and transmissions where there was no conversation at all.

The conversations between Balt and Judge Davis were usually short and to the point. The judge would give Balt an assignment, usually a delivery, and then on Balt's return confirm that the delivery had been made. The junior Time Detectives didn't find much of interest in these conversations.

The conversations between Balthazar and his father, however, were not as cordial. One in particular struck Xavier as odd.

"Let's hear that one again," Xavier said, leaning forward in the chair with his eyes closed. Xanthe pressed the button.

BALT: *I don't want to be here!*

ARCHIE: *It's for your own good. You'll thank me later.*

BALT: *There won't be a later, not for you, not for me, not for anybody! I can't do it! I'm not a fighter or a leader, regardless of what you saw . . .*

ARCHIE: *Quiet! Everything you say . . . !*

(*A long pause and rustling noises*)

BALT: (*Quietly*) *How about what I want? Don't you care about me?*

(*A long pause*)

ARCHIE: *Yes. Of course I do.*

BALT: *No, you don't.*

ARCHIE: *Balt . . . !*

(*Door slam*)

"So?" Xanthe said, pausing the recording. "They're having an argument. We knew Balt was in Bloomington under protest."

"Yes, but the way Archie stops the conversation suddenly, right when Balt is going to say what they're actually arguing about. Doesn't anyone else think that's kind of weird?"

"Maybe they were in Archie's hotel room and he didn't want the other guests to hear what they were saying," Rowan suggested. "Maybe he thought Balt was about to say something about time travel."

"There's another sound," Nina said. "Right after Archie stops him. It's a ringing noise."

"I didn't hear anything," Xanthe said. The boys shrugged; they hadn't heard the ringing noise either.

"It's hard to hear, but it's there. It's the sound of the alleviator keys."

"C'mon, Nina, the alleviator keys don't make sounds," Rowan chided.

"Yes, they do," she insisted. "They sound just like the alleviators, that chiming, humming sound, only softer. Anyway, I think right then, when he stops Balt from talking, Archie took his alleviator key out of his pocket."

"So . . . when he was trying to get Balt to shut up, it was because . . ." Xavier frowned. "Are you saying he was reminding Balt that the keys were picking up everything they were saying?"

"He wasn't trying to keep anything from the hotel guests. He was trying to keep it from you, Aunt Gertrude," Nina said, turning to the old woman.

Gertrude stared off into space for a long time. Finally she exhaled, shrinking slightly like a deflated balloon. It was a sign of defeat that the youngsters had never seen in her before.

"I sensed that something was amiss," she said, looking ruefully to Agatha. "I believe . . . Sister, I believe Archie has lost trust in me."

"Oh no, that can't be!" Agatha protested. "There must be some other explanation . . ."

"All these many years, even before Balt's disappearance, I've sensed a wall growing between us, that he was deliberately hiding something from me. This confirms it."

"Perhaps the children are mistaken. Perhaps their interpretation is flawed . . ." Agatha's voice trailed off until she was silent.

Xavier felt uncomfortable. Seeing Gertrude with her defenses down was like catching your father crying. It made you feel helpless and desperate to put a stop to it.

"Please, let's keep going," Xavier said. "I just thought of something." And indeed he had. It appeared suddenly in his head, the way ideas always do when you least expect them, like money on the ground, just waiting for somebody to discover it.

"We know that Archie and Balt were both aware of the keys, and of what they were transmitting back to the hotel. What if Balt used that to set up his escape?"

"You say 'escape' like he was in jail or something," Xanthe said wryly.

"I bet that's how Balt felt. Anyway, listen to this."

Xavier found a section of the recording and played it.

BALT: . . . *adventure of a lifetime! Fellows are leaving as farmers and coming back millionaires!*

UNKNOWN PERSON: *Believe me, I think about it constantly, I'm just not sure . . .*

BALT: *Just a moment. You can hold this, but you have to give it back.*

(*Rustling sounds and footsteps*)

JUDGE DAVIS: *I have a package for you to take over to the sher-iff. Be quick about it, it's important.*

(*Footsteps*)

(*Door opening and closing*)

(*Outside noises, birds, distant conversation, horse and wagon passing*)

"Did you hear it?" Xavier asked.

"Hear what? I didn't hear anything," Xanthe said.

"Exactly."

"Come on, Xave, quit goofing around."

"Balt's in the middle of a conversation that seems pretty excit-ing, then he suddenly stops, says, 'You can hold this, but you have to give it back,' then we don't hear him speak again for the rest of that particular golden hour. That's over forty-five minutes with-out saying anything! What happened to the conversation?"

"I did hear something," Nina piped up. "The alleviator key sound again, right when he said, 'You can have this.'"

"So . . . Balt was showing the key to somebody in the office?" Rowan asked.

"Not only that, but that same phrase, 'You can hold this, but you have to give it back,' happens twice. And listen to this; it's the last transmission where we hear Balt's voice."

Xavier started the machine again.

BALT: *You can have it, it's yours.*

(*Intake of breath*)

(*Rustling*)

(*Horse snorting and grunting close by*)

Xavier stopped the machine.

"You think Balt gave his key to somebody?!" Rowan cried. "But then he wouldn't be able to get back . . . oh, that's right. He didn't want to come back. He was running away."

"That would be a difficult thing to pull off," Agatha said. "Whoever took the key would have to refrain from speaking for a full hour; otherwise Gertrude would know that it had changed hands."

"There was somebody there who could easily have kept quiet," Xanthe said. "The other errand boy. Remember? Mr. Weber mentioned a 'Negro errand boy' who was mute. He also said the boy lived in Judge Davis's stable. That would account for all of those horse sounds."

"Goodness gracious, I saw that boy in Major's Hall," Gertrude said, eyes wide. "It had to be him. And to think that key was in his pocket all along!"

"Boy, that Balt was a sneaky guy," Xanthe mused. "By giving the key away, he bought himself time to disappear. He probably left right then, at the silver hour, and not after Lincoln's speech. He may have used the key to bribe the errand boy into delivering that note to Archibald Weber after he had already left, just to throw him off. But we still don't know where he went."

"He might not have cared where he went," Rowan said. "We should check the train schedules and see where they were going that early in the morning."

"I think I know where he went," Agatha said, shaking her head disbelievingly. "It's just a hunch, but that conversation . . . and I know Balt; with his wild spirit, I'm sure he couldn't help himself . . . after all, it was eighteen fifty-six, it's what everyone was talking about . . ."

"Agatha, do finish one thought before you start another!" Gertrude said, exasperated.

"I'm sorry, Sister. It's just that . . . Balt wanted to go as far away from Archie as he could. Well, he may have gone all the way to the other side of the country. If I'm not mistaken, Balt followed hundreds of thousands of other adventure seekers to the California Gold Rush." She turned to the four pairs of eager eyes facing her. "You may be going someplace a little more exciting than Bloomington after all."

+ CHAPTER FOUR +
WESTWARD HO

When the aunts, the Alexanders, and the Popplewells arrived at the Owatannauk Library, Jenny O'Neill, the head librarian, was waiting for them. She immediately whisked the group up to the fourth floor. In the elevator Xavier noticed that, though the building had five stories, there were several basement levels as well, twelve in all.

"Wow, this place is almost as big as the New York Public Library," he commented.

"In fact, it's bigger," Jenny laughed. "It's the largest library in the United States."

"Well, no, that would be the Library of Congress in Washington, D.C.," Xanthe said.

"I used to work at the Library of Congress," Jenny said with a little smile. "We're bigger. As of now we have one hundred and thirty million items on seven hundred miles of shelving."

"But the Library of Congress has almost everything that's ever been published . . ."

"I know. But we have things that have never been published."

The door opened and Jenny led them down a hallway to a windowless room lined with long tables, each with its own computer, printer, and desk supplies. People working on various projects tapped away at the keyboards, took notes, or stared intently at the screens. Some looked as if they might have been there for days. Three people had brought sleeping bags. Jenny led the group to a table in the corner.

"This is one of our research rooms. It helps to have some idea what you're looking for before you start on a trip; as you can see, research can be addictive." She gestured to one of the patrons with a six-inch-long beard and seven empty coffee cups in front of him, his eyes locked onto the glowing computer monitor, his fingers clutching the mouse like a lifeline.

"We're trying to find someone in the California Gold Rush in eighteen fifty-seven," Gertrude said. "If it's not too much trouble, we'll need you to pull some books on that era."

Jenny nodded her good-bye and departed, scooping up the empty coffee cups on her way.

Gertrude motioned to the chair in front of the computer. "Would somebody like to take the console? I tend to get shocks from the computers," Gertrude said, referring to one of the side effects commonly experienced by people who did a lot of time travel.

"Me first!" cried Xanthe. In an instant her butt was nestled in the seat.

Xavier curled his lip. *Me first* was like Xanthe's motto. As the eldest twin by twenty-one minutes (a fact she rubbed in his nose constantly), she was forever jockeying to be first in line, first to take charge, first first first. Sometimes it seemed like his life was an endless search for opportunities to squeeze by Xanthe, get out from under her shadow.

HOST: Hi, and welcome back to *Great Guys*. We're talking to Xavier Alexander. Xavier, let's talk a moment about your sister, Xanthe.

XAVIER: Yes, I thought you'd get to her eventually . . .

HOST: She's older than you by half an hour, smart, personable, resourceful. You've clearly been influenced by her. Would you say she is largely responsible for your success?

XAVIER: It's true that Xanthe is an amazing person in her own right. But to tell you the truth, she'd be nowhere without me. People think that since I'm younger—and by the way, it's only by twenty-one minutes, really almost negligible, scientifically speaking—that I follow her lead, or that I'm dependent on her. But it's the other way around. You see, Xanthe has a lot of issues. She's incredibly jealous, for instance. She has a bad temper. She overthinks things, and, little known fact, she is really messy. A pig! Her room looks like a tornado hit it. Did you know I once found a melted ice-cream cone on her desk? Mint chocolate chip smeared all over the place and ants crawling through it. Disgusting!

"Xavier, are you paying attention?" Gertrude asked. Xavier snapped back to reality.

"Huh? What is it?"

"Xanthe said she had a cramp in her wrist and asked if you could take over the typing."

"Oh yeah. Sure." Xavier slipped into the seat in front of the monitor.

Xanthe had already found the train schedules for Bloomington Station. The earliest train leaving the station on May twenty-ninth, eighteen fifty-six, was stopping in St. Joseph, Missouri. Gertrude pointed out that St. Joseph was the most popular launching place for people in Illinois heading to gold country.

"We need to find a database with information about anyone traveling through St. Joseph, Missouri. Let's start with hotels," Gertrude suggested.

"Good idea," Agatha agreed. "It took travelers quite a bit of time to buy supplies. A trip out west took about four months if you were lucky, and it required food, cooking utensils, buckets, shovels, lanterns, rubber blankets, guns, tents, and a good pair of boots, not to mention a wagon and something to pull it. Balt would have to spend at least a week getting all those things."

Xavier scanned through the names listed in the hotels' records; Balt's pseudonym, Walter Ebb, was not among them.

Jenny returned with a stack of books about the California Gold Rush. Xanthe, Rowan, and Nina each grabbed one, searching for any information that might help.

"I don't think Balt would want to spend a lot of time buying supplies. It would only slow him down," Xanthe said, thumbing through a book. "Xave, try finding the passenger list for the stagecoaches. It says here, 'The Pioneer Stagecoach Line was an option for those who preferred traveling light.'"

Xavier checked, but again he came up empty. Suddenly Rowan looked up from the book he had been flipping through.

"This book says that people traveling alone would join organized companies and associations to help them travel . . . you know, there's safety in numbers. Maybe if you could find the rosters . . . ?"

"Let's see, here's a list of some of the companies," Xavier said, scanning the screen. "Boston and California Joint Mining and Trading Company, Hartford Union Mining and Trading Company, Iron City Rangers of Pittsburgh, Yankee Argonauts, El Dorado Voyagers, Buckeye Rovers, Helltown Greasers . . ." Nina followed along on the screen.

"Wolverine Rangers?" She giggled. "Oh, there's a funny one: Miners of Temperance and Good Character."

"No Walter Ebb in any of them, though," murmured Xavier.

"Hey, what if he went by sea?" asked Nina after a moment.

"But the overland route was shorter by half," Xanthe countered.

"Yeah, and who would want to go by sea if you were already in Illinois?" added Rowan. "Look, it says here the sea route was even more uncomfortable than the land route," he said, consulting his book. "A lot of the ships were broken down, the captains didn't have any experience, the weather was stormy, the food was rotten, passengers were seasick . . . can you imagine having to deal with all that for nine months?"

"But Nina's got a point. If Balt was heading out west, he wasn't doing it to be a gold prospector, he was just trying to disappear," Xavier reminded them. "So he would take the most complicated path he could find. And he knew Gertrude would never try to land an alleviator on a crowded boat."

"And I don't know if anybody else noticed this, but the second train out of Bloomington was heading toward Boston . . . a popular port town," Xanthe added.

"It's certainly worth a try," Gertrude said.

Xavier's fingers were tired, so Nina took the next turn. Her fingers flew across the keyboard and almost instantly they found lists of ships in Boston that had embarked on trips to the West within the week of Balt's disappearance, as well as lists of passengers on the ships. They scanned the names three times; no Walter Ebb.

Xavier's eyes were getting tired. Time detection was not as glamorous as he thought it would be; so far it was just a lot of sitting and reading. Agatha suggested they all take a short break, so they moved to the kitchenette, where they found complimentary refreshments.

"What if . . ." Rowan started, stifling a burp from his ginger ale. "What if Balt was using his real name? We've been looking for Walter Ebb, but after Balt left Bloomington, maybe he didn't need to use the pseudonym anymore."

"I still don't understand why he needed to use it in the first place," Xavier said, but Gertrude was on her feet, gulping the contents of her cup.

"That's an excellent observation, Rowan. Quick, let's get back to the console!" she said. "We have to check those lists all over again!"

Xavier groaned. More lists! He dragged himself back to the computer. Rowan sat in front of the keyboard. The ships were still on the computer screen from their last search, so that's where he started. But instead of Balthazar Weber they found a different name: Oliver Weber.

"Strange," Gertrude murmured. "Why would Balt travel under that name?"

"Maybe it's just a coincidence," Xanthe said. "There could be hundreds of Webers in that area."

"Great heavens, that is no coincidence!" Agatha said, returning from the kitchen with a small pastry. "Oliver Weber is Archie's father!"

"Are you sure?" Gertrude said.

"Of course I'm sure! Archie wrote an essay about his father's service in the Civil War while he was at St. Ambrose. I remember it vividly. It was one of the most touching tributes I've ever read. Oliver Weber is definitely his father."

Xavier's eyes landed on something. He sat up straight.

"I found it!" he yelled. Several library patrons glanced up, alarmed, then returned to their own research.

"Found what?" Gertrude said, peering at the screen.

Xavier pointed at the screen, right above Oliver Weber. "There! Albert Web. And that's no coincidence, either. Albert Web is another anagram for Balt Weber!"

"How peculiar!" Gertrude said, tilting her head, as though reading it from another angle might somehow illuminate a deeper meaning. "I wonder . . . well, he and Oliver had to be traveling together."

"Oh, Sister, it all fits!" Agatha was so excited she hopped from one foot to the other like a puppy in a pet store. "That would explain why they used the pseudonyms! Archie must've known his father had heard Lincoln's speech, and that if he and Balt used the last name "Weber," people might figure out that they were all related. It would attract too much attention to them. It also helps pinpoint the moment when Balt changed history. Oliver Weber was supposed to get married to a young woman named Adelaide Clemens and have a son with her, a son named Archibald. I met Adelaide when I was Archie's teacher. I never met Archie's father, though, because he had already died in the Battle of Gettysburg."

"I see," Gertrude said thoughtfully. "So it appears that Balt coaxed his grandfather into going to the Gold Rush instead of meeting his destiny. Oliver must've been the unknown person that Balt was speaking to in the recording . . . why, what's wrong, Agatha?"

Agatha's excitement had drained away. She collapsed into her chair, her face in her hands. "He really was a devious fellow, wasn't he?" she said through her fingers.

"Sister?"

"Just think of all the plotting that went into this. Balt intentionally made Archie a victim of his own invention, the time machines, the thing Balt felt his father loved more than anything. It breaks my heart to think how that lovely little boy got so twisted . . ." Agatha trailed off, blinking back tears. She dabbed her eyes with a handkerchief.

"This is indeed disturbing," Gertrude said, placing her hand gently on Agatha's shoulder. "Obviously Archie knew his father was there in Bloomington, he had to. Why didn't he mention this to us? Again, I can only conclude that Archie doesn't trust us."

The two old women were silent, miserable in their thoughts, but the four junior detectives didn't notice. Rowan had pulled up more information. Albert Web and Oliver Weber had booked passage on the SS *Neptune* departing from Boston the day after the convention. Neither was listed among those who had died during the journey, and the ship arrived in San Francisco in ten months and seven days.

"San Francisco's the place!" Xanthe said. "When are we going? Are we going to go at the next silver hour?"

"Remember, you can only travel back in time to the same date on which you left," Gertrude said. "If you left today, you would arrive on June first, eighteen fifty-seven. Balt got there in mid-March. He would already have a few months' head start. Perhaps we should wait until next March to send you so you can meet the ship."

"But that's ten months away!" Nina whined. "We want to go now!"

"Please, let us go," chimed in Xanthe. "We can do this. Just give us a chance."

"I don't think it could hurt, Sister," Agatha sighed. "At the very least they'll get more information. And if we wait until March . . . well, as you said, we're running out of time."

Gertrude nodded. "You're right, Sister. Find Jenny and let her know we're ready. You kids have a lot of studying to do. I'm afraid you may have to pull an all-nighter on this one."

The last part of what Gertrude said was lost in the squeal of excitement. Agatha and Gertrude quickly escorted the foursome out of the research room.

The man with the six-inch beard watched them leave and shook his head. "Kids!" Xavier heard him say. The man pushed himself away from the desk and headed for the kitchenette to pour himself his eighth cup of coffee.

Jenny outfitted the four young time travelers with what she called "the essentials" in gold country. The boys each got a pair of Levi's pants with suspenders, some dark, loose-fitting button-up shirts, a white dress shirt, dark dress pants, a pair of tall black boots that went up to the knee, hats with wide brims, and dark coats. The girls each received three patterned cotton dresses with long sleeves, lace details around the collar and cuffs and bonnets to match, button-up boots, petticoats and bloomers that Nina described as "big balloon underwear," aprons, and cloth coats. They also received a variety of smaller props: lace handkerchiefs for the ladies, pocket watches and Bowie knives for the boys. They each received four hundred dollars' worth of double eagle gold coins.

"Coins were preferred then, before Federal Reserve notes existed and the States were all making their own paper money, which was easy to counterfeit," Jenny explained.

"What about guns?" Xavier asked.

"No guns," Jenny said.

"A lot of young men our age had guns."

"You two won't be among them. The gold towns are like your typical Wild West towns; there may be a sheriff, there may be vigilante justice, there may be very little law at all. But one thing everybody agrees on is that you don't shoot an unarmed man. Therefore, you will remain unarmed."

"But what if we need to defend ourselves against a bear?"

"Xave, what are you talking about?" Xanthe said. "You don't know how to use a gun!"

"You're forgetting laser tag," Xavier said.

"Oh, give me a break!" Xanthe said, rolling her eyes. "I thought you were against guns!"

"That's in the twenty-first century," Xavier answered. "I'm now going to be a man in the nineteenth century, and I think I should have one. It was just a tool back then, like a hammer."

"I'd prefer not to have a gun," Rowan said. "I know I'd only end up shooting myself. I whack my thumb with a hammer every time I use one."

"Forget it, Xave," Xanthe said. "No gun!"

When they arrived at the Owatannauk Hotel, it had already gone through its silver hour transformation. Otto was waiting by the alleviators, the twelve vestibules of time travel. Though they looked very much like elevators on the outside, they emitted a chiming sort of hum, like the sound of thousands of crystal glasses being played. He handed them each a sparkling alleviator key. Rowan put his key to his ear.

"I don't hear anything," he said.

"Maybe you've got wax in your ears," Nina said dryly.

Xavier walked up to Otto and peered into his eyes, moving closer and closer until their noses nearly touched. He knew Otto was a robot, but the craftsmanship was flawless. Otto's skin looked real, right down to the blemishes on his cheeks, the few brown hairs in his silver barbershop mustache, and the red blood vessels in the whites of his eyes, which had a peculiarity about them.

"May I help you?" Otto asked, unperturbed by Xavier's invasion of his personal space.

"Your eyes are different colors," Xavier said. "One's brown and one's blue."

"It is hereditary. Now, I believe it is time for your departure," Otto said, gesturing to the alleviators. "You'll be leaving from alleviator number two. Because of your new frequent-flier status your alleviator keys will allow you to travel for as long as a month, though twenty-eight days is probably a more precise number. If you need more time, you'll have to send someone back to recharge the keys."

"Xanthe! Xavier!" It was Nana, rushing up to the alleviators, waving for them to come out. While Rowan and Nina helped Gertrude set the coordinates, Xanthe and Xavier joined their grandmother outside the glittering machines.

"What's wrong, Nana?" Xanthe asked, her eyes darting toward the others. Xavier knew she wanted to be inside helping; it bothered her not to be in control.

"Listen," Nana said, drawing her shawl closer around her shoulders, "I wanted to talk to you before you left. To prepare you." Xavier and Xanthe waited for the old woman to gather her thoughts. When she lifted her face, her eyes were troubled.

"You kids know that you're going back to a time that was pretty tough for our people . . ."

"We know, we know, Nana," Xanthe assured her.

"No, I don't think you do know," Nana said sharply. Xanthe stopped glancing into the alleviator and straightened up, attentive.

"First of all, you're not used to being treated like you're lesser than," she said. "You two have grown up protected from all that mess. But you're going back to a time before the Civil Rights movement. Make no mistake; the fight over slavery was not a fight to give dark-skinned folks equality. A lot of the people who argued against slavery, even Abraham Lincoln for that matter, still thought that dark-skinned folks were inferior. The best you can hope for is that people you meet treat you like you're human, and you don't want to know the worst, but I'm sure you can imagine."

Xavier was quiet. He had a very good imagination. It was rare that he let his mind drift into those darker areas, images that turned his stomach and shriveled his guts. Even now it made him shudder, and he tuned her out. What was she trying to do anyway? Ruin the trip?

"You're gonna be called things you're not used to being called. *Colored* and *Negro* are acceptable terms for our people in that time. But you might be called some other things, things that will offend you. And you know what you're going to do about it? Nothing. Don't do a thing. Just let it roll off you like water off a duck's back. Our people had a lot worse things to worry about than name-calling. You hear me, Xavier?"

"Nana, I said I was listening," he answered, but she had hit a nerve. When he stepped into the alleviator, he could feel a heavy knot forming in his stomach, he could feel his shoulders sink, and at that moment he hated her for it.

+ CHAPTER FIVE +
GATEWAY TO GOLD

THEY ARRIVED IN SAN FRANCISCO AT THE SILVER HOUR. It was the first day of June, 1857, and though they had gotten little sleep, the four young time travelers arrived energized, focused, and ready to tackle their mission. They were also freezing.

Gertrude had set them at the end of a long pier that extended two thousand feet into the bay from the mainland, reasoning that there would be few people out there and that the San Francisco fog would provide excellent cover.

Seeing the fog through an eyepiece was one thing; standing in the middle of it was quite another. Xavier shuffled toward the others. They were only a few feet away, but in this thick mist a few feet made a big difference. All he could see were the wooden slats of the pier extending ahead into nothingness. He couldn't exactly see the ocean, but he could smell the brine, he could taste the salt in the air, and he could hear the water slapping against the pylons. The sound of boats knocking against the pier and the lonely cry of invisible seagulls seemed strangely haunting.

"I'm soaked!" yelled Xanthe, over the steady roar of the ocean. "Where's a good Windbreaker when you need it?"

"Yeah, I wish I had my down jacket!" Nina agreed through chattering teeth. "Why is it so cold? Isn't it June?"

"Mark Twain once said that the coldest winter he spent was a summer in San Francisco," Xavier yelled. "He wasn't kidding." He blew a few breath clouds to make his point.

"I think Miss O'Neill gave us each a good blanket," Rowan shouted, gesturing to the trunks they had brought with them. "We can use those . . ."

"No, don't!" Xavier said, stopping Xanthe, who had already lunged for the luggage. "We may be freezing, but we've got to play this right. We supposedly just got here after being on a ship for nine months. We should be used to harsh conditions by now."

"Oh, all right," Xanthe moaned, drawing her shawl closer around her. "I guess if we want to get warm, we'd better find a place to stay."

The friends dragged their trunks along the pier, which seemed endless, but as they approached the wharf the mist dissipated and gradually they were able to identify objects around them. They realized that the pier, indeed the entire bay, was crammed with hundreds of ships, stacked against each other in a maritime traffic jam.

Rowan gave a low whistle. "Wow. What happened here?"

"The Gold Rush," Xavier mused. "Who cares about the ships when there's millions to be made in them thar hills?"

Many of the ships were connected to each other with ramps, creating a floating community of sorts. Some looked as if they had been partially disassembled for wood, others had been resurrected as restaurants, hotels, even a prison. A few of the ships had been incorporated into the wharf as permanent fixtures, locked in by buildings that had gone up around them.

All along the wharf, merchants unloaded boats, fishermen prepared to go out, and shopkeepers started opening their stores.

The foursome had only gone a few feet when a broad-faced man rushed up to them.

"Any of you want a job as a cook?" he said. They looked at him blankly. "Come on now, it's with a decent hotel with plenty of high-tipping customers, you'll have a place to stay, food to eat, and I'll pay you twice what you would get wherever you're from. Where you from?"

"Boston," said Xanthe and Xavier.

"New York," said Rowan and Nina.

"We met on the boat," said Rowan, repeating the story they had been coached to tell.

"Well, I'll pay you twice as much as you can get in Boston or New York, or Timbuktu for that matter," the man said, mopping his damp face with his damp handkerchief.

"Why would you do that?" Nina said. "What's wrong with the job?"

"Nothing's wrong with it!" the man snapped. "It's just that every time I hire somebody, in less than a week off they go to the goldfields! Can't keep anybody around for a real job!" He peered at Rowan, narrowing his eyes. "I suppose you came here for gold, too."

"I was thinking of going in that direction," Rowan admitted.

"I thought so. Fool." He cocked his head, appraising Xanthe. "How about you, young lady?" the man said, mopping his face again. "Colored cooks are in high demand, and you'll get a lot of tips. Your people have a knack for food preparation."

"Ha! Not this one!" Xavier barked. Xanthe cut her eyes at him.

"Thank you, sir, I'll consider it. But right now I need to get my bearings. We only just arrived," Xanthe responded as elegantly as she could.

"You all are wasting my time," the man snapped. He rushed off, and seconds later they could hear him offer the position to someone else. Xanthe smacked Xavier in the head.

"Ow!"

"Stop making jokes at my expense!" Xanthe snapped. "I'm a perfectly good cook!"

"If you say so, but is fried chicken supposed to be burned on the outside and bleeding on the inside?"

"Shut up! That only happened once."

"All I know is even the raccoons stopped raiding our garbage cans for leftovers once you started cooking. And by the way, there's always a lot of leftovers."

Xanthe swatted him again, then glared at Rowan and Nina,

who were laughing. "It's not funny!" Xanthe fumed. She spun on her heel, marched into the street, and was almost run over by a young man dashing by with a torch. Rowan yanked Xanthe back just as two more torch carriers passed, followed by a red, silver-plated wagon with "Knickerbocker 5" painted on it in gold.

The wagon held what looked like an enormous boiler, with another metal piece shaped like a large light bulb in front of it. A long shaft extended from it with a handle that two men were using to draw it forward. Others helped to pull the heavy contraption with ropes. Xavier wouldn't have had any idea what it was except the men propelling it wore fire helmets and the crowd that followed was yelling, "Fire! Fire on Fourth and Mission!"

"It's a fire truck!" Xavier exclaimed.

"Well, duh!" Xanthe answered.

All around them men dropped what they were doing and joined the crowd. A young man with dark curly hair parted in the middle grabbed Rowan and Xavier.

"Come on, fellas! We can use all the hands we can get! It's a big blazer, three houses!"

"But we just got here," Rowan stammered. "We've got luggage . . ."

"Oh! Why didn't you say so?" The man grabbed two of the trunks by the handles and dragged them to the side of the road, parking them near a warehouse.

"Welcome to San Francisco. You're now honorary members of the Knickerbocker Five fire brigade. Let's go!"

"Meet us back here! " Xanthe called out to the boys as they were swept into service.

Xavier generally considered himself to be in pretty good shape, but helping to haul the fire truck up and down the unpaved streets of San Francisco winded him. In the distance smoke rose up like a black stain on the pink morning sky.

By the time they arrived at the scene, the flames had already claimed five houses—flimsy wood-frame dwellings. The street was crowded with volunteers from other fire companies. Several were hand-pumping water from a cistern through a fire wagon and out its hoses. This early fire truck was not as effective as modern-day fire equipment, but there was a respectable gush rising close to a hundred feet high.

But only about half of the volunteers were actually engaged in putting out the fire; the others were in heated argument.

"The men of St. Francis's have got this covered!" growled a man with a helmet that had "St. Francis Hook & Ladder" stamped on it. "Don't you Knickerbockers try to sweep in at the last minute and take credit for it!"

"Excuse me, but the Social Three got here first!" cried out a man with a helmet that read the same.

"You must be joking," the St. Francis man retorted. "Social Three's as slow as January molasses."

"Excuse me," Rowan shouted, tugging on the sleeve of one of the St. Francis men. "But the fire is spreading!"

Indeed the fire had claimed a sixth house. A middle-aged man and woman stumbled out in their nightclothes, dragging a hastily packed trunk.

Rowan grabbed Xavier by the arm. "Come on, let's help!"

They joined the other volunteers, who were rushing into the buildings and reemerging with furniture, paintings, and anything else they could salvage.

As Xavier carried out a box of china plates, he noticed one of the Social Three firefighters rummaging through one of the boxes that had just been saved. The man produced three bottles of champagne to a round of cheers from his fellow firefighters. He then proceeded to pop off the corks and pass the bottles around to the others.

Suddenly Xavier heard yelling and the clash of metal. A fight had broken out among the Sailor Eights, the Lafayette Hook and Ladder Co., and the High-Toned Twelve, who had just arrived wearing frock coats and stovepipe hats. They were bashing at each other with crowbars and pieces of wood and throwing rocks from the street. On top of that, a brawl had broken out among the Knickerbockers and the Social Three.

"The Social Three are only good for parades, glee clubs, and granny socials!"

"The Knickerbockers are nothing but villains and varmints!"

"Social Three's a bunch of dandies and drunkards!"

Meanwhile the fire raged on.

Xavier saw the dark-haired man who had recruited them leaning against a house on the other side of the street, writing in a small notebook. He struck a rather elegant figure in his striped gray pants, dark blue vest, and white shirt, which shone brightly compared to the sooty clothes of the other volunteers. Xavier ran over to him.

"Excuse me, but we're new in town. What the heck is going on here?!"

"Hmm?" the man said, looking up. "Oh. They're very competitive, you know. Always arguing over who's the best. They have a lot of pride in their organizations. Knickerbockers are New Yorkers. Sailor Eights are sailors, of course. Lafayette Hook and Ladder are Frenchmen . . ." He nonchalantly flicked a spark from his coat.

"But the fire! Nobody's doing anything about it!"

"Oh, it'll go out in time. See?" he gestured across the street. "They've contained it to this block. Not bad, considering the last fire took five blocks. That was two weeks ago. And the week before that we lost two blocks of houses on Telegraph Hill. That was the same week the Jenny Lind Theatre went up for the third time . . ."

Suddenly a large board flew out from the fighting men and landed in a puddle nearby. The young man looked down at his patent leather boots, now splattered with mud, and his lip curled in disgust. "Let's get out of here," he said. "It's getting dangerous."

As Xavier and Rowan walked back to the wharf with the man, he continued to jot things down in his notebook. Finally he put it in his pocket.

"I'm Francis Harte," he said, extending his hand. "My friends call me Bret."

Rowan's eyes lit up. "You mean the writer?"

"Yes . . . have you read my work?"

"I sure have! I'm a big fan! I must've read all of your short stories about the—Ow!" Rowan rubbed his arm where the hard pinch from Xavier had left an angry red mark.

"As a matter of fact I haven't written any short stories," Bret Harte said. "Just some poetry and a few articles . . . Do you read *The Golden Era* magazine? Or perhaps *Knickerbocker* magazine in New York? I've had a few things published there."

"Yeah, that must've been it," Rowan mumbled, glaring at Xavier who glared right back.

"It's funny you should mention it," Bret continued. "I was thinking of writing some short stories. That's why I joined the fire brigade. I wanted to get ideas."

"Well, you certainly weren't there to help," Xavier grumbled under his breath.

"Of course I helped. I recruited you two, didn't I?"

"Yeah? Well, how did you run up and down all those hills without getting dirty like the rest of us?" Rowan asked, wiping some of the grime from his eyes.

"Because I wasn't running up and down the hills," Bret chuckled. "I was perched on the back of the fire engine. You may have noticed it felt about a hundred and sixty pounds heavier at one point . . . that was me. I should apologize . . . normally I'm a hundred and fifty, but I had a big breakfast."

The boys laughed, and Bret joined them. He offered Rowan his handkerchief but Rowan declined. "What I really need is a place to take a bath," Rowan said. "We should find the girls and a hotel room."

"There are plenty to choose from," Bret said. "That is, if they haven't burned down yet . . . I'm kidding," he said when he saw Rowan's alarmed look. "My hotel's pretty nice, the Mark Hopkins. It's five stories—tallest building in the city. A little pricey, though, twenty-eight dollars a night. If that's not to your liking there are plenty of other hotels and flophouses. I don't recommend those for the ladies, though, not unless they like to bed down with bugs, and plenty of them." He turned to Xavier. "You'll probably find a place to stay between Clark's Point and Telegraph Hill . . . they call it Chili Hill. Lots of good places run by your people." It took Xavier a moment to understand his meaning.

"Oh. Yes, of course. A Negro hotel."

"And I happen to know a good one. It's a boardinghouse run by a woman by the name of Mammy Pleasants. She'll take care of you and your . . . was that your wife?"

"Sister!" Xavier corrected quickly. It never ceased to amaze him how people always mistook him for being older than he was. He and Xanthe were only fourteen! But then it occurred to him that childhood ended much earlier for kids in the eighteen hundreds; once you hit adolescence you were basically a young adult, eligible for marriage and capable of making a living on your own. This was, after all, what they were pretending to be: four young people hoping to make good lives out west.

Bret had opened up his notebook. "Can you read?" he said, jotting down the address.

"Of course I can read! What do you think I . . ." Now it was Rowan's turn to pinch Xavier's arm. Xavier shot him a look, which Rowan answered with a smirk.

"I mean, I learned ciphering and such from a kindly gentleman who frequented my pa's barbershop," Xavier said humbly. Bret ripped the page from his notebook and handed it to him.

"Good. Here's the address, then." Bret turned to Rowan. "Perhaps I'll see you later, if you choose to stay at the Mark Hopkins. I suppose you all are only stopping here until you can get up to the gold mines."

"To tell you the truth, my sister and I are here looking for our uncle, who we think might be out in the goldfields, but we don't really know where he is. Xavier and his sister, Xanthe, just happened to be on the boat with us . . ."

"I was ship's steward," Xavier interrupted. He suddenly imagined himself the polished and efficient caretaker of the captain's needs, a behind-the-scenes expert on everything about the operation of the ship.

"Took us only three and a half months on the clipper ship," he continued, warming to his story. "Had some pretty rough storms around Cape Horn on the tip of South America, almost lost a few men, including Mr. Popplewell here. One huge swell just toppled him right over the side, and the ship had gone pretty far before anyone noticed. To make matters worse, a shark was heading right for him. Folks didn't know what to do;

his sister was beside herself. So I hitched a life ring to the end of a whale harpoon, aimed it at the beast, shot it right into his cold, black eye, and killed him. We pulled in Mr. Popplewell and had shark steaks for supper."

"Well!" Bret said. "That's some tale!"

"Yeah. Some tale," Rowan muttered. "We'd better be going. It was nice to make your acquaintance." He held out his hand. Bret shook it.

"Good luck." Bret took his notebook back out of his pocket as he strode down the dirt street.

"What was all that about?" Rowan said as they walked back to the warehouse where they had stowed their trunks.

"What?"

"That crazy story! Clipper ships? Sharks? Harpoons? That's not what we agreed on!"

"It's just to make it more interesting. If you're going to tell a story, you might as well make it a good one."

"Well if you want to paint yourself as a hero, that's your business," Rowan said. "But don't make me the dope, all right? And we're supposed to be inconspicuous, you know; we don't want to attract attention. Just keep the stories simple—"

"All right, all right, I hear you," Xavier said, cutting Rowan off. Rowan was a good guy, but he had a habit of sucking the fun out of an adventure. He was forever playing it safe.

They found the girls coming out of a shop near the warehouse.

"We found the Ghirardelli chocolate shop!" Nina squealed,

holding out a bag full of the confections. "And the original Levi's pants store. And dry goods stores and fancy clothing shops, banks, restaurants . . . and tons of places to buy mining supplies!"

"Yeah, and we found a lot of crackpot inventions, too. Like an ointment you can spread all over your body that's supposed to attract gold dust," Xanthe laughed. "And a submarine suit to help you get any gold that's underwater. I bet it drowns anyone who tries to use it."

"Are you hungry?" Nina asked. "Because there are all kinds of restaurants around. Chinese, Spanish, French, Italian, Mexican . . . just like the food court at the mall! But no smoothies," she added with a giggle.

"I'm starving," Xavier said. "How about that fish place down the block? We can leave the trunks for a couple of hours more. They seem pretty safe here."

The "fish place" was owned by a Portuguese chef. They were seated immediately by an eager waiter who spoke little English but who understood Xanthe's Spanish well enough to take their orders. After the boys described their firefighting ordeal and their meeting with Bret Harte, the food arrived. It didn't resemble in the least anything they thought they'd ordered, but they were too hungry to complain, and settled into discussing their next move.

"First we have to figure out if Balt and Oliver stayed in town or if they went to gold country," Xanthe began.

"I'm guessing gold country, for the adventure," reasoned Xavier. "And it's easier to lose yourself there. I say we just hit each town, one by one."

"I just thought of something," Rowan said. "What if they struck it rich and already went home?"

"I doubt that happened," Xanthe said. "First of all, it doesn't matter what Oliver decides to do—we know Balt isn't going back to Bloomington. Secondly, we're close to the end of the Gold Rush. All the easy pickings are gone. People out here now are here for the long haul. Hopefully Balt and Oliver signed up with a crew somewhere. It'll make them easier to find."

"We don't even know what Oliver Weber looks like," Nina added.

"Well, somebody does," Rowan said. "We'll just get them to point him out to us."

When they returned to where they'd left their trunks, the fog, which had been gone for most of the afternoon, was beginning to roll in from the water, covering the sky with a uniform gray gloominess and making it difficult to discern the time of day. It felt like evening, however, and they were all stifling yawns.

"I think Nina and I will give the Mark Hopkins a try," Rowan said. "And don't worry, I'm not going to bug Bret Harte. I know he's an important writer and I shouldn't do anything to alter his history, blah blah blah."

"You'd better not," cautioned Xanthe, remembering the mistake she made on their last trip. "He's going to be huge in

about ten years . . ." Rowan waved her off, simultaneously sig-
naling a passing carriage, which stopped. The driver jumped
down from his perch and hoisted the two trunks into the back
of the carriage.

"We'll see you guys tomorrow. Eight o'clock at the stagecoach depot." Rowan turned to the driver. "Mark Hopkins
Hotel please." The driver nodded. Rowan turned back to the
twins. "You guys are gonna be OK getting a ride?"

"Us? Of course!" Xanthe laughed.

"Yeah, the Alexanders can take care of themselves," Xavier
added with swagger. "Go on, get out of here. Get some sleep!"

With a crack of the whip Rowan and Nina's carriage
whisked them off.

After the dust settled, Xavier turned to Xanthe. "What do
you think the chances are that we'll be able to flag down a nice
big carriage like that one?" he said doubtfully.

"Let's buy a cart," his sister sighed. "I know a store that sells
them."

They picked up their trunks by the handles and dragged
them down the street.

+ CHAPTER SIX +
A PLEASANT EVENING

Xavier and Xanthe weren't sure what to expect of the Pleasants Boardinghouse. They were pleased to discover a three-story clapboard-style house, with pink daisies brightening up the window boxes and a bed of purple snapdragons along the footpath. Xavier had to admit he had expected the businesses and living quarters of brown-skinned people in this day and age to be meager and shabby. This house looked downright inviting. The sign on the door stating "Come on in" expressed as much.

Inside, a young woman with a round face and skin the warm color of cocoa sat behind a small table reading a newspaper called *North Star*, another surprise as far as Xavier was concerned.

"Hello," he said, removing his hat. The girl looked up. Her high cheeks shone in the lamplight.

"May I help you?" she asked. Xavier grinned.

"Yes, you may indeed. My sister and I are looking for a place to stay for the night."

"Just one night? That's a shame."

In that instant Xavier also felt it was a shame and considered maybe staying for more than one night. The sour look on Xanthe's face nixed that proposition. He turned back to the girl. "Yes, just one night," he sighed.

"We have to leave tomorrow," Xanthe said. "We're going to gold country."

"A lot of people are," the girl said, writing something in a ledger. "I wish you luck. Mr. Frederick Douglass says if the Negro is going to ever amount to anything in this country, he's got to stake his claim in the land along with everybody else. If we don't get ours while the gettin's good, we'll be out in the cold." She caught herself, smiling as an apology for her passionate outburst. "Would you like two rooms with one bed or one room with two beds?"

Xavier was feeling bold. "Two rooms, please." He enjoyed the surprised look on Xanthe's face. The girl handed him two keys, one of which he passed to his sister.

"I'm Xavier Alexander, hailing from Boston, Massachusetts. Am I speaking to Mrs. Mammy Pleasants?"

The girl's eyes widened. She shook her head as if in warning, but it was too late.

"Mammy *what*?!" A voice howled. "Don't you ever refer to me by that slave name!" The parlor doors flew open and there stood a thin, honey-colored woman in a black dress with a high, white collar. One of her eyelids was half closed, giving that side of her face a sort of sleepy look, but the other eye was fierce, and bore into Xavier like a drill. It was difficult to tell how old she was; she had the hardened, timeless look of petrified wood.

"I beg your pardon," Xavier said, bowing humbly. "I meant no disrespect. That was the name given to me by the person who recommended your establishment."

"Must've been a white fella then," the woman sniffed. "You call me by my Christian name, Mary Ellen Pleasants . . . though you look like you *should* be calling me 'mother.' How old are you anyway?"

"Sixteen," Xanthe and Xavier lied in unison.

"Well, from the looks of you, you're not runaway slaves. You don't have the attitude. What brings you to San Francisco? I like to know who's staying in my house."

"Our parents passed away from sickness," Xavier said. "Our father's dying wish was for us to come out and make something of ourselves in the West."

"That's right," added Xanthe. "Many a time he told us this was a land of opportunity."

"Did he now?" Mary Ellen appraised the twins for a moment. "Well, if you really want to set yourself up, you'll forget about being gold miners and open up a store that *sells* to gold miners. The big rush is over but there's still plenty of greed to go around. People pouring in by the droves. And they all want a place to stay, a place to eat, clothes, equipment . . . that's where the money is."

"I'd like to try my hand at mining first," Xavier said.

Mary Ellen shrugged. "Makes no never mind to me. Do what you want." She started back into the parlor, then hesitated and turned back to the girl behind the table. "Lucy, have somebody take those trunks," she said, and then, turning to the twins, said, "Why don't you two come with me? You might be interested in what's going on in here."

They followed her into the room. There sat a group of dark-skinned businessmen, all elegantly dressed in suits. Three of them wore silk vests, and they all wore crisp white shirts with straight collars and ties that wound around the neck to be knotted in a bow. Xavier felt that the only shabby thing in the room was himself.

"Gentlemen, these two young people are new in town, just got off the boat from Boston," Mary Ellen announced.

One of the men rose. He held his cigar aloft as he hooked his thumb in his suspenders. "I'm from Boston. What's your name?"

"I'm Xavier Alexander, this is my sister, Xanthe," Xavier said.

"Can't say I know that name," the man said. "But I'm John Bowen. President of the Athenaeum Institute. Welcome. We were in the middle of a meeting."

"I'm sorry, we don't mean to interrupt . . ." Xanthe began.

"Nonsense," Mary Ellen said, steering them both toward a free sofa. "If you want to get anywhere out here, this is the place to be. This here is the headquarters of Negro activism in California."

"Well, not *here*, Mary Ellen," corrected a man wearing a minister's collar. "We're only meeting here until we get a new building," he explained to the twins. "We used to be located on Washington Street, right over the Athenaeum Saloon, but to tell the truth, it seemed out of place to have our respectable organization perched on top of a den of gambling and spirits. We Negroes have to be mindful of our image. White folks already think little enough of us as it is without our people hooting and hollering, drunk and destitute from gambling."

A round of *hear hears* erupted from the group.

"Reverend, as long as I own a piece of that saloon and those Negroes pay for their drinks, they can hoot and holler all they like," Mary Ellen retorted. "We colored folks may have to be mindful of our image, but there should be a place we can go to let down our hair."

"You've got places for that, Mary Ellen," said another man, this one with a white beard. "They say the ladies there let down a lot more than their hair." Mary Ellen turned her sleepy eye on him, a smile tugging at her cheek.

"You would know, Samuel. You would know all about it."

"Let's get back to what we were discussing before the interruption," John Bowen said quickly. "We need to set the agenda for the next Colored Convention."

"Colored Convention? What's that?" Xanthe asked.

"What's that? You haven't heard about the Colored Conventions? We've already had three! Wasn't it reported on the East Coast?"

"They're young," Mary Ellen said. "Maybe they can't read." She turned to Xavier and Xanthe. "This is why I wanted you to come in. You've got to become a part of this. We're all out here on a mission, you understand? I don't care if you're out here for gold, if you're running away, or if you were dragged here. We've all got the same mission, and that is to survive.

"Now, you may think you're safe in California because it's a free state, and we have some successful Negroes running businesses out here, but our work is far from over. Just this year the Supreme Court passed down that horrible Dred Scott decision . . . says that Negroes in this country have no rights that a white man has to respect."

"It's outrageous that a black man can't testify against a white man in court!" the reverend muttered bitterly. "Doesn't matter that there are murderers walking around who could be in jail where they belong. Oh no! A black man is lower than a white murderer, I guess."

"With the Democrats in charge, I'm not sure another convention is going to do any good at all," one of the businessmen said. "We're going to have to pray for a miracle."

"We're not praying for anything," Mary Ellen snapped. "The Lord helps those who help themselves. If we just sat around trying to pray our problems away, young Chester Lee here wouldn't be with us today. He'd be picking tobacco somewhere in Mississippi." She hooked her thumb at the young man with soft gray eyes, sitting in the corner.

"Not true," Chester said. "I'd be dead. I'd kill myself before I'd work on another plantation."

"What happened?" Xavier asked, always eager for a good story.

"Well, I'll try to keep it short, but it's been a long journey to be sure. See, I was a slave, brought out here from Mississippi by Mr. Charles Stovall, who was the son of my owner. Mr. Stovall settled in Sacramento and hired me out to people, pocketing the money for himself, of course. He opened up a school where he taught for a few months, but then he started getting worried. See, the law says that a man cannot own a slave in California unless he's just passing through. Stovall realized that if he stayed much longer, he might have to set me free. Well, he didn't want to go back to Mississippi himself, but he tried to send me back, and I didn't want to go. So I ran off and hid . . . anyway, he searched me out and had me arrested.

"Now, it was apparent to just about everybody that Mr. Stovall was not just 'passing through' California. The law was on my side. But when the case went to court, the judge found for Mr. Stovall, saying that since he was inexperienced and young, he had obviously just made a mistake, and I should be given back to him and shipped out to Mississippi. Well, that put the colored community in an uproar. Stovall knew he was on thin ice and tried to sneak me out secretly by boat. Little did he know, members of the Negro community, some of these people right in this very room, were patrolling the wharves and the docks every night, looking for any sign of my leaving."

"That's right," the reverend broke in. "We found out Chester was being held on Angel Island, ready to be smuggled onto the *Orizaba*, heading to Panama. When they tried it, we were right there. We had Mr. Stovall served with a writ for keeping a slave illegally. That started a whole slew of legal battles, but this time we hired better lawyers . . ."

"They cost a pretty penny, but it was worth it," added Mary Ellen.

"The whole community paid for it. It was a beautiful thing," said Chester. "I owe a debt of gratitude to every Negro in San Francisco and Sacramento. For the first time, I've got real freedom—to go where I want, do what I want . . . it's a blessing."

"And that Fugitive Slave Law is dangerous for us, too," John said grimly. "Kidnappers snatch up Negroes and ship them back to the slave states, even if they were never slaves to begin with! If a black man can't produce a piece of paper that says he's legally free, those scoundrels haul him out, bound and shackled, hidden in the cloak of night, and off he goes to the South."

"And heaven forbid someone thinks you're guilty of something," the reverend added. "You'll find yourself dangling from a noose before a judge even gets his robe on."

"We've obviously got a lot of work to do," Mary Ellen said, turning to the twins. "You better get some rest. Stagecoach leaves early. Don't want to catch the afternoon stage if you can help it. It's a lot dustier in the heat of the day."

She led them back to the reception area, where Lucy had returned to her newspaper.

"I must say, ma'am, that is an impressive group of people in there," Xavier said.

"What did you expect?" Mary Ellen answered, slightly annoyed. Xavier gave her an embarrassed smile. As they mounted the stairs, Mary Ellen called after them.

"Just remember, like it or not, you're part of this mission. You're one of us."

"Yes, ma'am," Xanthe said.

"Breakfast is between six and nine in the dining room. Get there early if you want the cinnamon buns."

"Yes, ma'am."

The old woman disappeared into the parlor. Xavier and Xanthe climbed the stairs and went to bed.

+ CHAPTER SEVEN +
A HARD RIDE

THE CINNAMON BUNS, DRIPPING WITH HONEY AND brown sugar, were worth the early wake-up. Xavier gobbled up three, and then stuffed two more in his pockets for later. Chester was also at breakfast, having decided to take the stagecoach to the gold mines as well.

"Now that I'm a free man, I may as well try my luck," he said. "I'm not much for owning a business. I like working outside, in the fresh air."

They departed with a terse nod from Mary Ellen Pleasants, whom Xavier thought in many ways resembled Nana. Soon they reached the depot where Rowan and Nina were already waiting by the ticket window.

"We went ahead and bought your tickets," Rowan said as they walked up.

"Thanks," Xanthe said. "This is Chester Lee. He may be joining us." They all introduced themselves.

"We brought somebody, too," Nina said just as Bret Harte exited the depot. Unlike the serviceable clothing that the rest of them wore, he was dressed in pinstriped gray slacks, a boiled white shirt and red vest, a black frock coat, and a top hat. *The word* dandy *was created just for him*, Xavier thought.

"Good morning!" Bret cried out. "How was your stay with Mammy Pleasants?" Xavier sensed Chester bristling.

"She doesn't care for that name, sir," Chester said politely. "She prefers Miss Mary Ellen."

"Oh, well, I'll have to remember that," answered Bret. "I do apologize. But however she is addressed, she runs an elegant house. Once you eat her cinnamon buns, you feel like you've died and gone to heaven. I do believe if I close my eyes I can still smell their sweetness."

Xavier closed his hand over the secret stash in his pockets.

"I decided to roam back through the gold country to tickle my muse," Bret continued. "I've already tried my hand at mining; dredging gold from the ground is too laborious for my tastes. But it occurred to me that I could probably dredge up some excellent stories. Folks on the East Coast wouldn't believe some of the rollicking adventures people have had out here in gold country. Those stories could turn into a gold mine of their own."

As Bret ambled off to light his cigar, Xavier pulled Rowan aside. "I thought you said you weren't going to get involved with him!"

"This was totally his idea! I didn't say anything—honest!

He was here at the depot before we were!" Rowan's eyes twinkled. "Come on, it'll be fun! We just have to be careful, that's all."

Xavier relented. Who was he kidding? He'd love to hang around with Bret Harte. He was more surprised that Rowan, who was usually cautious, was willing to take the chance. Perhaps the spirit of the Wild West was having an effect on him.

"Hey, look at this!" Nina said, pointing at a sign on the wall. They all gathered around. It was a large poster that read:

TIPS FOR THE STAGECOACH TRAVELER

1. The best seat on the stage is the one behind the driver.

2. In cold weather, don't ride with tight-fitting gloves or boots. Do not grease your hair or dust will stick there in sufficient quantities to make a respectable 'tater patch.

3. Don't growl at the food received at the station—we provide the best we can get.

4. Don't keep the stage waiting. Many a

virtuous man has lost his character by so
doing.

5. Don't smoke a strong pipe inside the
coach.

6. Spit on the leeward side.

7. If you have anything to drink in a bottle,
pass it around.

8. Don't lean or lop over your neighbors
when you are sleeping.

9. Never shoot on the road—the noise might
frighten the horses. Careless handling and
cocking of weapons makes nervous people
nervous.

10. Don't discuss politics or religion.

11. Don't point out where murders have been
committed, especially if there are women
passengers.

12. Expect annoyances, discomfort, and
some hardships.

"Pretty funny," Nina giggled.

"I'm not laughing, little miss," Chester said. "You should pay close attention to these rules. Stagecoach travel is not for the faint of heart."

"Take a look at these," Xanthe said, perusing an array of Wanted posters tacked to the wall. Xavier took a look.

WANTED: DEAD OR ALIVE
FOUR FINGERS MARKHAM
a.k.a.
THREE FINGERS MARKHAM
For the robbery of banks and the murder of three good men. Description: Six feet five inches, heavyset, black hair, beard, missing one or two fingers on right hand.
$5,000.00 REWARD

WANTED: ALIVE
LARRY "THE RATTLESNAKE" DOOLAN
For robbery of banks and horse thievery. Description: Six feet six inches tall, lean. Yellow hair, yellow eyes, yellow teeth. Long knife scars on both cheeks.
$3,000.00 REWARD

WANTED: ALIVE
LEW "BLACK RABBIT" RABBET
For robbery of stagecoaches. Description:
Five feet six inches, black hair, clean
shaven. Known to wear black clothing, rides
a black horse. Crazy eyes.
$3,000.00 REWARD

Just as Xavier finished reading the last poster, a thunderous sound filled his ears. In the distance he saw a coach approaching fast, pulled by six powerful-looking horses, their manes flapping wildly. Xavier felt giddy, almost as though it were Santa Claus's sled pulling up and not a clattering stagecoach.

As they drew closer, the man in the driver's seat pulled back on the reins, and the horses slowed to a quick trot. They halted with almost perfect precision in front of the depot, followed by a cloud of dust.

Immediately a flurry of teenage boys appeared, leaping up from the various benches where they had been biding their time, waiting for this momentous occasion. Two of them raced over with a team of fresh stallions and started to unhitch the sweating horses, while two others helped the passengers out of the carriage.

The driver jumped from his perch, pulling down the kerchief that covered his jack-o-lantern grin. Every other tooth seemed to be missing, and when he spoke a kind of whistle played among the holes in his mouth.

"I've faced down robbers, scallywags, and bloodthirsty savages, but I have never seen a band of hooligans as uncouth and coarse as this bunch right here," he said, jerking his thumb at the hostlers, who howled and slapped their knees, laughing convulsively at a joke that Xavier was certain they'd heard a million times.

One of the boys handed the driver a canteen, and another passed him a lit pipe, and the driver sat on the bench and enjoyed a smoke as he watched the young men scurry about.

"How you folks doing?" he asked the four friends, who were gawking at all the activity. "This your first time on a stagecoach?"

"Yes, sir," Rowan answered. The others nodded as well.

"Well, you're in for a treat. See this?" he said, pointing at the gaps in his mouth. "Lost most of 'em from hitting bumps in the road. The vibrations rattled them right out of my head!"

"Good morning, sir," Bret Harte said, extending a hand, which the driver shook. "You been traveling all night?"

"Just about, just about," the driver grinned. "I'm Jim Canby, but my friends call me Curly. We're going to get to know each other real good, so you go ahead and call me Curly."

"All right, Curly," Bret said. "Though it's a strange nickname for someone with hair as straight as yours."

"It describes my lip duster," Curly said, twisting the tips

of his mustache, which were curled into impressive spirals. "Though some say it's a fair description of my brain." With that he let out a whistle and a cackle that convinced all present that the name was clearly based on the latter.

"We'll get you folks set up right quick. This your luggage?" he asked, pointing to the collection of bags. "You're allowed twenty-five pounds each, that's all the space I can spare."

"This is a beautiful coach, sir," Xavier said, and he meant it. Even under the dust the body of the maroon-and-gold coach gleamed from the varnish, and somebody had gone to the trouble of painting a detailed landscape on the door: a flock of sheep grazing on a bright green meadow. Two lamps hung on the sides of the coach, and the interior was upholstered in padded leather and damask cloth.

"It's a Concord Coach, young man, made in New Hampshire," Curly said proudly. "It's the best there is, and I've ridden all kinds of broken-down heaps. And Mr. Butterfield, the man who owns this operation, provides the best horses. Big, rollicking beasts they are, up for anything. That's considerably different from my previous employers. With those folks I'd come in from a long ride and all they had to refresh my team was a few mangy mules. Made me look like a clown on a circus wagon." He turned to the station agent. "Got anything I can toss down my gullet before we move on?"

"Of course, Curly. I wouldn't let you starve."

The station agent snapped his fingers and one of the boys ducked into the depot, then reappeared with a plate filled with something that could've been beef stew. Xavier didn't inspect it too closely; the strong unappetizing smell wafting from it kept him at a distance. Curly didn't bat an eye, however, and started scooping the mess into his mouth with great slurps of enjoyment. In no time the plate was empty.

"Let's get a move on," Curly said, suppressing a burp. The hostlers had already loaded the luggage onto the top of the coach, and so Xavier, Xanthe, Rowan, and Nina scrambled in the carriage, fighting for the seat behind the driver. Nina won, easily slipping her petite frame under the traffic jam at the door. She settled into the coveted spot while the others watched helplessly, their shoulders wedged up against each other. After that it didn't seem to matter where you sat, so Bret and Rowan sat next to her, and Xavier, Xanthe, and Chester sat across from them. The coach was about four feet wide, so it was a tight fit, but at least nobody had to sit in the center seat, which had no back at all, only a leather strap for support.

With one leap Curly was up in his seat, whip in hand. "I suppose you've got some mailbags for me," he called down to the station agent.

"That I do," the agent replied. He shouted out and a youth emerged from the station lugging two huge sacks. Then a second came out with two more. There was no room on top, so the bags were tossed inside the carriage, forcing the passengers to lift their feet and rest them on top.

With a crack of the whip, the coach lurched forward and careered down the road.

The annoyance, discomfort, and hardship began almost immediately. Rowan described the ride as akin to sitting inside an earthquake-simulation machine. Nina likened it to being inside a snow globe while it was being shaken. Xavier thought it felt like they were trapped in a toy wagon that a giant baby was bouncing off the ground. To make matters worse, one of the mailbags had opened, spilling its contents. Now the passengers had to be on the lookout for flying envelopes and packages.

Conversation was impossible. The pounding hooves and clattering wheels drowned out all but the loudest exclamations, such as, "Ow! That stupid box smacked me in the eye!" and, "Hey! Get your elbow out of my ear!" Not that anyone wanted to talk. If you opened your mouth, it was instantly filled with the dust swirling through the windows. It didn't matter what you looked like at the start of the trip; in less than an hour everyone was the same gray color. Every once in a while Bret dusted off his jacket with his handkerchief, but it was a losing battle; the handkerchief was just as filthy as everything else. Eventually he copied Chester, who had taken his handkerchief and tied it around his mouth. This reminded the time travelers to check their pockets. Sure enough, Jenny the librarian had the forethought to provide them with kerchiefs. In no time they looked like the most ridiculous band of outlaws in the West.

The fact that they were wedged into the seats made up for the lack of seat belts, but if a wheel hit a particularly deep rut, they would pitch forward with such force that they sometimes switched seats with whoever was across from them. After an hour of the bone-jarring trip, Xavier had just about had it. His eyes felt gritty, his mouth felt gritty, even his brain felt gritty. As he rubbed his eyes he noticed that the windows had curtains. "Rowan, close the curtains!" he yelled, sliding the black leather covering across the window on his side.

Rowan did the same, plunging them into darkness.

Now the flying boxes were even harder to dodge. The dust hung in the air with a depressing staleness. Without being able to see the countryside, the swaying of the coach made Xavier queasy. He prayed for an instant, painless death.

"This is—Ow!—worse," moaned Xanthe, grabbing Xavier's hand. She suffered from acute claustrophobia, and this wasn't helping.

"Which . . . is . . . worse . . . Ow! The . . . dust . . . or . . . the . . . dark?" said Rowan.

"I . . . vote . . . for . . . the . . . Whoa!" cried Xanthe, thrown into Bret's lap. "Sorry, Mr. Harte . . ."

"Quite alright, my dear," Bret said, steadying her.

"Open the window!" Xanthe gasped, pulling down her kerchief. "I'm going to be sick!"

Rowan lifted the curtain, and the dust poured in. Fortunately, the carriage rolled to a stop outside a depot. The four friends staggered out for a breath of fresh air while the station agent came to greet them and the hostlers went about their chores.

Xavier ached all over. It felt as if all his joints had popped from their sockets. Rowan, Nina, and Xanthe also looked crooked and misaligned. The only people who didn't seem bothered by the ride were Chester and Bret, who eyed the four friends with a fair amount of amusement.

"I suppose I should have warned you, country roads are not as well maintained as city ones," Bret said. "If you think this is fun, wait until we hit the mountains."

"There's usually a basin on the side of the station," Chester said, leading the way.

The water revived them somewhat, and Xavier was surprised to feel the pinch of hunger. Bret and Curly were already inside the depot and so he, Rowan, and Nina joined them while Xanthe took a walk, still trying to settle her stomach. Chester lingered behind, confirming what Xavier had suspected, that the former slave was smitten with his sister.

The station was an adobe building, made of sun-dried mud bricks. The roof was constructed with grass and mud, and there was a window that was basically a square hole cut into the side of the building, with no glass. Inside there was a fireplace and a table, where Bret and Curly were eating from tin plates and cups.

"What's for lunch?" Xavier asked.

"A recipe of my own. I call it 'bull chowder,'" the station agent said matter-of-factly.

"Sounds . . . delicious," Xavier lied.

He and Rowan sat down to a bowl of the thinnest, sorriest-looking soup Xavier had ever seen. It had chunks of what may have been meat, but then again, they may not. Rowan kicked Xavier under the table and nodded his head at their companions, who were clearly avoiding the chunks of "bull" and spooning up only the broth.

Xavier tried it. He had never tasted old laundry water before, but he was certain he was now. Starvation would be a slower and more pleasant death, so he excused himself and went outside. He hoped that doing some yoga stretches might help realign his body.

Curly finally emerged from the building smoking his pipe. The horses had been replaced and the travelers had resigned themselves to getting back into the carriage. The mailbag with the particularly vicious pointed package had been dropped off at the station so there was slightly more room; at least they wouldn't be seated with their knees bent up to their chins.

"Where you all headed?" Curly said in between puffs.

"I'm not particular," Bret said, coming out after him. He had lit a thin cigarillo and sat on the bench outside the station. "Where do you recommend a man go who is looking for some good stories to tell?"

"Well now, that's an interesting question. There's been adventure and excitement in almost every Gold Rush town I know of. Lemme see, there's the town of Rough and Ready . . . they seceded from the United States in eighteen fifty to get out of paying the mining tax. 'Course, after three months they changed their minds—didn't want to miss out on the Fourth of July celebrations." Curly peeled off a cackle and scratched his patchy beard.

"There's the proud town of Gouge Eye; you can guess what

happened there. Then there's Fiddletown, Squabbletown, Brandy City, Humbug, Drytown, Yellow Jacket Mine, Poverty Hill, Bummerville, Poorman Creek, Jackass Creek, and my favorite place, Hangtown. They've had fine distinction of performing the most hangings in a month. Twelve."

"I'll be stopping off at Negro Hill, sir," Chester said.

"I thought as much," Curly said.

"Is that where a colored man struck it rich after the place had already been scoured by forty-niners?" Bret asked, wagging his cigar at Chester.

"Yes, it certainly is," Chester said. "The whole area's been settled by colored folks now, and they are still finding enough gold to keep them there."

"How about the rest of you?" Curly said. "You're all together, right?"

"To tell you the truth, sir, we're looking for someone," Rowan said. "We just figured we'd start in the northern towns and work our way south. Or vice versa."

Curly hoisted himself up to his perch. "We'll be going to Hangtown, then, if it's all the same with you. I know a gal there who's got a voice like a rusty saw and a body like a potbellied stove, but she's my sweetheart and I haven't seen her in a month."

"Hangtown it is!" cried Bret, stubbing out his cigar. He climbed inside the carriage.

"Hangtown it is," Rowan repeated with much less enthusiasm. He climbed in after Bret, followed by Chester and Xanthe.

"Aren't there any towns with happy names?" Nina asked, stopping at the door. "Like Richtown? Or Motherlode Hill? Or Big Bags of Money Meadows?"

"Sure there are, little lady. There's the town of Gold Bar. That's a nice name."

"Well, why don't you drop us off there?"

"You wouldn't like it. It's a ghost town. Folks thought there was gold there, but there wasn't. They nearly starved, searching and searching. Finally a fire burned most of the place down, gave everyone a reason to leave. Nice name, though."

Nina stepped into the carriage. Xavier was about to follow her, but then he got an idea. "Say, can I join you up there?" he asked Curly.

"You sure can," Curly said. "I'd enjoy the company." Curly pulled up his kerchief.

Xavier eagerly clambered up next to him and pulled his kerchief up as well. Curly cracked the whip only once and the horses charged forward.

+ CHAPTER EIGHT +
A COUPLE OF STORIES

THE VIEW WAS MUCH BETTER FROM THE DRIVER'S SEAT, and the lurching wasn't as bad either, for you could see the terrain and anticipate when the carriage was going to dip or sway. After a while, Xavier was able to relax, though relaxing on the top of a stagecoach still required a strong grip on the seat and keen sense of balance.

"Who are you looking for?" Curly yelled over the clatter of hooves. "Friend or foe?"

Xavier frowned. "I'm not sure," he yelled back.

"You might want to figure it out before you find him," Curly cackled. "You wouldn't want to be surprised by something like that. He could be a changed man, you know. Sometimes gold fever catches hold of someone and changes them. I've seen many a man ruined by the draw of gold. Hope it doesn't happen to you."

"Believe it or not, we're not here for the gold at all, just the friend."

"So it is a friend after all."

"I hope so."

"Me too, for your sake."

The day yawned ahead of them and the monotony of the stagecoach ride began to take its toll. The passengers became used to the rocking motion, the seat ejections, and the occasional flying packages, and so were able to take naps to fill the time. Everyone figured out that Xavier had found the true "best seat," so they switched off whenever they reached a depot, giving Curly a chance to regale each with stories of his adventures through gold country.

Bret spent his time taking notes, though the sudden jolts loosened several pens from his grip. Chester didn't mind staying in the carriage. He brought out a harmonica and played it for a while, and they all sang along to "Oh! Susanna" and "Camptown Races," but they didn't know any of the other songs, so Bret had to sing those solo.

Xavier looked forward to riding on the top, not just because it was less sickening, but because of the extraordinary view. All around them were rolling hills of tall, green grass sprinkled with wildflowers. Curly knew them all: goldenrod tall enough to get lost in, tufts of blue lupines, delicate buttercups, soft purple clover, bright white star lilies, fiery Indian paintbrush, and the gorgeous California poppy, a flower of the deepest orange that looked like its tips had been dipped in liquid gold. Massive live oak trees lined the hillsides, with their knobby, gnarled trunks, branches twisting like a witch's fingers, and leathery, dark green leaves. Each one guarded its hill like a lord. Xavier was itching to climb one.

There were also streams and brooks that ran along their route, crisscrossed by rough wooden bridges. Xavier wished they could stop to have a drink, dangle their feet in the water, and skip stones, but they were on a schedule and Curly wasn't about to ruin his reputation for punctuality just so folks could get their feet wet.

Xavier judged that at the rate they were going they would get to their destination in about fifteen hours. When the sun got low and Curly pulled into a lonely depot to stop for the night, Xavier figured they were three-quarters of the way there.

The station agent, a humorless fellow who seemed annoyed that his solitude had been interrupted, served them a dinner of bacon, which was only slightly rancid, and salty soup, which covered the flavor of the bad bacon. There was also slightly stale bread with butter, which is what they primarily used to fill their stomachs. The agent offered them the use of the beds in a back room, then retired to the back himself. After he left, Curly warned the travelers that the beds were most likely as not filled with fleas. Instead, they all laid their bedrolls and blankets out on the porch. Chester had already built a campfire and settled on the steps to play his harmonica. Curly started drinking something from a small canteen, which he offered to Bret, who took one sniff and politely declined.

As Chester continued to play, Curly stretched out his stockinged feet and breathed in the night air like one who is satisfied and hasn't a care in the world. He glanced up at the Wanted posters on the wall, the same array of posters that they had read at the depot in San Francisco.

"That's some bad company up there on that wall," he said.

"It is indeed," agreed Bret. "They sound like a desperate bunch."

"That they are, that they are," Curly said, taking a sip from his canteen. "Only last month I was robbed by Black Rabbit himself."

"You don't say?" said Bret, rubbing his hands in front of the fire. The night air had gotten chilly, and they all gathered closer to its flickering warmth.

"Black Rabbit seems like a silly name for an outlaw," Nina said wryly.

"Silly or not, he'll take everything you own and the clothes off your back," Curly said. "He's mad as a March hare, and the way he looks at you with those crazy eyes . . ." Curly shivered.

"What did he do?" Xavier asked, sensing a story. Chester stopped playing and moved closer to the group, interested in hearing Curly's tale.

"Well, let me start at the beginning," Curly said, easing himself into the story as if he was putting on a favorite pair of pants. "I was taking some folks up to Hangtown, same as I'm taking you. From there I'd go south to Drytown, Angel's Camp, Columbia, all the way to Chinese Camp, then turn back west and head to San Francisco. It's a big circle. Now, I'd been

driving this route for two years, and I reckon I know every stone, every blade of grass along the way. I've run up against mountain lions, coyotes, even a bear or two, not to mention my share of shady road agents stopping the stagecoach to lighten its load, so to speak. I keep a Winchester rifle under my seat next to the strongbox for just such interruptions. I don't tolerate these kinds of individuals. They're mean and heartless, and if one of us has to die, I'd just as soon it be them.

"Anyway, that's a long way of my saying that I feel pretty confident about driving this coach, and protecting the people and its contents. It helps if other men have brought firearms . . . by the way, do any of you fellas happen to be carrying?"

Xavier, Rowan, and Chester shook their heads. Xavier gritted his teeth, wishing that he'd been able to convince Jenny to give him a gun. Curly was looking at them like they were babes in the woods. Bret reached inside his jacket and produced a small pistol.

"I'm armed. It's mainly for show, though," he admitted. "The man who sold it to me informed me it sometimes misfires, and he was in fact missing a thumb. But I'll use it, if I have to."

"Friend, you'd probably have more luck throwing that thing than shooting it," Curly said with a high cackle. "But thanks for the offer. If we face danger I'll hand you the rifle. I've got a pretty little revolver in my holster. Picked it up after the robbery . . . but now I'm getting ahead of myself. Where was I? Oh yes, I was on my route. I'd heard there was a new stagecoach robber aggravating drivers between Angel's Camp and Murphys, so when I made it down there I had my eyes peeled for any trouble. I'd just picked up some passengers, two fellows who had about ten thousand dollars' worth of dust that they wanted transported to a bank in San Francisco. I told them it might be safer to take it to a nearby bank and let the bank do the transporting, but they argued against it, and to tell the truth I don't think they were planning on putting the money in a bank at all, but in the hands of card dealers and loose women.

"As they say, a fool and his money are soon parted. Sure enough, just about sunset, as I was crossing the bridge of the Stanislaus River heading toward Columbia, a man comes galloping from the other direction, blocking my path. Now I was going pretty fast myself, probably faster than I should've over a bridge, but he doesn't slow down. I have to pull up, and that is no easy feat with six horses. They all start tripping over each other and falling down . . . it was a mess. By the time I had everything settled I was staring down the barrel of Black Rabbit's pistol.

"It was a long barrel, too. It was no ladies' gun; he meant business. He was dressed head to toe in black, and his stallion was black. He even had a black kerchief covering his face, all except his eyes, which were dark and wild. I can't exactly put my finger on it, but they were startling eyes, and I could feel myself become ill at ease just from his stare.

"'Hand over the gold in your safe box,' he said in a strangely calm voice. There was no emotion in it, just the expectation I would do as he said. There was no point in arguing with him; he seemed to know that we were carrying a considerable amount, and he knew where it was. He didn't even bother to rob the fellows in the coach; didn't ask them to step out or anything. I was spitting mad, but I was stuck. If I made the wrong move on this fellow, he'd kill one or all of us. I was the one he was pointing the gun at, so I figured I was the poor sucker who'd go first.

"You start thinking differently about things when you are facing your own mortality. Suddenly simple things, like breathing and seeing a blue sky and hearing birds sing, those become more precious, while big things, like maintaining your reputation and protecting somebody else's gold, those things become less important. Before you know it you're undoing the latch of the strongbox, and watching the bags of gold dust packed into the saddlebags of a horse that is now showing you his flanks and galloping away like a bat out of hell.

"I hadn't heard from the fellows in the coach, but I knew they'd be mad at me. I was worried I might lose my job if people thought I was too much of a coward to fight off a bandit. But I had nothing to worry about. Wouldn't you know, when I looked in the coach those two scallywags were climbing out of the mailbags, shaking like a couple of wet dogs. They'd hidden in there to save their own skins, leaving me to fight for myself! And one of them had unleashed his bladder all over the mail, too, making my next delivery an unpleasant one. They had no idea what happened out there between me and Black Rabbit, so needless to say, I told them a much different story than the one I'm telling you.

"When I got to San Francisco I bought a revolver and practiced till I was quick on the draw. I've used it three times since
I bought it—not against Black Rabbit, mind you—but it sure
makes a big scary bang when it goes off, and it's gotten rid of
some of the more sniveling sort of robbers. My reputation is
secure. And I'm looking forward to seeing the Rabbit again. I
surely am. I've got a little surprise for him."

Curly patted his holster and spit a stream of tobacco, which
evaporated with a hiss in the embers of the dwindling fire. He
laughed and settled into his bedroll. The others lay back as well.
Without the warmth of the flames, the cool night air envel-
oped them and they had to snuggle deep into their blankets.

As the others succumbed to slumber, Xavier found himself
staring at the big, black sky, following the path of the Milky
Way through the constellations, trying to come up with a
story he could tell Curly tomorrow to shore up his own reputation. He fell asleep thinking of outlaws, fast horses, and
sharpshooting.

By the next morning, Xavier had come up with a doozy of
a tale. The surly station agent served them a breakfast of por-
ridge with "nuts" ("Do nuts have wings?!" Curly cackled after-
ward), and by the time they got on the road, Xavier was dying
to tell his story.

His turn to ride up top wouldn't come until after Nina's,
so he bided his time in the coach, watching Bret jot notes and
laugh to himself, watching Xanthe and Chester talking to each
other about who knows what, and watching Rowan's head

droop into half slumber, only to be jarred by a bump that sent it snapping back again.

"Bret, how do you know if you have a good story?" Xavier asked, just to make conversation.

"That's a good question. If I knew the answer, I guess I'd be a famous writer instead of a hopeful one." He thought for a moment. "I suppose a good story is a true one. Oh, I don't mean absolutely true, but it's got to have that core of honesty. Otherwise it's just a bunch of nonsense."

Xavier nodded and turned to look out the window, but Bret continued, wound up.

"Another thing. A good story has a life. It has a beginning, a middle, and an end, like birth, life, and death. That middle should be stimulating, thrilling even! And worthwhile . . . it should have a purpose . . . a point. And a good story always has a surprise ending. You lead the reader in one direction and then give them a good twist.

"The worst kind of book is one where you already know the ending before you start. Then what's the point of reading it? It becomes a chore. Life should never be a chore. What a hopeless sort of life that is, just going through the motions, trudging toward something dreary and predictable. A good surprise ending—one that makes sense, mind you—gives a person joy and satisfaction."

Xavier nodded again. He hadn't expected Bret to get so philosophical, but he shouldn't have been surprised; Bret was a man who could talk, a man who liked the sound of his own voice. They had that in common.

They stopped at the depot in Sacramento to change horses and freshen up. Then it was Xavier's turn to ride up top, and he scrambled into the seat next to Curly, who gave him a welcome nod, flicked the reins, and sent the fresh team charging ahead.

"Funny thing. That story you told us about Black Rabbit last night," Xavier yelled over the pounding hooves, "it reminds me of a run-in I had with another outlaw, a fellow they called the Ghost Rider."

"Never heard of him."

"You haven't? Well, he doesn't travel around these parts—he's out in the plains. But who knows, he may make it out here yet. It happened a while ago . . ."

"I thought you said you just got to San Francisco from Boston."

"That's true, but this is a different trip I took with my uncles, to Indian country." Xavier was irritated that Curly was poking holes in his story. "You want to hear it or don't you?"

"Sure. I'm sorry, I'm a natural nitpicker. Go ahead with your story."

"All right, then. This was about three years ago. There were five of us: my two uncles, my two older cousins, and myself. I had joined them because my father had recently passed away and my mother had too many mouths to feed. We were traveling in a covered wagon, following the Oregon Trail to gold country.

"One of our wheels broke and we knew we needed to fix

it, but the sun was going down. There was an outcropping of boulders, and as the moon came out we started to hear howling coming from those rocks. Turns out it was the lair of a pack of wolves.

"Well, we made a big bonfire to keep them at bay, but the only thing we had for fuel was the wagon and whatever was in it. First went the broken wheel, then our clothes, then another wheel, and so on. The wolves were surrounding us and we just hoped we could keep the fire going until dawn. Suddenly, we spotted a figure riding up on a gray dappled horse . . ."

"You could see the color of the horse that far away at night?"

"Sure I did; it kind of glowed as he came closer to the fire," Xavier shot back. "At first we thought he'd come to help us, but as he got closer we thought otherwise. On that horse was the strangest fellow I've seen. He had a light gray hat with an eagle feather poking from the brim. He wore gray pants, black boots, and a white duster that flapped behind him like a cape."

"Feather, huh? Maybe he was an Indian who pinched the clothing off his last victim."

"I believe he was at least part Native American," Xavier said. Curly frowned.

"Native American? You mean like a pilgrim?"

"Uh, no. I mean Indian."

"Why didn't you say so? This story sure is confusing," Curly said, scratching at his chin.

"Anyway," Xavier continued, "my oldest cousin suspected something was amiss and told me to unhitch one of the mules and get help. So I started doing just that, but I snuck a peek at what was going on with the others.

"The man approached my uncle and said, 'Give me your gold.' I'll never forget that voice: raspy, like the sound of the whipping wind. 'We don't have any gold,' says my uncle. 'Then give me what you got, or I'll feed you to my friends,' the stranger says, meaning the wolves. 'We don't have much,' my uncle replied. Actually we did have some money in a strongbox in the wagon. I wonder to this day if my uncle had handed it over right away whether we could've avoided what happened next.

"Before my uncle could get another word out, the stranger pulled a huge knife and flicked it at him, hitting him right in the heart. Down he went, dead as a doornail."

"Great horny toads! Those Indians would attack an unarmed man!"

Xavier was beginning to feel a little bad for the Indians. Curly obviously had a strong bias against them. "I'm not sure he was Indian," he reminded Curly. "Anyway, my other uncle goes for his gun, but this fellow also had two pistols in some side holsters and he pulls them out lickety-split, twirls them like a trick shooter, and takes out my uncle and oldest cousin at the same time. One shot each, right in the forehead. How he could aim so accurately, I can't figure out to this day.

"Now, my younger cousin scoots over with me and helps me undo both mules, and the two of us take off. A mule isn't too fast, but it's hardy, and I guess the stranger was too busy to take notice of us, or maybe he didn't consider us much of a threat as we skedaddled like two jackrabbits with our tails on fire.

"My cousin and I made it to the nearest town and found the sheriff, who collected a few other men. We all rode back to the wagon, but of course it was too late. My family had been slaughtered, our valuables stolen, and the vultures had already arrived to pick over what the wolves had left. Later, when the sheriff put me and my cousin on a stagecoach heading back home, he told us that the stranger was known only as the Ghost Rider, and that he had attacked hundreds of covered wagons along the trail, but no matter how hard they tried to track him, he left no clues behind. He just disappeared like the morning mist."

"My, that is some tale! I'm surprised you decided to make your way out west again."

"Well, Curly, the way I see it, life is about taking chances," Xavier said. "I'm not one to play it safe."

"I agree with you there," Curly cackled. "There's no fun in safety. I know another fellow who didn't play it safe . . . they hung him about two weeks ago, but he sure had fun while he was living . . ." Curly launched into a whole new story, and then Xavier came up with one, and Curly had another, and they traded tales back and forth until about noon, when they pulled into the Hangtown Depot.

+ CHAPTER NINE +
LILY ROSE

ONCE THEY WERE IN HANGTOWN, IT WAS CLEAR THEY would be staying a while. As soon as they stopped, Curly told the station agent not to hurry hitching up a new team, and then he practically skipped down Main Street to a business with a sign out front that read "Baths—$1.00." The passengers didn't mind stretching their legs a bit either, and headed for a much welcome stroll down the covered boardwalk in front of the shops.

After passing through so many sleepy small towns, Hangtown seemed like a bustling metropolis in comparison. Its Main Street stretched at least ten blocks, and from it radiated several side streets, also lined with shops. Beyond these were blocks of residences dotted with churches, as well as a white clapboard schoolhouse, a livery stable, and a firehouse. Even farther out sat a small jail that looked like a stone cube, and a stable that housed the undertaker's Clydesdale horses and hearse. Next to that was a graveyard with a white picket fence surrounding it, the tombstones still white and clean like rows of baby teeth.

Main Street, however, was where the action was. There were several saloons, restaurants, and dry goods stores, which sold clothing, mining equipment, and candy. There were hotels and boardinghouses, two banks, two pharmacies, business offices for doctors and dentists, and barbershops. All of these were set side by side, so that where one shop or business ended the other began.

In front of one of the saloons was a grand oak tree with wide spreading branches. Again Xavier felt the itch to climb.

"Boy, I'd love to get up into that tree," he said to Rowan. Bret, who had overheard his comment, laughed.

"I don't think so," he said. "That's the hanging tree. It's what gave this town it's name. Vigilantes caught a gang of five thieves. They tried them, found them guilty of course, then hung them in that very tree on different branches, like Christmas ornaments."

"OK. Well, I guess I won't be climbing that particular tree," Xavier mumbled.

"There's a low tolerance here for crime of any kind," Bret warned them. "You know, a little while ago they changed the name of this town to Placerville to try and erase its grisly reputation, but reputations have a way of sticking like a bad smell. No matter what it says on the books, this place will always be Hangtown."

Bret disappeared inside one of the clothing shops and Chester went hunting for some boots, but the time travelers decided that what they wanted was candy, and they found what they were looking for in Dilly's Candy Shop. Big round lollipops swirling with rainbow colors greeted them as they entered, and barrels of taffy, caramels, licorice, and hard candies lined every wall. The glass case displayed huge slabs of fudge, fluffy white balls of divinity, and chocolates filled with nougat, nuts, creams, and fruit.

After buying enough sweets to keep their teeth bathed in sugar for a week, they decided to eat lunch at one of the restaurants. As they walked down the block they noticed a crowd had gathered under the hanging tree.

"Oh no, I hope it's not an execution," Rowan groaned.

"Let's take a side street," Xanthe suggested. "I am not in the mood to see a dead body."

"Hold on a minute," Xavier said. "I don't think it's a hanging." He edged his way into the crowd, which had given their attention to the rotund man standing on a barrel under the tree.

"Ladies and gentlemen," the man shouted. "I am Mr. Craigmiles, and I have with me one of the most villainous, murderous, bloodthirsty individuals ever to poison our good towns with his presence! Where is he, you might ask? Why, right here, in this wooden box!" A murmur ran through the crowd as Craigmiles motioned to a wooden box that was no more than two feet high.

"Who is it, Tom Thumb?" a voice called out from the crowd, followed by laughter.

"No, it is not Tom Thumb, nor any other midget," Mr. Craigmiles said. "Rather, it is the head of that most infamous criminal, Joaquin Murieta!" A louder murmur ran through the crowd. Mr. Craigmiles held up his hands.

"Do you remember that Mexican bandit? The Robin Hood of El Dorado, who, in eighteen fifty, after the brutal killing of his girlfriend by white bandits, and after being flogged nearly to death himself, vowed vengeance on all Americans? The man who then embarked on a three-year spree of robbery, murder, and mayhem? And do you remember how, in eighteen fifty-three, the governor hired Captain Love and his Rangers to hunt down this outlaw, which they did, cutting off his head as proof to claim their reward? Ladies and gentlemen, I have purchased that head. It is right here, residing in this box, which I will be taking on tour through the midwestern and eastern parts of the United States. Mr. Murieta's head has toured these gold towns in the past, but I am here to tell you that this is your last chance to gaze upon this terrifying face of evil! It will be on display at the Motherlode Saloon for the next two days, just one dollar apiece for five full minutes of horror! Thank you very much!"

Mr. Craigmiles hopped down from the barrel, picked up his box, and marched toward the saloon, followed by most of the men in the crowd. The ladies drifted back to the shops. Xavier wanted to take a peek, but from the disgusted looks of everyone else in his party he knew it was a losing proposition.

They ate at a Swedish restaurant, then split up to see if they could find anyone who knew Oliver Weber or Albert Web. Not sure how people would respond to queries from Negroes, Xavier and Xanthe each went with one of the Popplewells.

Xavier and Nina tried the establishments on the east side of the street and Xanthe and Rowan were assigned the ones on the west. Most people were kind but dismissive: "Sorry, can't help you" was the phrase most used; however, those of a more playful nature suggested that they check with the undertaker. More than one shopkeeper suggested that they ask a woman named Lily Rose, the Spanish Rose of Hangtown, who ran the saloon at the end of Main Street.

Xavier and Nina caught up with Rowan and Xanthe, who were waiting for them with big grins on their faces.

"Any luck?" Xavier asked.

"No, but we know a good place to look," Rowan said.

"Lily Rose's!" they all sang out. They walked across the street, past the Huckleberry House Hotel, a cozy-looking establishment with its merits painted right on the shutters: "Beds with springs," it boasted. "Latest styles for comfort. Most favorable terms. Seasonal delicacies on hand."

Next door was the Lily Rose Saloon. Unlike the other dusty, dimly lit bars they had visited, this place had a bright, carnival atmosphere. Inside, the sounds of tinkling glasses, laughing, cheerful conversation, and piano music could be heard.

Nina winced. "Whoa, that piano player stinks. He's hitting one clinker after another."

"I'm sure they're barely aware of the music," Xanthe mused,

studying the bright pink building. "Figures that the only decent place in the whole town would be run by a woman."

"Oh, here we go . . ." Xavier said, rolling his eyes.

"I'm serious! This saloon is an oasis of civilization. Men who came out west didn't realize what life would be like without women around. They didn't know what they would become when they had complete freedom to do what they wanted."

"So what *did* they become?" Nina asked.

"Smelly, loud, violent, and greedy," Xanthe sniffed.

"You're exaggerating," Xavier protested, feeling the need to defend the masculine sex. "Look around, it's not like this is some crazy, rootin' tootin' town."

"Hah! Need I remind you that the name of this place is Hangtown? And that there's a severed head only a hundred yards away, being shown off for entertainment?"

"All right, all right, men are pigs," Rowan said. "Let's just go inside."

Bright lights, glittering chandeliers, tablecloths the color of cotton candy, and mirrors on every wall gave the Lily Rose Saloon its cheerful atmosphere. Young women with sweet faces served drinks, swishing between the tables in colorful dresses, and wearing their hair pinned up in careless buns so that here and there a strand bounced down the sides of their faces or the backs of their necks. Xanthe gave Xavier a poke in the arm and pointed to a corner table. There sat Curly with his sweetheart, who bore little resemblance to his homely description.

One woman was the most popular by far. She stood on the

first step of a staircase that led to a second story, elevated above the circle of men vying for her attention. As she spoke, the men laughed heartily. Then one of them would say something back to her and she would laugh, a high, throaty peal, like an exotic jungle bird. Her black hair, pushed back into smooth waves, gleamed in the light, and her eyes were like two shiny black olives against her golden skin. She wore a large amethyst gem at her neck and another on her finger. They all knew this must be the one and only Lily Rose.

Xavier suddenly became aware of Rowan's heavy breathing. He turned and saw his friend had broken into a sweat.

"Relax, kid!" Xavier said. "They're just women. They're not going to attack you!"

"I know that," Rowan snapped. "I just . . ." He heaved a big sigh. "I hate this."

Sometimes Xavier felt sorry for his friend's social ineptitude. Wherever he went, Rowan stuck out like a potato in a fruit salad. Not only that, but you could read every thought, every emotion he had on his face. He and Xavier couldn't be more different; it was surprising they got along as well as they did.

Xavier kept everything close. He was a chameleon, as changeable as the weather. He could make himself fit perfectly into any group, molding himself within minutes, adjusting his posture, his speech, his manner, until you almost wouldn't recognize him.

HOST: Tell me, Xave, if I can call you that, what exactly is the secret to your incredible popularity?

XAVIER: My grandmother thinks I was just born blessed, and I guess there might be something to that! (Laughs) But in all seriousness, I have a theory, which I will now relate to you. I call it "Xavier's Four Steps to Success," or, "How to Get What You Want." Write this down, it's priceless! (Laughs) OK. First of all, people will help you if they like you. Second, people will like you if they feel comfortable around you. Third, and this is very important, people feel comfortable around other people who are like themselves. Which brings us to number four: therefore, make people think you are just like them.

HOST: But how do you do that? It sounds difficult.

XAVIER: Well, I have to admit, I do have a sort of genius for this. I've done it so often that now I barely know I'm doing it. It's a matter of making slight adjustments to your behavior. For instance, if I'm talking to somebody who speaks with an accent, I subtly try to match that accent. I use the same phrases and words they use. I adjust my intellectual level to theirs. If they have their hands shoved into their pockets, or if they're rocking on their heels, I do the same. If they wave their hands while they talk, so do I. If they shift their eyes around, so do I. If they make piercing eye contact, I don't flinch. If they're pious, I thank the Lord. If they're crude, I can pass gas as easily as a bean-fed horse. You see how it works? The trick is to do it without letting them know you're mimicking them. If they think you're making fun of them, you're finished.

HOST: That is truly amazing.

XAVIER: I know.

Xavier studied Lily Rose like a lion eyeing its prey. He could see that her beauty and charm masked a savvy, tough-as-nails businesswoman. He noticed the way she tilted her head and flashed her eyes, how she tossed her hair back when she laughed, and how all of these subtle gestures got the men surrounding her to jump like marionettes on strings. Something told him that she cared little for these men, these panting dogs, desperate for feminine attention. If he wanted to impress Lily Rose, he needed to be the opposite.

Xavier sidled up to the bar and pretended he hadn't seen her, even though she was less than six feet away from him. Xanthe, Rowan, and Nina had moved toward a window, not wanting to interfere. Lily Rose's eyes flicked to them for a second, but she was much more intrigued by the solitary stranger at the bar. And why wouldn't she be? He couldn't have cared less about her.

She left her circle of sycophants to join Xavier. The other men, realizing their time was up, dispersed to look for other young ladies who would giggle at their jokes.

"Well hello, stranger. I don't think I've ever seen you in here before," Lily Rose said. Xavier turned with feigned surprise, then tipped his hat.

"Good afternoon, Miss. You haven't seen me 'cause I've never been here before. Can I buy you a drink?"

"You cannot," she laughed. "Don't you know me? I'm Lily Rose. The proprietress of this place."

"You? No!" Xavier laughed. "A fine woman like you has no need of work! Why, from across the room I took you for a princess or an empress or something." Lily Rose threw her head back and laughed.

"You're a liar and a flatterer," she said. "But you're a good one. You can call me Lily. Sit down at my table," she said, motioning to an empty table with a floral centerpiece. "What are you drinking? You look a little young for whiskey."

"Only young in years, Miss Lily. I'll have a sarsaparilla."

"Hmm. That's sweet." Lily Rose signaled the bartender. "A mint tea and a sarsaparilla, Joe," she said. Xavier pulled a chair out for her and she took a seat, and then he did as well, removing his hat. The piano struck a particularly sour note, drawing hoots from the crowd.

"Those your friends?" Lily Rose nodded at the awkward threesome by the door.

"As a matter of fact, they are. We're looking for someone and were told that you might know his whereabouts. A fella who goes by the name of Albert Web. Or his buddy, Oliver Weber. You know where we can find either one of them, Miss Lily?"

"Maybe I do or maybe I don't," she said coyly. "Either way, I'm not in the habit of talking about who or where my customers are. Not to strangers anyway."

"We're not looking to hurt him, just ask him some questions."

"He doesn't sound like a friend."

"To tell the truth, we're not sure what he is."

"I'm sorry, stranger. I like your face, but a lot of scoundrels have pretty faces."

Suddenly a shot rang out and the mirror on the stage shattered into hundreds of shards. A man stood near the stage, pistol smoking.

"What's the meaning of this, Tyler?!" Lily hollered as she flew across the room. "I hope you know I'm charging you for that mirror!"

"I do apologize, Miss Lily, but I could not stand one more minute of that god-awful piano playing!" A round of cheers went up from the feisty crowd.

"I can't help it!" the piano player shot back. "I lost my pinky two days ago. My hand still hurts like the dickens, too!"

"Well, my ears hurt like the dickens!" the man called Tyler shouted back. "If you sit your arse back down at that piano, you'll be missing more than a pinky. I'm gonna put a hole right between your eyes."

"Tyler, you've got no right shooting up my place," Lily scolded. "How long have we known each other? And here you are frightening my girls and causing a ruckus ..." She gestured at the waitresses who had huddled together near the bar. "Now I want you to get out, or I'm gonna have Big Jake come over and throw you out!"

Big Jake appeared at the top of the landing on the second floor. His heavy footfall challenged the construction of the staircase. His head was the size of a prize-winning pumpkin and his hands were curled into fists. Tyler stuffed his gun back in its holster.

"I'm just saying, Miss Lily, you need to get yourself a better piano player. I can't have a conversation with that horrible racket going on in the background."

"My dog can play better!" yelled one of Tyler's cohorts.

"So can mine, and he's dead!" yelled another.

"Come on, fellas, let's go to the Swede's place," Tyler said, grabbing his hat from the table. "He's got a Mexican who can play a banjo."

The group of men rose and shuffled toward the door. Jake grabbed Tyler's arm and the young man reluctantly dropped a gold nugget into the huge outstretched palm. Jake let him go.

"Max, play something!" Lily pleaded to the piano player, who had left the stage.

"I don't think so, Miss Lily," Max said, brushing bits of glass off his sleeves. "I'm gonna give up music. It's gotten too dangerous." He picked up his bowler hat, pressed it onto his head, and walked out the door.

The party atmosphere had dampened considerably. A few other men rose from their seats and started for the door.

"Oh, wonderful," Lily fumed to nobody in particular. "There goes my business."

Just then a sweet ragtime tune tinkled from the piano. The men stopped in their tracks and turned to the stage. A slip of a girl, with a blue ribbon holding back a mass of bouncy black ringlets, sat at the piano, her fingers dancing along the keys. All the anger, frustration, and disappointment in the men's faces melted away and color came to their careworn cheeks. In that second, Nina had become the daughter they'd always wanted.

In the next second, Lily was by the stage. "Look at the customers!" she whispered loudly. She batted her eyes and smiled broadly, encouraging Nina to do likewise. Nina nodded and gave the men a sugary smile. The men sighed; their fantasy daughter was returning their affection.

When Nina finished the piece the men pounded their hands together and stomped the floor, roaring their approval. Lily urged her to get up and curtsy, which Nina did, stumbling slightly, which only added to her innocence.

Then the men started throwing small rocks at her. Rowan jumped forward, alarmed, but Xavier was at his side pulling him back.

"It's gold, Rowan," he said. "They're throwing gold."

Rowan's eyes widened. "I don't believe it." But it was true. As the men chanted for more, Lily motioned for Nina to play, so she sat back down and started playing "Turkey in the Straw," which started the men grabbing for dance partners.

Lily Rose drew Rowan aside. "Excuse me, young man, but is that your sister?"

Rowan nodded dumbly then managed to stutter, "Yes. Yes, I am . . . I mean, she is." He got his bearings and removed his hat. "Rowan Popplewell, ma'am. That's my sister, Nina."

"Call me Miss Lily. Mr. Popplewell, how would you feel about your sister performing for my customers? She can make a lot of money here, and I sure need some entertainment. My goodness, she's better than little Lotta Crabtree, and that girl's the most popular attraction around!"

Xanthe held up her hand. "Excuse me, Mr. Rowan," she said. "I've been looking after Miss Nina since she was a wee-un, and I have concerns about her being in a place . . . like this."

Lily drew herself up. "What kind of a place do you think this is? Don't answer that. I know what you think. Well, it's not that kind of place. Lily Rose runs a clean establishment. There's no funny business going on with my girls, I see to that."

"Just a moment, Miss Lily," Xavier interrupted. "The way I see it, we can help each other out. You need entertainment, we need information. What do you say, Miss Lily, are we still strangers?"

Lily smiled and crossed her arms. "I don't know any Albert, but Oliver Weber is camping in Glitter Gulch . . ."

"That sounds nice," Rowan said aside to Xanthe.

". . . Right along Cutthroat Creek."

"Maybe not so nice," Xanthe murmured back.

"It's a bit of a hike. You might want to get a couple of mules. Meanwhile, you're welcome to sleep in Huckleberry House. I own it. It's the place next door, but it's also attached to the saloon by that staircase," she said, pointing behind her.

"That sounds just fine, Miss Lily," Rowan said, taking her hand.

"Your sister's a star, young man. You'll see. You're going to be very rich."

Rowan said nothing, answering her only with a crooked grin.

+ CHAPTER TEN +
GOLD CAMP

As Nina played for the enthusiastic crowd, Lily offered Xanthe a job as a cook in the Huckleberry House Hotel.

"My last cook lit out for the mines. I'd rather have a woman cooking—more dependable. And I pay well here, twice as much as you can get in San Francisco. It's just breakfast and lunch, and you get help from some of the girls. They take turns serving and helping in the kitchen."

"That would be fine, Miss Lily," Xanthe said, giving Xavier a smug look. "You'll be surprised by what I can make."

"Yeah, one big batch of stomachaches, coming right up!" Xavier whispered to Rowan, who doubled over in a coughing fit to cover up his laughing.

By the time Nina finished playing, she had a fistful of gold nuggets. She jumped off the stage to show Rowan, and the two exchanged secretive glances as Lily Rose led the time travelers up the staircase to the bedrooms. She left them there to get settled and sent one of the girls to collect their bags from the stagecoach depot before Curly left.

"Nina, I think it's great that you've been discovered and all," Xanthe said after Lily went back to the saloon, "but you already know you're a superstar!"

"I'm hardly what you could call a superstar," Nina laughed. "OK, I've won a bunch of contests. I've played with a few symphonies. I've cut two CDs, which I would be surprised anybody bought, except for maybe my relatives. I really haven't made much money from them."

Rowan turned one of the nuggets over in his hand, then held it up to the light. "I wonder how much this is worth?" he murmured. Then he tossed it on the bed where Nina had dumped the other nuggets she had collected from the stage. There were ten tiny rocks. Rowan moved them around on the blanket, the crooked grin on his face again.

Because they were all anxious to follow up their one and only lead, they decided that Rowan and Xavier would buy a couple of mules and ride to Cutthroat Creek to see if they could find Oliver Weber before nightfall. The girls would have to stay at Lily Rose's, now that they had jobs to do. Though disappointed, the girls knew from their research at the Owatannauk that very few women were at the mining camps, and if they showed up there they would most likely draw too much attention.

As the friends discussed the plan, Lily dropped in to give Xanthe money to buy supplies for breakfast and three new dresses for Nina.

"The more bows and ruffles the better," Lily added.

Nina made a face. "Sounds like baby clothes. I'm eleven years old."

"Well, we're going to say you're eight," Lily said. "Look, sweetie, these men don't see little girls very often. Just your being here is a treat, even without the piano. Can you sing?"

"Not according to anyone who's heard me."

"You might want to give it a shot. I can assure you, no matter what comes out of your mouth, those heartsick fellas will think they hear an angel. All you have to do is smile and scoop up the money."

That sounded just fine to Nina. She and Xanthe went on their errand and the boys packed some food and their bedrolls, then went to the livery stable to purchase transportation for their trip to Glitter Gulch.

They bought two long-eared, barrel-bodied mules. Xavier felt like he was a little kid on a pony ride at the park, the way his legs hung over the side of the animal. He had wanted to buy a couple of smart-looking horses, but the liveryman warned them that horses were not as sure-footed on the trail, so of course Rowan insisted on taking the safe route, despite Xavier's pleas and attempts to bribe him with candy.

Once they were on their way, Xavier was glad Rowan had stuck to his guns. Following the trail was difficult for it was constantly changing. Parts of the trail were rocky, parts were muddy, parts had collapsed into the ravine, and parts had disappeared altogether, covered by fallen trees or a rockslide.

It was late afternoon and the woods were already growing dark. As the sounds of nighttime creatures rustled around them, it suddenly occurred to Xavier that he and Rowan were literally in the wilderness, armed with only a couple of knives, and that if they didn't find the camp soon they would be lost.

"Rowan, did you ever join the Cub Scouts or the Boy Scouts or anything like that?"

"No. You?"

"Yeah, I spent a summer doing survival training. Hopefully we won't have to make a fire; I wasn't so good at that. But I can make a shelter if I have to. And I think I can catch a rabbit. By the way, you didn't bring food, did you? Because it attracts bears."

"I thought you brought candy!"

"I lied. I would've given it to you when we got back."

"Well, I have candy."

"Then why did you want *my* candy?"

"Xave, you can never have too much candy!" Rowan said, exasperated. "And I don't want to throw mine away!"

"I guess it doesn't matter. After all, to a bear, *we're* food."

"Xavier, would you mind shutting up?"

"Not at all. Not at all."

Ten minutes later the stars were visible through the pine branches. The boys heard laughing and smelled roasting meat, and as they pushed into a clearing they saw a small campfire with six men seated around it, cooking. One of the men was tuning a fiddle.

In the flicker of the fire the men all looked very much the same. They wore the popular Levi's pants with suspenders, rough cotton shirts, hats with wide brims, and boots. Their faces were grizzled and bearded, their hair shaggy and long. Their skin had the hard, tanned, creased look of people who spend a lot of time in the sun.

The smell of the meat drew the boys closer. As they approached, the men stopped talking and looked up, eyeing the newcomers suspiciously.

"Good evening," Rowan said. "How are you fellows doing?"

"Who are you?" one man said, rising. He was about six feet five inches, with a full black beard, a gun in a holster, and hands like two large hams.

"My name's Rowan," Rowan answered. "And this is Xavier."

"Is that your slave?" the man asked.

"Of course not!" Rowan sputtered. "Xavier is . . . he's a free man."

"You sure? 'Cause we don't cotton much to slave drivers," another man said, standing next to the first. This one was blond, with a short red beard. "Every man keeps what he works for, whether he be white, black, red, brown, yellow, or green," he added.

"We're not here to work," Rowan said.

"Then what are you here for?" the first man said, narrowing his eyes. "We don't cotton much to thieves, either." He pulled out his revolver and pulled back the hammer with a click.

"Look, we don't want any trouble; we're just looking for someone. Lily Rose said we might be able to find him here."

The tension broke and the men eased back into their seats around the fire. The man with the black beard slipped his gun back into its holster.

"Lily Rose? Why didn't you say you were friends of Miss Lily? Any friend of Lily's is a friend of ours. The name's Ed Lansky. Who are you looking for?"

"A couple of fellows who go by the names of Albert Web and Oliver Weber."

"My my, so you've come looking for me and Albert. Welcome. I've been expecting you," said the man who was tuning the fiddle. He put the instrument down, hitched up his pants, and sauntered over to Rowan and Xavier. They gasped.

"Otto!" the boys murmured together.

"I beg your pardon?" Oliver Weber said.

Xavier peered into the man's face. It was uncanny. He was younger and rougher, but his features were the same— the slight build; the long, pointed nose; and the eyes: one brown, one blue. The only difference was the look of worry in Oliver's expression. Then Xavier felt something hard against his stomach. He looked down to see a revolver pressed against him.

"I don't want to hurt you, young man, but you're getting awfully familiar. I suggest you back off," Oliver said.

Xavier backed away slowly, his hands raised. "I'm sorry, sir. You just look a lot like someone we know."

Oliver lowered the gun and rubbed his neck at the base of his beard. "It's funny. Ol' Albert said it was a giant, scary-looking old crone who'd be on his tail. You fellows don't fit that description at all."

"Mr. Weber, we really need to talk," Rowan said. "It's a little complicated."

"Can it wait till after dinner? We've got some quail if you haven't eaten yet. There's some beans, of course—there's always beans. Pete made some biscuits that are a little tough, but not so bad if you soak 'em in coffee." The second man, with the blond hair and red beard, grinned and tipped his hat.

"We'd be happy to join you," Rowan said eagerly. "And we've got a whole bag of candy, if you fellows would like something sweet for dessert."

The men cheered and shifted over to make room for the boys around the campfire. The quail disappeared in no time. Nobody touched the beans. After dinner, coffee and whiskey were passed around, followed by Rowan's bag of candy. Each man selected a piece of fudge, taffy, or hard peppermint. Some of them popped the candy in their mouths immediately, while others saved theirs for later, clutching them like small treasures.

The candy and the whiskey put the men in such a good mood that when Oliver tucked the fiddle under his chin and started playing, the men jumped to their feet and danced, stamping their boots, locking arms, twirling, and kicking up their heels. Xavier and Rowan joined in, and pretty soon men from some of the neighboring tents came over to join the party. More whiskey was poured, and then the storytelling began.

Every miner knew a friend of a friend who had dug up the largest gold nugget ever found. There were run-ins with desperadoes to be discussed and chewed over. There were Indian raids to be reported, and memories of traveling entertainment that were worth resurrecting. And everybody had a grizzly bear story.

Xavier told his tale of the Ghost Rider in a hushed whisper, this time adding even more haunting details. The miners listened, slack-jawed, hanging on his every word. After he finished, several men nodded knowingly, claiming that they, too, had heard of this same mysterious man. Some of them even swore they had a friend of a friend who had been robbed by the Ghost Rider. *This is how legends begin,* Xavier thought to himself.

The revelry lasted late into the evening. By the time the miners drifted back to their tents it was after midnight. Xavier and Rowan caught Oliver watching them as he leaned against a pine tree, smoking a thin cigar.

"All right, let's talk," he said. "I'm curious. What do you want with Albert . . . or should I say Walter Ebb? That's his real name. He changed it to Albert to throw his pursuers off his trail, which I'm sure you know already."

"Is he here?" Rowan asked.

"You first."

Rowan looked at Xavier, who shrugged. "Albert . . . Walter's father asked us to look for him. When Walter asked you to come with him to California, he was running away."

"That explains a lot," Oliver said, spitting out some tobacco that had stuck to his tongue.

"Like what?"

"Well, I met Walter only five days or so before we decided to leave. Judge Davis hired him. He was a moody fellow, but for some reason he took a liking to me, perhaps because our eyes are the same. It's unusual, just ask your friend," he said, motioning to Xavier.

"Yes, I'm sorry about that," Xavier said, sheepishly.

"Anyway, I had been toying with the idea of heading out west for a while, but a few things kept me from going. First of all, I felt I had an obligation to the judge. I'm his best clerk; I have an eye for detail, so to speak," he laughed, pointing at his brown eye. "But my other eye is always on the door, you know. I've got a wild streak. Sometimes I feel torn in half. My responsible, dependable side was working with Judge Davis, but my adventurous side yearned to explore the wilderness of the West. Walter recognized that side of me and urged me to grab the chance while I could. It seemed to mean a lot to him. I couldn't make up my mind, so I left it to fate. I was waiting for an answer to a question, maybe the most important question of my life. I had asked my sweetheart for her hand in marriage."

"Adelaide Clemens," Rowan said.

"That's right. How do you know Adelaide?"

"We've been tracking Walter. She's part of the story."

"Well, you certainly are thorough. If Adelaide said yes, then I would stay in Illinois; if no, then I would go. Adelaide knew me well. She was afraid of my wild side, so she had reason to ponder the possibilities of her future. Finally, the day before the Republican Convention, she sent word back through one of our delivery boys, Benjamin."

Oliver reached into his shirt pocket and pulled out a small leather package tied with a piece of twine. He untied it and removed a folded piece of paper, which he handed to Rowan.

"May I?" Rowan asked. Oliver nodded, looking off in the distance. Rowan unfolded the paper and began reading. "My dearest Oliver, I have considered your proposal. It has been my greatest wish to be married to you, to bear your children, to keep your house. But with sadness I must decline your kind offer. I hope one day you will find it in your heart to forgive me. Do not try to contact me. I am heartsick but firm in my decision. With tender affection, Adelaide Clemens."

There was silence while Oliver took a long drag on the cigar. "Broke my heart. But I can't blame her, poor girl. She must've gotten broken up when she was writing it. See how her writing gets shaky where she finally gets to the business of turning me down?"

"And you didn't contact her before you left?"

"Well, she was pretty clear about that, wasn't she?" Oliver said. "I didn't want to offend her. And besides, look how she ended it ... 'Adelaide Clemens.' Usually in her letters to me she just signs her name 'Addie.' But writing her whole Christian name out, 'Adelaide Clemens,' with that cold formality, is like pounding the last nail in the coffin. Walter and I left the next morning."

The boys exchanged looks. They were both thinking the same thing.

"So, then what happened?" Rowan prompted.

"From the beginning, Walter was as jumpy as a leapfrog. He insisted we take the sea route, which was fine with me since I could afford it, and it allowed me to bring a lot of my equipment. Passage was a little rough, but we had a grand old time despite the weather, making plans, talking about our hopes and dreams. But as we neared San Francisco, Walter admitted he was on the run, a fugitive of sorts. He told me he'd keep in touch, but the day we landed he disappeared. I haven't seen him since."

Xavier frowned. Something was bothering him about this whole thing. He couldn't put his finger on it, but there was a notion glinting in the back of his mind, and whenever he tried to focus on it, it zipped off, like a fly evading a flyswatter.

"Thank you for your time," Rowan sighed, handing the letter back to Oliver. Oliver tossed the remains of the cigar on the ground, stubbing it into the dirt with his foot.

"Sorry I couldn't be more help. Do you know the giant woman? The one Walter was worried about?"

"Yes. But she's not bad. She wants to help him," Rowan said.

"You mean she wants to help his father."

"Yes, that is what I mean. But somehow I think it will turn out to be the same thing."

It was late so the boys laid their bedrolls out under the stars. Xavier was so exhausted from hiking and dancing, he was sure that as soon as his head hit the ground he'd be out like a light. Rowan had gotten his second wind, however. The gold camp seemed to energize him. The last thing Xavier heard before he drifted off was Rowan pressing Ed Lansky to say how much gold he'd found in Glitter Gulch, and how much more he thought was still in the ground, waiting to be discovered.

In the morning they packed up their mules and set off back to Hangtown.

"What do you think of that letter? The one Oliver got from Adelaide Clemens?" Xavier asked Rowan as soon as they left the camp.

"I think the second half of it was forged," Rowan said. "I think Adelaide accepted Oliver's proposal, then Balt bribed Benjamin into giving him the real letter, wrote the part turning Oliver down, and had Benjamin deliver it. That's why the handwriting changed."

"But he made a mistake in signing it with her full name. And that part telling Oliver not to contact her was just to keep him from getting it all straightened out."

"Boy, this kid is a jerk," Rowan said, shaking his head. "How low can you get?"

"I know. He's screwing around with his own grandpa!"

The boys reached a section of trail that was covered with a mound of small rocks that had slid down the side of the mountain. They dismounted the mules and carefully led them over the pass.

"So, I wonder how hard it is to mine for gold," Rowan said, out of the blue.

"I don't know, it looks kind of boring to me."

"Boring until you strike something. Then you'll be yawning all the way to the bank . . ." Suddenly Rowan looked up, alarmed. "What's that?"

"What's what?"

"I thought I saw something moving."

"Do you think it's a bear?"

"Oh man, I hope not!"

"Look, don't freak out. It might be a bear or a mountain lion. If it is, just try to make yourself look bigger. Wave your arms. Yell at it. Throw something. But whatever you do, don't run. If you run it will think you are prey!"

"Wait, I thought with bears you're supposed to lie on the ground and play dead."

Xavier frowned. "You know, I think you're right. But for a mountain lion, definitely don't lie down."

"Well, what should we do? It's getting closer!"

"Rowan, it's probably just a deer. You're getting scared of nothing."

But it was neither a deer, a mountain lion, nor a bear. As

they got to the end of the landslide, a black horse trotted from behind the brush, blocking their path. Its rider, a man dressed entirely in black with a kerchief covering his face, pointed a revolver at the boys. It was Black Rabbit.

"Stick 'em up," he said.

+ CHAPTER ELEVEN +
BLACK RABBIT

XAVIER AND ROWAN SLOWLY RAISED THEIR HANDS. Their mules, now loose, wandered a few feet away to munch on some grass.

"Give me your gold," Black Rabbit said flatly.

"We don't have any, honest!" gulped Rowan.

"You're leaving a gold camp empty-handed? What kind of fool do you take me for?"

"He's telling the truth, we don't have any gold," Xavier said. "Just a little money. A pocket watch."

"I'll take those then. And take off your clothes."

"What?" Rowan said, blinking.

"Remove your garments. Boots, too. Or I'll kill you and remove them myself."

The boys quickly stripped down to their long johns.

"Now put everything in the saddlebags and toss them over here."

The boys gingerly stepped through the prickly grass and tried to unfasten the saddlebags from the mules, but the animals kept turning around and hitting them with their tails. The whole operation was taking a lot longer than it should have. Finally, they unbuckled the saddlebags and brought them to Black Rabbit, who swung them over the back of his horse.

"Hey, watch out for bears," he said mockingly.

Then he aimed his pistol at Xavier and cocked the hammer. Xavier's stomach sank right to his bowels. His body started to shake. He prayed so hard he thought his head would explode: *Please, God, don't let this be the end of me, please, God, I'm not finished . . . I'll do better, I'll stop being selfish, I'll help my family more . . . I'll help everybody more . . . I'll dedicate my life to . . . to . . . just, please . . . not yet . . . not now . . .*

At the last minute, Black Rabbit turned and fired over the mules. The animals bolted, crashing wildly through the brush. Then Black Rabbit spurred his horse and streaked upward into the hills.

Xavier and Rowan stood there, frozen, for several minutes.

"I've never looked down the barrel of a gun before," Rowan finally croaked.

"Me either," Xavier said. "It sure is a lonely place to be."

They started down the path, each lost in his own thoughts. That night they lay under a small lean-to that Xavier built by laying a few branches against a bush, but it didn't protect them from the mosquitoes, which made a hearty meal of their tender flesh.

The next morning the boys trudged for hours, shivering in the dew and ravenously hungry. When they saw the undertaker's stable on the outskirts of Hangtown, they quickened their pace. They were so happy to be back, they barely heard the townspeople pointing and laughing at them as they stumbled down Main Street.

They pushed through the swinging doors at the Lily Rose Saloon and fell into the arms of the first woman they saw.

The next thing Xavier knew, he woke up on a large, soft mattress in the Huckleberry House Hotel, bathed and dressed in a flannel nightshirt. There was balm on his mosquito bites and one of his feet was bandaged. Rowan was asleep next to him in the same bed. His pulse was being taken by a man whom Xavier took to be a doctor. Bret was there, and his eyes brightened when he noticed Xavier was awake.

"I brought the doc as soon as I heard what happened," he said. "Is it true then? You were robbed by Black Rabbit?"

"Yeah. How did you hear about it?" Xavier mumbled.

"News travels fast, especially when it's about two fellas running through town in their underwear."

"Well . . . he caught us off guard," Xavier muttered as Rowan's eyes fluttered awake. Rowan sat up in bed in time to get a spoonful of medicine from the doctor.

"He's caught a lot of people off guard," Bret said, brushing lint off of his trousers. "Some of them didn't turn out as lucky as you. All you lost were your clothes."

The doctor prescribed for Xavier the same thing that he had given Rowan: a healthy dose of something called "Dr. Bell's Peppermint Chill Tonic," as well as "Dare's Elixir Mentha-Pepsin Reconstructive Tonic for the Stomach, Liver, Nerves, and Blood," and "A. Wertheim's Safe Rheumatic Remedy." They all tasted pretty nasty, and Xavier was happy when the doctor picked up his black bag and left.

Bret fetched Xanthe and Nina, then left the four friends alone for privacy. The girls fretted over the condition of their brothers for several minutes, then sat on the side of the bed as the boys told them about their harrowing encounter with the outlaw Black Rabbit and then their meeting with Oliver Weber. They started with his resemblance to Otto and ended with the depressing news he had given them, that Balt's whereabouts were still unknown.

"I don't care about that!" Xanthe said. "You guys were almost killed! Maybe we took on too much with this assignment. Maybe this place is too dangerous . . ."

"Xanthe, we're not going back without finding Balt," Xavier said. "The aunts, the Owatannauk Board of Directors . . . *everyone* is trusting us to do this. It's important."

"And we're not hurt," Rowan added. "Just some sore feet and a case of poison oak." He scratched his neck where the rash had started to spread. "Look, I'm the first one to bail on a risky scheme. But I agree with Xavier. This is too important."

"How do you know?" Nina said.

"It just is," Rowan said. "We may not fully understand

what's going on, but we do know the Board is desperate to find Balt. They've been searching for him for years. Years! I have the feeling we're their last hope."

"But Oliver told you Albert . . . I mean Walter . . . well, Balt . . . whatever his name is . . . disappeared in San Francisco," Nina said. "I think we've run out of leads."

Lily Rose appeared at the top of the stairs. "Xanthe, I've got some bedsheets and towels I need washed . . . Oh, you're awake," she said, noticing the boys. "How are you feeling? You looked pretty worse for wear when you stumbled in here this morning. I trust my girls took good care of you."

"Yes, ma'am, they did," Xavier said, suddenly aware of who must have bathed him and put him to bed.

"I'll have a doctor come and give you something for your fever," Lily said.

"That's all right; there was a doctor just here."

"You mean Arnold Lempkin?" Lily snorted. "He may be a doctor this week, but he was a dentist last week, and before that he was a card dealer in Sacramento. No, I'll get you a good doctor. This one's Chinese. Those Chinese are thorough." She turned to Xanthe. "Remember the sheets." Xanthe nodded.

"I'm confused," Xavier said to Xanthe after Lily went back downstairs. "Why are you doing laundry? I thought you were the cook."

"That was until the hotel guests got a taste of breakfast . . ." Nina giggled.

"Nina! Shhh!" Xanthe said, giving her a light shove.

"Xanthe made jawbreaker muffins, raw sausage, and . . . and the pancakes . . ." She started giggling again, unable to control herself. "The pancakes bounced! Boing! Boing!"

"What did I tell you?" Xavier laughed.

"I'm not used to this kind of stove!" Xanthe snapped. "And I wouldn't be so quick to laugh—you arrived here in your underwear, after being robbed by a . . . a rabbit!"

"He's a strange one, that's for sure," Rowan said, sitting up against his pillow. "I mean, he was scary all right, but he seemed more interested in making us look stupid than taking our money."

"Hmm. He's tricky. Like a rabbit," Nina said.

"Tricky?" Xavier said. The pieces fell together in his head so fast he could hardly keep up with them. Then it happened. His mind snatched the elusive fly of an idea buzzing in the back of his head. He threw the covers back, jumping out of bed.

"Wait a minute, what did that wanted poster say about him?"

"Let's see," Xanthe said, trying to remember. "It said, 'Lew "Black Rabbit" Rabbet, five foot six, black hair, crazy eyes . . .' Oh, Xave, you don't think . . . ?" Now she was on her feet.

"Yes! Yes! It's the same guy! The black hair, the crazy eyes— one brown, one blue—and the name! The *name*! Lew Rabbet is another anagram for Balt Weber!"

"Wow!" said Rowan. "Wow, Xave. That was impressive."

"And now we've got a lead!" squealed Nina.

"Yes. We know who he is. We practically know where he is.

We just have to figure out how to get him," Xavier said, rubbing his hands together.

"Whoa there, cowboy," Rowan said. "You had me, but now you lost me. You're not seriously thinking of trying to capture Black Rabbit, are you?"

"Rowan, it's not Black Rabbit, it's Balt! We're so close, if we could just . . ."

"No, Xave, it *is* Black Rabbit. Uh, hello? Do you remember that little robbery that happened yesterday? Big gun? Us running through the woods in our long johns? So what if it's Balt, he's also a dangerous criminal . . . maybe even a murderer!"

The other three exchanged glances. Rowan had a good point. They had done what they had set out to do: find Balthazar. It was time to call the aunts.

Xavier and Rowan stayed in bed for most of the day, nursing their wounds. Bret, who had also rented a room at the Huckleberry House Hotel, came to visit. He brought Chester with him.

"I was sorry to hear what happened to you," Chester said. "But I'm glad to see you're still breathing. Anyway, I'll be leaving shortly, so I wanted to say good-bye. I'm heading out for Negro Hill. If you ever find yourself there, come look me up."

Chester seemed to direct his invitation to Xanthe more than anybody else. She smiled and nodded, and when Chester took her hand and kissed it, she blushed.

When the Chinese doctor arrived, he applied compresses and herbs to their cuts and bruises, and supplied them with a tea that they were told to drink five times a day. It had a foul, bitter taste, but because it was always served by one of Lily's lovely ladies, Xavier started to look forward to receiving his dose. As he and Rowan slept off and on, they could hear Nina playing the piano in the saloon to applause and stamping feet.

A short time before sundown, Xanthe and Nina entered the bedroom. Xanthe threw herself into a chair, exhausted.

"I thought pioneers lived the simple life. There's nothing simple about it," she complained. "I've broken about ten dishes, and I don't know how anybody can sew anything with thread that keeps knotting up," she said, holding up her thumb, which was riddled with poke marks from a needle. "I've lost at least a pint of blood from this thumb alone. I think Lily is fed up with me."

"How can you tell?"

"Well, after I ruined my third dress, she grabbed it out of my hands and yelled, 'I'm fed up with you!' I admit it; I'm not cut out for the domestic household arts. It's the golden hour. Let's call the aunts."

They all held up their alleviator keys, which shimmered in the waning light. Xavier put his to his mouth like a microphone. "Testing, testing, one two three . . . this is Mission Gold Rush, do you read me? Over."

"Xave, just get to the point. They're not going to answer back." Xanthe spoke into her own key. "Aunt Gertrude? Aunt Agatha? If you can hear us, we need to talk to you right away."

"We've found Balt," Rowan added, speaking into his key. "What do we do now?" They all looked at each other for a moment. "Well, I guess that's it," Rowan said, putting his key back in his pocket. "Now we just have to wait."

Fifteen minutes later they heard a commotion downstairs. The foursome dashed to the saloon in time to see Lily trying to calm an elderly woman who was red with rage.

"Mark my words, madam, whiskey is the devil's brew! It leads to loose morals, lasciviousness, loud laughter, and other behaviors ill fitting a society of serious and sober God-fearing citizens!"

Xavier had to stifle a laugh. It was Aunt Agatha, dressed in a severe black dress that was straining to cover her figure. As soon as she saw the children, she waggled her finger at them.

"How old are those children? Why, I am shocked! Shocked! That you would draw these innocents into this house of sinfulness!"

"They came here of their own accord, madam," Lily sniffed. "And there is nothing sinful about my business!"

"Oh my, I'm getting the vapors," Agatha said, fanning herself with her pamphlets. "I can't bear to be in here one more second! Show me to a doctor!" she cried, reaching for Xanthe. Xanthe looked over at Lily, questioningly.

"Take her to the doctor," Lily said.

"The Chinese one?"

"No. The other one."

Xanthe nodded and took Agatha by the elbow, steadying

her as she stumbled out the door onto the street. They were soon joined by the other three.

"How was I?" Aunt Agatha whispered conspiratorially. "I love pretending to be a member of the temperance society. So against my normal personality . . . not that I condone heavy drinking, but they were such finger-shaking party poopers, you know."

"Aunt Agatha, we've found Balthazar," Rowan said. "But getting him back to the Owatannauk isn't going to be easy."

"I know. But don't say anything yet. We need to have Gertrude with us, and we couldn't both come here at the same time. Counting Balt, that would make seven people from the future in the same location, and that's one too many. I've parked an alleviator outside the livery stable. We're going to the Owatannauk."

+ CHAPTER TWELVE +
RISE OF THE GHOST RIDER

GERTRUDE PEMBROKE SAT IN HER LIVING ROOM watching the eight eyes that shifted slightly under her unwavering gaze. "It's worse than I thought," she said finally. "This is going to make things very difficult. Very difficult indeed."

She fell into silence once more. The children fidgeted in their seats, waiting for her to explain what she meant. After a minute or two, Agatha cleared her throat.

"Perhaps, Sister," Agatha began delicately. "Perhaps it is time that we told the children exactly what is going on."

"That would only be possible if we knew," Gertrude said with an ironic smile. She sighed and rose from her chair. "But I suppose you're right. They've gotten us much farther than I ever imagined they could . . . no offense," she said, turning to the four young people, who were not offended in the slightest. "But we are dealing with a very sticky situation here, and I have run out of ideas. So. Here it is. The Owatannauk Twilight

Tourist Program is in trouble. Only a few people are aware of this. We have a potential disaster on our hands."

"Is it because of Balt?" Xavier asked.

"Yes," Agatha said. "But you need to know a little more about Balt to truly understand what's going on." She looked to Gertrude, who nodded, and Agatha continued.

"As you already know, Balthazar is Archibald Weber's son, and he's an angry, bitter young man. What you don't know is that Balthazar is not just some spoiled juvenile delinquent. He's as gifted as his father. More so. As you know, I taught Archie in high school for a short period of time; that's how we met. When Balt was eight, Archie asked me to tutor him, and his abilities were nothing short of remarkable.

"It must've been strange for Balt to grow up at the most popular resort hotel of its time. There was always something interesting going on, and celebrities were showing up on a daily basis. He had hundreds of acres to explore, not to mention the facilities—boats, horses, golf, tennis—a child's paradise, I'd imagine. But as Balthazar grew up, I could see that he was not as carefree as his father. He was a serious boy with a sensitive soul, an easily bruised heart, and the poor thing didn't have any friends. If that wasn't bad enough, when Balt was eleven, his mother passed away.

"Archie did not take her death well; he withdrew from the world, spending even more time with his inventions. It devastated Balt, for other than myself his mother was his only real companion. I tried to fill the hole in his life that her death had created. I spent more time with him outside of studying. We took walks, read poetry, played music. Somehow he came to terms with it, but it affected him deeply. All his mischief, his childish merriment, disappeared. In its place was a serious and sober young man.

"Then, the very day Balt turned twelve, Archie informed me that my tutoring services were no longer needed. He was going to instruct the boy himself . . ."

Agatha hesitated, turning to Gertrude. "Go on, Sister," Gertrude prompted.

"Well, it was at this point that Balt took a turn for the worse. He became sullen. It was not uncommon for him to have angry outbursts. Often I'd catch him off in a corner somewhere, muttering to himself. He and Archie would disappear into Archie's study, and you wouldn't see either one of them for days. Days turned to weeks, weeks turned to months."

"Wait, go back a bit," Rowan said. "What did you mean when you said the Twilight Tourist Program was in trouble?"

"There are dark forces at work," Gertrude said. "Forces that threaten to use the hotel and its alleviators for self-serving purposes. As troubled as he is, Balthazar is the only one who can keep those forces at bay."

"Er . . . what does that mean?" Nina asked.

"I don't really know," Gertrude admitted. "I'm only repeating what Archie told me. It seemed he didn't want to entrust me with too much information."

Then Xavier remembered something. "Aunt Agatha, the Balthazar that you knew . . . would he be capable of murder?"

"Absolutely not," Agatha responded staunchly. "Sure, he had a reckless side, but he would never . . ."

"Balthazar is a criminal, Sister," Gertrude interrupted. "It may be that we're too late. We may have already lost him."

"Nina and I know what it's like to lose a parent suddenly," Rowan added quietly. "That anger . . . anger at the whole world . . . at God . . . it can twist you."

"No. I don't believe it," Agatha said, hitting the arm of her chair sharply. "We can't give up on him yet. We have to have faith that some part of his goodness can still be reached . . ." Agatha sighed. She was having trouble convincing herself.

A pall hung over the room. Rowan scuffed his shoe on the floor. Xanthe twisted her apron strings around her finger and stared into space. Nina cracked her knuckles. Xavier relaxed and eased himself into The Zone. Sometimes finding an answer was frustrating, like catching a fly, but other times it was like riding a glider, coasting over the landscape of his thoughts, scanning the whole terrain. Then one detail would pop out from the others, and with hawklike precision he'd turn toward that detail, swoop down, and grab it. Xavier looked up.

"I've got it." All eyes turned toward him. "I know how we can lure him in."

"Go on," Gertrude said.

"Well, the way I figure it, Balt is running from his former life: his father, Aunt Gertrude, even from Aunt Agatha. So it's got to be one of us who convinces him to come back," he

said, gesturing to the younger people in the room. "We have to make friends with him, get him to trust us, maybe find out why he's so angry. Then, when the time is right, we can reveal who we are and why we need him to come back."

"Xave, think about what you're saying," Xanthe said. "He's an outlaw! How are we going to get close to him?"

"Outlaws have friends," Xavier said.

"Yeah, right. Other outlaws," Xanthe said sarcastically.

"Exactly."

She frowned. "You aren't saying we're going to become outlaws? That's . . . that's crazy!"

"All of us becoming outlaws is crazy. But I'm only talking about one of us. Me."

The group erupted in protestations.

"You can't be serious!"

"This isn't a game!"

"Are you nuts?"

"It's too dangerous!"

"You're no outlaw; you've never even stuck gum under a table!"

Xavier waited for the noise to die down. He noticed that Gertrude was the only one who had kept silent.

"I am serious," he said. "And I know it's dangerous, but from what I've heard, it's worth it. Balthazar doesn't sound like a killer, so let's assume that part of his reputation isn't true and that he's not going to murder me."

"Xavier, how are you ever going to pass yourself off as a

criminal?" Xanthe said. "You're a fair mimic, a so-so actor, and a big liar, but come on! He'll see through you in an instant!"

"I don't think so. First of all, he's sort of a fake criminal himself. It's like a game to him. And secondly, I've got a persona just waiting for me to step into. The Ghost Rider."

"That goofy character you made up?" Xanthe scoffed.

"He may be goofy to you," Xavier said, slightly hurt, "but he's no more ridiculous than any of the other legendary outlaws of the West."

"I think Xavier has an excellent idea," Gertrude said. Xanthe stopped laughing.

"Really?" Xavier said, surprised. It made him a little nervous that Gertrude agreed with him.

"We need to lure Balthazar in. As we are all aware, Xavier seems to have a knack for . . . shall we say, making friends."

"But what would the rest of us do?" Nina said.

"Well, for us to make the Ghost Rider real, he needs a reputation," Xavier said. "You have to help me build it. I need to have some actual robberies under my belt. If you can help set them up so that I can make a big splash, the legend of the Ghost Rider will be off and running."

"So you want us to help you look like you're a notorious stagecoach bandit," Rowan said, warming up to the idea. "I guess you rob a coach that has a couple of us in it, and a few civilians . . . people not likely to fight back."

"We can hang a handkerchief out the window of the stagecoach so you'll know we're ready for you," Xanthe added.

"What if we set the alleviator nearby, so you can disappear into thin air!" Rowan added excitedly.

"Those are all great ideas," Xavier said. "And see if you can get Bret Harte to be one of the civilians. He's a good storyteller. Once he gets a handle on the Ghost Rider, the story will spread like an Internet virus."

"I still don't see how this is going to lure out Balt," Nina said, folding her arms.

"Well, I'm no psychologist, but I'll bet that one reason Balthazar turned to crime is because he wants attention. He was lonely. No friends. Then he even lost his teacher," Xavier said, indicating Agatha. "And look at how he's dressed himself, all in black with a black horse. It's a costume! And it's kind of juvenile, if you think about it. Real bandits don't care what they wear, they just want money. Balthazar is putting on a show."

"OK, so he's got a big ego . . ." prompted Nina.

"Somebody who has spent all this time turning himself into one of the most talked-about outlaws is not going to like hearing about another guy doing the same thing he's doing in his own territory, grabbing all the attention. Believe me; I know what I'm talking about. Xanthe and I go through this all the time!"

Xanthe laughed. "That's for sure. If Balt's anything like me and Xave, he's going to want to get rid of the Ghost Rider for good." She grinned and punched Xavier playfully. "Or at the very least, check out the competition."

"Or maybe he'll be scared off, and go somewhere else," Nina said.

"No, no, he's not going anywhere," Rowan said thoughtfully. "He's sticking around Hangtown for a reason, and that reason is Oliver Weber. Remember, Oliver is his family. I think Balt genuinely likes him and wants to be near him. Just a feeling."

"Once Black Rabbit comes out of his hole, I'll try to charm him, get to know him," Xavier continued. "Maybe offer to join forces. I don't know, I'll have to see what kind of state of mind he's in. I'll come up with something. I always do."

"But listen, Xave, you've got to check in with us, every day if you can," Xanthe warned. "I don't want you out there alone. We need to know what's going on with you and vice versa."

"Yeah, yeah, I know," Xavier said, waving her off.

"She's right, Xave," Rowan added. "You have to check in with us."

"I heard her!"

"It's decided then," Agatha said. "Xavier will stay here so that we can prepare him for this new role that he is to play. But the golden hour is almost up. The rest of you need to get back to Hangtown. I believe Nina has an eight o'clock show, and you don't want to disappoint Miss Lily."

"Oh, you know about that?" Nina said, embarrassed.

"Of course, my dear. As a representative of the Christian Temperance League I make it my business to know all of the purveyors of scandalous behavior! And by the way, I would stop playing ragtime music, my dear. Ragtime didn't become popular until after the Civil War."

As they walked through the lobby of the Owatannauk Resort Hotel, Xavier noticed Otto behind the reservations desk, talking with what appeared to be a Japanese samurai. Otto certainly looked like a real person, but when compared to his prototype, the gracious, thoughtful, and very human Oliver Weber, Otto definitely fell short.

The friends said good-bye at the alleviators and wished each other luck, then Xavier and Agatha continued on to the Owatannauk Library. When they pushed open the heavy doors, Jenny O'Neill was waiting for them.

"Gertrude called and told me you'd be coming," she said, leading them to the dressing rooms. "Xavier, if you're going to embody this Ghost Rider character, you need to tell us what he looks like. Then we'll see what we can do."

Xavier described the Ghost Rider to Jenny the same way he had to Curly. In less than an hour Jenny had pulled together his outfit, a Western costume in light gray and white. Xavier started to put on the ensemble, but Jenny stopped him.

"Before you get dressed, you need to put on the appropriate underwear."

"The long johns I have are fine."

"Perhaps, but they're not bulletproof. These are."

Jenny handed him a pair of long johns that were slightly thicker than the ones he was wearing. Xavier ducked behind the changing screen and slipped into them. They felt a little stiff and had a rubbery texture, but they were lightweight and comfortable. He twisted around and touched his toes.

"We use them for travelers who anticipate getting into violent situations," Jenny said. A worried tone had crept into her voice. "Remember, this only protects your body. Your boots are reinforced to protect your feet. The crown and brim of your hat are also bulletproof, but your hands and face are still exposed. Now try on the rest."

Xavier did, donning the white shirt and gray trousers, the black boots, the hat with the feather, and the long white duster that floated behind him as he twirled in front of the three-way mirror. He tried to be nonchalant, but he couldn't mask his pleasure; this outfit was a million times snazzier than the shapeless clothing he'd been given at the beginning of the mission.

"Those clothes suit you," Jenny said. She hesitated, then pushed a box toward him. "Here. You'll need this to complete the look."

Xavier opened the box. Inside was a pistol with a gleaming silver barrel. He picked it up and turned it over in his hands. The gun was heavier than he expected, and cold. He was certain his parents wouldn't approve.

"Maybe I shouldn't carry this," he said ruefully.

"Well, you don't have to," Agatha said. "But Gertrude and I talked it over with Annabelle, your nana, and we all agreed that you need something to defend yourself with. It's not a typical weapon, however."

"This gun shoots heat-seeking tranquilizer darts," Jenny explained. "If you aim within three feet of a living target, the darts will find it and hit it, and within five seconds the target will fall fast asleep, but only for about fifteen minutes. It's a safeguard to keep you from accidentally changing history. There is no possible way to kill anyone with it, and any injury should be slight; at worst, you'll only make the victim late for an appointment . . . but try not to do that, either. Also, according to your legend, the Ghost Rider carried a gun and was a remarkably accurate marksman."

"Nana said it was OK?"

Jenny nodded. Xavier spun the gun and slipped it into his holster. It felt strange there, like it was a living thing he was carrying on his hip. His hand kept knocking against it, and the weight made him walk differently.

"You'll get used to it, my dear," Agatha said. "I've had to carry guns on a few of my trips. Just remember to pull it out of the holster before firing. I know that sounds obvious, but once when I was camping in the rain forest with the poacher police, we were suddenly attacked by a jaguar. I reached for my weapon, and the next thing I knew I was under a bush and a monkey was poking me with a stick. Not a pleasant way to wake up, I must say. Anyway, I know you don't need to hear this, but please be careful."

"You should probably practice using it," Jenny said. "We have a firing range downstairs in the basement, but before you do that, there's one last thing you need."

Jenny led Xavier and Agatha down the hallway to a door that opened to an enclosed courtyard in back of the library. The walkways were illuminated by low lanterns that created large white polka dots throughout the garden. At nighttime most of the flowers were colorless, their fragile silhouettes barely visible. Only the white flowers shone like fallen stars nestled in the dark shrubbery.

At the end of the garden Jenny unlatched the gate to a large, round wooden building, which turned out to be an exercise arena for horses. There in the middle, standing perfectly still, was a gray Appaloosa stallion.

"Is this . . . for me?" Xavier gasped, turning to Agatha.

"The Ghost Rider has to ride something," Agatha said, her eyes twinkling.

Xavier walked toward the animal, which followed him with its soft brown eyes. When he got close enough, Xavier placed his hand on the horse's muzzle, which was velvety soft.

"His name is Sky Dancer," Jenny said. "But we just refer to him as Dancer. He's a very special horse—a robot, programmed to follow your every command. You ride him the way you'd ride any horse. I understand you've had some experience . . . ?"

"At a couple of summer camps," Xavier said. "Is he really a robot? He doesn't look like a robot." Xavier scratched Dancer's ears. The horse shook his mane.

"No, he doesn't," Agatha agreed. "But like the other inventions you've been exposed to at the Owatannauk, it is a technology available only to people in the Twilight Tourist Program."

Jenny whistled sharply. Dancer walked toward her and stopped.

"You're not the first person to need a reliable animal," Jenny explained, putting her foot in the stirrup and swinging her other leg over. "And by *reliable* I mean an animal that not only responds to your commands, but also won't die on you. Dancer will take care of you."

Jenny clicked her tongue and Dancer trotted around the ring. He broke into a canter, and then eased into a full gallop. Jenny's ponytail flew behind her. The third time around she dropped her feet from the stirrups and tucked them under her so that she was crouching in the saddle. The next moment she was standing, with Dancer's stride never breaking. He galloped around twice more and Jenny jumped back into a straddle. When she tugged back on the reins slightly, Dancer stopped almost instantly.

"Sorry about showing off," Jenny grinned. "I took a trip back in time to Romania in the early nineteen hundreds and fell in with a circus. But I wanted to show you how smooth he is. Nothing will frazzle him. Not even the alleviators, which would certainly freak out most horses." She swung her legs around and slid off the saddle.

"Whistle, and he'll lock in the pitch and frequency," she said. Xavier did, and Dancer nodded and snorted, stamping his hoof twice.

Jenny handed Xavier the reins. "Here. He's all yours."

Xavier placed his foot in the stirrup and hoisted himself up. With a click of the tongue, he was off.

Agatha and Jenny went back into the library while Xavier practiced. He rode for hours. Though he was only an intermediate-level rider, Dancer made him feel like an Olympic gold medalist. He galloped in circles and figure eights, executed sudden reversals, jumped hurdles, and stopped on a dime. Then Xavier tried riding bareback, mounting Dancer at a run, and standing on the horse as he raced around the ring, just as Jenny had done. Then Xavier dismounted and walked to the other side of the ring. When he whistled, Dancer galloped up to him and stopped. Xavier experimented, adjusting the whistle to make the horse approach him at a walk, a trot, or a canter.

Once Xavier felt confident about Dancer, he found Jenny and Agatha at the main desk in the library. They escorted him to the firing range. He was surprised at how difficult it was to shoot a gun. Squeezing the trigger required real effort, and when the gun went off, the explosion startled him and his whole body was thrown backward. After firing six shots, Xavier's shoulder was sore and the target was just as clean and bullet free as when he'd started.

"Hopefully you won't have to use it," Agatha said kindly.

"And remember, the bullets will seek out living targets themselves," Jenny added. "These practice targets aren't heated in any way . . ."

"I want to keep trying until I get it right," Xavier said.

"Suit yourself. I've got work to do in the library."

"The sound of gunfire tends to rattle my brains a bit," Agatha said. "I'm going home. When you're finished, ride Dancer to the Owatannauk, go inside the resort, and into alleviator number twelve. Gertrude said she'll have it set for a location in the foothills just outside of Hangtown. Apparently there's a six o'clock stagecoach leaving Hangtown every day that should pass by it during the golden hour. Good luck, and be careful."

After Jenny and Agatha left, Xavier spent the next several hours practicing his gun skills. At last he was able to draw with a clean, smooth motion and shoot two bull's-eyes in a row. He went back outside to the arena and found Dancer in the exact position that he had left him. He put his old civilian clothes into the horse's saddlebag and set off for the resort.

As they walked, Xavier wondered if Dancer could understand English. It occurred to him that whoever had designed and built the horse had also probably designed Otto, and could've given Dancer the ability to speak if he'd wanted to.

(Applause)

DANCER: Welcome back to *Good Guys*, I'm Dancer, your guest host . . . or guest *horse*, as the case may be. (Laughs) Now tell me, Xavier, you have a lot "riding" on this mission, if you'll excuse the pun. Everything depends on you at this point. Doesn't that make you nervous?

XAVIER: Not at all, Dancer, not at all. You see, I am destined for greatness. Everything in my life has been building toward this.

DANCER: So are you saying that you are the leader and your friends and sister are supporting players?

XAVIER: Not to diminish their contributions in any way, but sometimes you just know that fate has something important in store for you, Dancer. And let's face it, not everybody has the skills, or the guts, that one needs to truly be considered great.

DANCER: Fascinating. Thank you for being so candid. I'm honored to have you as my rider.

XAVIER: My pleasure.

Xavier reached the driveway outside the Owatannauk Resort Hotel just in time to see it transform. In an instant, the whole building seemed to brighten and sit up, as though nudged out of a long slumber. He walked Dancer through the lobby and down the hallway to the alleviators, then into the twelfth time machine, passing a small group of Victorian phantoms who were outfitted for a fishing expedition. They didn't give him a second look.

+ CHAPTER THIRTEEN +
EUREKA!

THE ALLEVIATOR SET XAVIER DOWN IN AN AREA NOT far from Glitter Gulch, near the same trail where he and Rowan had been robbed by Black Rabbit. He rode Dancer up and down the path, taking note of the trees and boulders and the curve of the creek so that he would be able to find the alleviator easily. There was a spot where the trail overlooked the road, which he thought would make an ideal location to wait; from that vantage point he'd be able to see the stagecoach coming from either direction and still remain hidden by the huge rock formations.

Once satisfied that he knew the area well enough, Xavier took Dancer up into a thick part of the woods and made camp. As part of his personal training to be prepared for anything, Xavier had taken a survival course. The participants had all been given a sleeping bag, a canteen of water, a pocketknife, and a backpack containing a blanket, a rope, a first-aid kit, and protein bars, and then were left to fend for themselves for three days. He learned a lot in that class. For instance, he learned that he preferred a bed to sleeping on the ground, and that food prepared on a stove usually tastes better than anything stuck on a stick and hung over a fire, and that mosquitoes were the worst creatures ever created. Xavier put these thoughts in the back of his mind and set about cutting branches to make a shelter in case it rained. Fortunately, he had a canvas tarp to use as a roof and a warm bedroll. He set these up, then dressed himself in his civilian clothes and hiked toward the Glitter Gulch camp, hoping to grab a bite to eat.

When he reached the camp, it was early afternoon. The men had already finished breakfast and were hard at work, mining the creek. Xavier found Ed and Pete, who were just cleaning up the dishes. They recognized Xavier from his earlier visit and offered him some leftovers: a plate of greasy beans, beef jerky, and a cup of coffee. It looked awful, but he hadn't eaten anything that morning, so he choked it down. As he ate, he was asked to tell the story of his robbery at the hands of Black Rabbit. Somehow they already knew many of the details, and filled in the parts that Xavier tried to skip. Also, the story had grown to include Black Rabbit making off with several thousands of dollars in gold, and giving Xavier and Rowan a whipping.

"Well, that is some wild adventure," Ed said after Xavier finished. He picked up a shovel. "I'm surprised to see you fellows again. If that had happened to me, I'd stay in town for a while."

" 'You fellows?' "

"Your buddy Rowan showed up this morning," Ed said, resting the shovel on his shoulder. "He's out working the Long Tom."

"Really?" Xavier hadn't expected to find Rowan at the camp. That wasn't part of the plan.

"I'll take you to him. We were just heading over there."

They walked to a wide part of Cutthroat Creek that was brown and silty from agitation. Men shoveled gravel and dirt into long, shallow wooden flumes that were built at the edge of the water. They didn't look up when Ed greeted them but only gave a cursory *hey*, their eyes scanning the runoff for the glint of gold.

"Take a good look, Xavier; you're not going to see this anywhere else. We're the last of a dying breed."

"What do you mean?"

"Most men are joining the companies now, blasting mountains with water to break 'em down, using dynamite to open up holes. That's where you have to go now to get the gold; there's not much you can get this way anymore." He jerked his thumb at the men laboring in the creek.

"Well, why are you here then?" Xavier asked.

"I didn't come out here to be some hired hand making a salary," Ed said. "Heck, that's what I was doing in the New Hampshire shipyards! Nope, I came out here to work for myself."

"I was a lawyer in Philadelphia," Pete broke in. "There's a

difference between working alongside good, honest men, splitting everything you find evenly, and working for some pasty-
faced businessman with his feet up on his desk, raking in the
dough without getting his hands dirty. But I guess pretty soon
it's all going to go to the businessmen. That's when I'm going
home."

"Aw, Pete, you're never going home," Ed joked. "We're
gonna bury you right next to your pickax with a rock overhead that says, 'Here lies a fool who died of gold fever.' How
long you been away from your wife anyway?"

"Five years," Pete mumbled. "I swear I'm going back. I
reckon my baby girl's not a baby anymore . . . But I just need to
make one good strike . . . I know it's here somewhere. My bones
are telling me this hill still has a lot to give up."

They reached Rowan, who was working a sluice with Oliver
Weber. Rowan jumped, startled, when he saw Xavier.

"Hey, Xave," he said nervously.

"Hey, Rowan, I didn't know you were here."

"Yeah, well, uh, Oliver was at Lily's last night and mentioned that they could use a hand out here, so I volunteered."

"Oh. I thought you had something else to do." Xavier raised
his eyebrows meaningfully.

"I think I can do both," Rowan said pointedly. He picked up
a shovelful of gravel and dropped it into the top of the sluice
flume, which was really a series of connected troughs, each
about two meters long. There was a large tray at the top where
the gravel and dirt went in and was spread around with a shovel

head. Water, which had been diverted from the creek, rushed over it, moving the mucky material along. Xavier noticed that there were wooden slats along the body of the flume and that dirt was getting caught against them.

"You're welcome to join our group," Ed said, wading into the creek and shoving his shovel into the gravel. "But you don't get a share unless you put in the work. No slacking off."

"Thanks, fellas, but I've got some business to take care of first. Maybe later."

"Make sure you come back," Pete said. "I hear Negroes are good luck."

Xavier almost laughed out loud. Considering everything that was going on in the East and the South in eighteen fifty-seven, that seemed like a bizarre sentiment.

"Rowan, can I talk to you a second? About that business?"

Rowan hesitated, then shrugged. "All right." He turned to the other men. "I'll be back."

Xavier led him far away from the camp before turning. "What the heck do you think you're doing?!" he yelled. "You can't start gold mining! We've got to flush out Black Rabbit!"

Rowan crossed his arms stubbornly. "I have to do this, to keep up our story. When we came we said we were here to mine gold. I have to act like I'm interested."

That made sense, but there was a strange look in Rowan's eye that bothered Xavier, an expression he had never seen there before. Then he realized what it was: insincerity.

"All right," he said, after chewing it over. "I guess what we can do is have you carrying some of your gold somewhere . . . maybe pretend to be taking it to a bank in the next town when I rob the stagecoach."

"You'll give back what you steal, won't you?" Rowan said. "I'm only asking because you might accidentally change history if you take the fortunes of the innocent bystanders we have riding with us in the coach." Again, the shifty look.

"I didn't think about that," Xavier said. "Yes, I have to figure out a way to get the money back to them. Try not to bring anyone with you who is carrying very much."

"Yeah yeah yeah," Rowan said, then got to the point. "But if I've got gold, I want it back, too."

"Of course."

"Good."

They both heard a rustling in the bushes. Xavier saw a black figure slipping behind a clump of pine trees.

"Shh!" Xavier whispered. "It's him again! Black Rabbit! Shoot, I can't meet him like this! It's too soon, and I'm dressed all wrong!"

"I can't believe we're going to be humiliated again!" moaned Rowan.

"That's not going to happen," Xavier whispered. "This time, I've got this." He pulled back his jacket to reveal his gun.

"You've got a gun?" Rowan gulped.

"Don't worry. I know how to use it. And it just shoots tranquilizer darts anyway . . . I've got it!"

"What are you doing?" Rowan hissed as Xavier removed the gun from the holster and crept toward the clump of pines.

"I'm going to put him to sleep before he gets a good look at me," Xavier murmured back.

"What if he does see you, and he shoots you?"

"I'm wearing bulletproof underwear."

"But I'm not!" Rowan almost shouted.

"Oh yeah. Well . . . hide."

The black figure was huddled behind the trees. Out of the corner of his eye, Xavier saw Rowan dive behind a boulder. With a sudden sweep of his hand, Xavier pulled back the branches . . . surprising a five-hundred-pound black bear.

Xavier dropped the gun. It slid several yards down the ravine.

"*Bear!!!*" Rowan screamed, jumping up from his hiding place. The bear sniffed the air, then lumbered toward him.

"Don't panic!" Xavier yelled. "Just wave your arms and make loud noises! Or play dead! I have to get the gun!"

Xavier slid down the ravine. The bear glanced at him for only a second, but then went back to Rowan, sniffing his face and coat. Suddenly his teeth were pulling and tearing at Rowan's jacket.

"He's eating my pocket!"

"What's in your pocket?"

"Candy!"

Rowan tore off his jacket, threw it at the bear, and fled. Xavier found the gun under a bush, but the bear was already charging after Rowan. Xavier was surprised at just how fast it could move. There was no way Rowan would be able to outrun it.

Then there was a large crack, a yell, and a crash and the sound of rushing rocks. Rowan had slid down the ravine.

The bear stopped before going over the side, and Xavier almost ran into him. As the animal turned and drew itself up, Xavier staggered back and pulled the trigger. The dart hit the bear and it howled, raising every hair on Xavier's body. Not only was the bear not asleep, now it was angry.

Xavier backed away slowly. Play dead? Make himself seem bigger? He couldn't decide, so he ran.

The bear bounded after him, close on his heels. Xavier grabbed a low tree branch and swung himself up. He climbed a few more branches for good measure. The bear was up on its hind legs, clawing at Xavier's leg, but then it staggered, lost its footing, and fell with a thud that shook the earth.

Xavier slowly climbed back down and pushed the bear with his foot. It was out cold. Then he raced to the spot where Rowan had toppled over the edge.

"Rowan! Rowan!"

"I'm over here."

Fortunately, it was not a cliff but just a steep slope. Xavier scrambled in the direction of the groans. There, scratched up and bruised, sat Rowan, his hand still clutching the bush he had grabbed, his feet braced against a boulder. Next to him a spring of water trickled from a hole made by a dislodged rock, which Rowan held in his hand. He looked dazed.

"Are you all right?" Xavier said, scooting closer to his friend.

Rowan nodded slowly. His eyes were strange and wild. "Look," he croaked. He held up the rock in his hand. Through the mud Xavier could see glittering, sparkling gold.

+ CHAPTER FOURTEEN +
THE GREAT STAGECOACH ROBBERY

On the way back to the camp Rowan had been very quiet. They talked about what they needed to fake a stagecoach robbery, but Xavier could see his friend's thoughts were elsewhere. The glittering rock was shoved in Rowan's pocket, and his hand seemed glued to it. Xavier told Rowan where the alleviator was stationed, near the place where they had been robbed by Black Rabbit. Before they parted, he made Rowan promise to go back into town immediately. Rowan promised, but then turned around and made Xavier promise not to tell anyone about what he had discovered, not even Xanthe and Nina, and that's when Xavier knew something had changed in Rowan.

That left the rest of the day for Xavier to think about how he was going to manage to rob a stagecoach, an idea that seemed more and more ludicrous as the day went on. His mind kept constructing disastrous scenarios in which he'd end up making a fool of himself, or worse. He reminded himself that this was his idea, so he had to make it work. If he didn't, Xanthe would have something to tease him about for the rest of his life. That thought slapped the reluctance right out of him. He focused on what he needed to do.

What *did* he need to do? He had to convince people that he was a ruthless outlaw. He needed to cloak himself in mystery, and impress whoever was in that stagecoach so strongly that they would talk up a storm, until the Ghost Rider became larger than life. More than anything, he needed to get Black Rabbit's attention.

But no, that wasn't right. He needed to get *Balthazar's* attention. Because Black Rabbit was a fake. He closed his eyes and relaxed, easing his mind into The Zone. Then, as always happened when he gave it enough time, a germ of an idea wriggled its way up like a green shoot pushing through soil. Xavier chuckled to himself. He had something that would work. It would take time, but it would certainly work.

It seemed like it took forever for the golden hour to come. He sat on Dancer, watching the sun slowly make its descent, and he was struck but the beauty of the West, the wild nature of it all, the red rocks, the giant trees, the smell of dust and sagebrush, the breathtaking mountains, and the wide open plains with boulders scattered randomly about, as though a giant had flung them around like so many marbles. It was too bad it couldn't stay this way. For so many years the natives had taken care of the land, living with it, not changing it. Now strangers were digging it up, destroying its natural state, all for the sake of money. The miners didn't intend to stay, only to grab what they could out of the ground and go.

Xavier spied the stagecoach coming around the bend. It had a white handkerchief fluttering from the window. That was the sign. He clicked his tongue, pressed both heels sharply into Dancer's flanks, and charged down the path to the road. He pulled his kerchief up over the lower part of his face and drew his gun.

Later that night when Xavier recalled the event, he realized it really could not have gone better. It was one of those moments in time when either God is smiling or all the planets are aligned correctly, or Lady Luck is in your corner, or you've been imbued with superpowers, or as in Xavier's case, you are in The Zone.

As soon as the stagecoach appeared, he shot his gun in the air. The crack it made split the atmosphere and resounded through the canyon. The stagecoach driver pulled back on his reins, the horses reared and whinnied, pawing the air. When the driver finally got them quiet, Xavier realized it was Curly, and he was reaching for his six-shooter.

"Don't touch that gun, old man, if you value your life . . . what's left of it," Xavier growled. At first he was afraid that the old stagecoach driver would recognize him, but he soon realized that Curly really didn't see him at all; all he saw was the image, the costume. And Curly was afraid.

"Throw down your gun," Xavier ordered. "And get those nice folks out of the coach."

Curly did as he was ordered. As he climbed down from his perch, Xavier could see he was shaking. Xavier had never had this kind of power over someone before. It felt ... scary.

Two middle-aged women and a young girl climbed out of the wagon. Xavier relaxed when he saw the girl was Nina. Xanthe and Rowan were not there. At first that troubled him, but then he realized that it was better that way, to include only one of their group in each coach that he robbed. That way no one would have to be robbed more than once. And Xavier was very glad to see Curly. The old man would certainly spread the news that a new bandit had come to town. Then, when Bret Harte climbed out after Nina, Xavier knew he had hit the jackpot.

"All right, little lady," Xavier growled at Nina. "How about you collect what you can from your friends and put it in this here bag." He tossed her his saddlebag.

Nina didn't move. She looked like she was about to cry. Xavier was impressed. "Do it!" he barked. She jumped, then stumbled over to the bag. Bret made a move to stop her, and Xavier twirled the pistol, firing a shot in the dirt in front of him.

"Stand your ground," he drawled, "unless you want a couple of new nostrils."

"You leave her alone," Bret said, his voice strained.

"Or what?"

"Or you'll have to deal with me."

"Shut up, pretty boy," Xavier snarled. "And put your valuables in that bag. Including that prissy little gun you've got in that fancy vest of yours."

Bret's eyes widened. Xavier knew he was taking a chance, but it was clear Bret hadn't recognized him. Besides, the performance wasn't over yet. Bret would have a lot more to think about once Xavier was finished.

Nina had already collected a few things from the ladies. When she reached Curly, he gave up his knife, but Xavier noticed he hadn't revealed the rifle yet. Bret dropped in a variety of things. A snuff box, handkerchiefs, rings, a pocket watch, a pen, a knife, a small bag of gold, and the dainty pearl-handled pistol.

"Now unhitch the strongbox, old man," Xavier said, motioning to Curly with his gun. Curly reached for the box under the driver's seat. Xavier knew what was coming next. In a flash, the old man whirled around with the rifle, but before he could pull the trigger, Xavier fired a shot into his shoulder. Curly fell backward, dropping the gun. He was able to get up and stagger a few steps before dropping slowly to his knees and then falling on his face.

Nina screamed and ran to Bret. The older women hid their faces. The effect was so believable that even Xavier's heart skipped a beat. Had he really shot Curly? Was he dead? But there was no blood coming from the hole in the old man's shirt. Xavier had to trust the technology of the Owatannauk and press on. He walked Dancer over to Bret and stared down at him.

"You best empty that strongbox into my bag, unless you want what he got," Xavier said.

Bret found the key in Curly's pocket and unlocked the box. It held several medium-size bags of gold, which, by the looks on their faces, belonged to the older women. They comforted Nina, who sobbed uncontrollably. Xavier would have to compliment her when this was all over; she was a natural. Bret put the gold in the saddlebag and handed it up to Xavier.

"One last thing," Xavier said. "I'm taking the old man."

"Why?" Bret demanded, outraged. "He needs medical attention! Either that or a Christian burial!"

"Maybe you didn't understand me. I said I'm taking the old man. Hand him up here." Xavier twirled the gun and pointed it at Bret's forehead. "Now."

Bret fumed but lifted Curly up and draped him over Dancer's back.

"Now, everybody get back in the coach," Xavier ordered.

They followed his instructions. Xavier spurred Dancer to gallop up the path where he could now see the alleviator waiting. He was aware that Bret was running after him and was close behind. Then, with a leap, Dancer was in the alleviator. Xavier turned the horse, which reared up, and kicked the button on the wall to close the alleviator door. The invisible time machine would hide them until the golden hour was over, even without having to travel anywhere.

Sure enough, Bret spun around, searching for the outlaw on horseback who had seemingly disappeared into thin air. He stood for a moment, listening, then slowly backed down the path.

Xavier knew he had to work quickly. The thick pine cover overhead had made it hard to see whether sunset had begun, but by his estimation the golden hour was almost over. He leaped off Dancer, pulling Curly down with him, and gently laid the old stagecoach driver on the ground. Then he searched through the saddlebag and found Bret's pen. Unfortunately, there was no ink. He gritted his teeth, took his knife, and drew it across his hand. A thin line of blood appeared.

Quickly he took the quill and dabbed it in his blood. The sharp point stung against his broken skin, but he steeled himself and wrote a message across Curly's forehead. Then he opened the door, pushed Curly out, and quickly hit the alleviator button. There was a flash, and he felt himself tingling, getting light-headed, and falling into the dizzying vortex of time space.

Xavier and Dancer arrived at the Owatannauk just as it settled into its dilapidated state. It was cold in the hotel at dusk, and fairly dark. Xavier knew he should probably get some rest, so he tied Dancer to a nearby railing and plunked himself down on a sofa, raising a cloud of dust. It was not going to be a pleasant place to spend the night.

He couldn't get settled anyway. He was too pumped up from the robbery. He opened up the saddlebag and took out the contents, laying them in front of him. A blush of shame crossed his face. He really had stolen these things. Right away he knew he had to find a way to return them.

Then Xavier remembered something. The Fibonacci numbers. He decided to explore the rooms upstairs.

He left the horse in the lobby and ran up the stairs to the second, secret hallway that he had explored with the others. It was illuminated by the moonlight shining through the stained glass window at the end of the hall. The only thing he could see clearly was St. Francis of Assisi's face, his eyes shining brightly. He slowly walked down the hallway until he was outside the door with a brass twenty-one on it. He opened the door.

It was one of the dead ends, a trompe l'oeil painting of prison bars.

Fibonacci numbers. Zero. One. One. Two. Three. Five. Eight. Thirteen. Twenty-one. Add the number to the number that comes before it to get the next number. That was the pattern. And in this second hallway, the one where St. Francis was wide awake, each of the doors that corresponded to these numbers had an actual room or rooms behind it. All except this one: room twenty-one.

Xavier stared at the prison bars painted on the wall for a moment. Then he went to the janitor's closet, behind door zero. There he found a large wrench. He picked it up and carried it back to door twenty-one. He lifted it in the air and swung with all his might.

The first impact only chipped at the plaster. The second made a bigger crack and much of the plaster fell away, revealing brick. But he kept swinging. He pounded the wall again and again, getting into a rhythm, each whack getting him closer to . . . what? He probably should've waited and told the others; he probably should have had them there with him. But curiosity had gripped him. He couldn't resist. He kept swinging.

Finally the bricks crumbled away and he was punching a hole through wood—a wooden door. He pushed the broken splinters through the hole he had created and peered into the blackness. Then he broke away more of the bricks and wood until he had made an opening large enough to crawl through. He went back to the janitor's closet, where he had seen matches and a candle in a candleholder. He brought these back to the hole he had made, lit the candle, and climbed through.

When his eyes adjusted to the light he saw that he was in a suite of rooms. He was standing in a large living room area. A sofa, a coffee table, and an overstuffed chair sat next to a fireplace on one side of the room; on the other were a bookcase and a small writing desk with a Tiffany lamp. On the wall were clocks. Hundreds of clocks.

Xavier walked slowly around the room. It was distinctly different from other rooms in the hotel. The furnishings in those rooms were ornate and Victorian, but these were natural. Artistic. Even by the glow of candlelight he recognized them as being from the Arts and Crafts movement, a period in architectural history that he'd read about in a book, in his unending effort to know a little bit about everything. The movement was a reaction against the industrialization of the early twentieth century, which was threatening time-honored manual crafts into extinction, replacing them with inferior, shoddy results of mass production.

He tried to turn on the Tiffany lamp, but the bulb was out. Then he realized that this was the first light bulb he'd seen in the entire hotel. All the other fixtures in the hotel used gas. This room was different indeed.

He also discovered that the suite was really more like an apartment. There was a hallway, which he followed to a small kitchen, a bathroom, and several bedrooms. Another room had no furniture at all, but was filled with clear pipes, too many to count. They were lined up in rows, climbing the wall and disappearing into the ceiling. Xavier deduced that they must be pneumatic tubes, a way of sending information from one room to another. He had seen them in other rooms in the hotel, but this room was clearly the hub of that system.

The largest room of all was a study . . . no, not a study . . . a laboratory. A room filled with long worktables cluttered with what looked like electrical experiments: wires, batteries, bulbs and meters, metal clamps, generators with strange dials and hundreds of switches.

Xavier quietly walked among the tables, up one aisle, down the other, and up again, careful not to touch anything. The only sound was his footsteps on the stone floor, which echoed in the deathly silence. In the corner of the room was a large architectural easel with blueprints laid out carefully on top.

By now it was beginning to dawn on him where he was,

even before he saw the leather-bound book on the easel. The cover was soft with wear. He opened it to the first page and held the candle close to the page so he could read the graceful handwriting:

Archibald Lewis Weber, Notes, Volume 12

He flipped through the book. It looked to be some kind of diary, riddled with doodles, notes, mechanical drawings, a hodgepodge of things. This was Archibald Weber's apartment. But why had it been sealed behind a brick wall? A shiver went down his spine.

He looked out the window and realized that the pitch black of night was softening to gray. He felt a tingle throughout his body, and he was hit with the sudden realization that it was the silver hour and he had to get out of there. Fast. Once the silver hour began, the hole he had made in the wall would disappear until the hour was over, and until then he'd be trapped, locked in with whatever was contained in this apartment.

Xavier stuffed the notebook in the back of his pants and ran. As he ran, the candle went out.

The tingling intensified to numbness. He stumbled into the sitting room, dropping the candlestick, his hands stretched out ahead of him. He banged his hip on something hard, then tripped over an ottoman, whacking his forehead on the edge of the chair. He grunted and crawled along the floor, trying to remember what objects might be near the door. When his head hit the wall, he reached out and found some broken bricks and other debris on the floor, and then, finally, *finally* he found the hole!

He dove through it, praying that the hole wouldn't seal up with him halfway through; how horrible that would be, to be chopped in half by a brick wall suddenly materializing within his body. But he was through, and in a wave of light and color the hole was gone, the trompe l'oeil painting was back, and the resort was bright and cheerful, the coming dawn promising a beautiful day of recreation for the hotel phantoms.

Xavier quietly retraced his steps, back through the door that led to the first hallway, and then back down the hallway to the lobby, where Otto was waiting with Dancer.

"Good morning, Mr. Alexander. Will you be having breakfast?"

"Yes, I think I will, Otto, as long as I have time."

"The restaurant is down the hall. They should be able to get you out within the hour. Just don't order the eggs Benedict. The hollandaise sauce takes some time to prepare."

"Thank you, Otto."

Xavier ate breakfast. The waffles with fresh fruit were heaven compared to the rancid food he'd eaten in gold country. In forty-five minutes he had a full stomach, and set out with Dancer to alleviator number twelve, and infamy.

+ CHAPTER FIFTEEN +
NOTORIOUS

Wanted: Alive

The Ghost Rider

For robbery of stagecoach and assault.

Description: Dark skin, possibly Negro or

Indian. Dressed in gray and white, gray

dappled horse. Six feet tall, cross-eyed and

hunchbacked.

$2,000 Reward

XAVIER READ THE WANTED POSTER IN THE EL DORADO
stagecoach depot with some confusion. Was this supposed to
be him? Six feet tall? Cross-eyed and hunchbacked? The six
feet tall part was all right; he was five foot seven and he had
never dismounted Dancer, so it would be hard for anyone to

really know how tall he was. But he was extremely disappointed with the rest of the description. The Ghost Rider was supposed to be cool! Not some dopey-looking thug!

Xavier left three packages with the El Dorado agent, who would send them with the next stagecoach going to Hangtown. The packages, addressed to Rowan, Nina, and Xanthe, contained the personal effects that he had stolen, and a letter saying to return them to their owners. He also included instructions for when the next robberies should occur.

It had been two days since the first robbery. After he had returned from the Owatannauk, Xavier had gone to Negro Hill, where he'd remembered Chester said he would be. He figured he'd be able to blend into the black community without attracting too much attention. When he got there, he discovered Negro Hill was actually a multiethnic community, with blacks, whites, and immigrants from all over the world.

He had found Chester in town and checked into the same boardinghouse where he was staying, the Civil Usage House, run by a stout woman named Joanne Chambers. It was similar to Mary Ellen Pleasants's place, though not quite as pretty. Xavier told Chester he had given up on getting fair treatment in Hangtown but that Xanthe had stayed behind, and he could see the disappointment on the young man's face. Nevertheless, Chester introduced him to some of the other boarders. They were relaxed and convivial, and politics was always as much the subject of conversation as gold.

Xavier got back from El Dorado just in time for dinner.

Joanne had prepared a hearty meal of beef stew, biscuits, and gravy. Xavier could see why blacks had a reputation as good cooks. Many of them had been employed as cooks back east or in the South by their previous employers, or owners, as the case might be.

"You hear anything else about the stagecoach robbery out by Hangtown?" Chester asked, helping himself to some collard greens.

"Nothing new," Xavier said.

"Crazy, isn't it? Black fella taking that kind of chance. He better hope he's caught by bounty hunters. If the vigilantes catch him, he'll be strung up and skinned like a jackrabbit."

Xavier gulped. "Why? I saw a Wanted poster that said to bring him in alive."

Chester raised an eyebrow. "You kidding me? The way he humiliated that driver by scribbling all over his face?" He gave a low whistle. "It was right there on the old fella's forehead, written in blood. 'Borrow or rob?' I don't know what it means, but it sounds like a warning."

"Maybe he's like Robin Hood," suggested Joanne.

"Maybe," Chester shrugged, mopping up more of the gravy with his biscuit. He took a big bite and dusted off his fingers.

Xavier was tempted to add his own two cents, but he remembered that too much talk was the biggest mistake a criminal could make. The best tactic was to pretend to be mildly interested, but ignorant.

"Well, I don't know," Xavier said blandly.

"I heard he disappeared into thin air!" Joanne Chambers said, buttering a biscuit. "He's called the Ghost Rider. Maybe he's the spirit of righteousness, come to pay back all the grief we've suffered."

"She's talking about the riots we had a few years ago," Joanne's husband and partner, Roland, said to Chester and Xavier. "We used to have a flourishing Negro business community here. That was before some rowdy white folks came in and shot up the place, then settled right here in town. Suddenly we couldn't put our children in the public school anymore. We can't testify in court, we're not allowed to homestead . . . it's a crying shame."

"That's all we need, some colored fella riding around stirring things up and drawing their ire," an older man in the corner called out, eavesdropping on the conversation. "That's not going to help nobody."

"Yup," said Xavier.

"Huh. I'm glad he's sticking it to them. I hope he does it again," Joanne sniffed. "And I bet they never catch him. He's an idea. A dream. You can't lynch a dream."

Xavier kept his head down. He was already plotting the second appearance of the mysterious Ghost Rider.

It was important to be consistent. During each robbery, Xavier shot the ground in front of somebody's feet. He chose the weakest person in the group to collect the valuables and load them into the saddlebag. At the end, he always shot somebody, kidnapped them, disappeared into thin air, and then left the victim near the trail with a message written on their body. The only difference was that he had purchased a bottle of red ink to use instead of his own blood; otherwise there was a familiarity to each robbery that made them easier as he went along.

Xanthe was at the second robbery, wailing like a fire engine, a pathetic attempt to draw attention to herself, but it didn't matter. Nothing topped the Ghost Rider. With his flapping white duster and cool demeanor, he transcended mere criminal. He was becoming a legend.

The second message, which he wrote on the arm of a boy who looked to be barely older than himself, was as inscrutable as the first: WAS IT A RAT I SAW?

For his third message he chose a pudgy, spectacled, middle-aged man, writing on his leg, NAME NO ONE MAN.

Something bothered Xavier, however. At the third robbery, a red handkerchief was wedged in the door instead of a white one. When he ordered everyone out, he discovered that Rowan was not among them, though according to the plan, he should have been. Where was he? Xavier hadn't seen him since he'd left him at Glitter Gulch. It ended up not making a difference, but still, Rowan's behavior bothered him.

With the fourth robbery, Xavier chose a wiry man missing most of his teeth. He wrote in his best penmanship on the man's back, NO EVIL I DID, I LIVE ON.

His legend continued to grow. The Ghost Rider was on the tip of everyone's tongue. Who was he? Why did he always strike at sunset? What did those peculiar messages mean, and what happened to the kidnap victims between the time they were taken and the time they reappeared half an hour later? And why were the victims getting their stolen goods back? What was the point?

The reward for capturing the Ghost Rider soared to four thousand dollars. Not because he was dangerous but because he was a nuisance, and from the conversations he overheard, Xavier could tell that the humiliation of white people at the hands of a black man rankled the white community.

After the first four robberies, Xavier left the Civil Usage House and returned to camping in the hills. If Black Rabbit was going to find him he had to be in a place where he could be found. At the same time, he knew that with a bounty on his head, there would be others looking for him. He changed the location of his camp every night. Sometimes he laid his bedroll on the ground, then slept in a nearby tree. Sometimes he would create a booby trap with twine and cans as an alarm for intruders. If he saw bounty hunters before they reached his camp, he would shoot them with the dart gun, then pick up and leave before they woke up. And he used the alleviator as much as he could to keep himself invisible.

It had been a while since he'd seen the others, but he was having so much fun playing the outlaw he didn't want to ruin it by having to listen to Xanthe yammer about being careful and not taking chances. He liked being a lone wolf for a while. He trusted his own instincts more than anybody else's, and besides, he was doing just fine. In fact, he was doing great!

Only once was he surprised by someone coming upon his camp. The night before, he had just finished an unsatisfying meal of beef jerky and cold beans, and had decided to crack open the leather diary he'd found in Archibald Weber's laboratory. So far, he'd been unable to find anything in the book that made much sense to him. First, the handwriting was sloppy and hard to read. But even more perplexing was the content. It took him a while to realize that whole sections of the book were written in different languages: Ancient Greek. Arabic. French. German. Chinese. Italian. Spanish. Russian. And more that he couldn't even identify.

He'd been flipping through the book, looking for any English passages he could find, when he'd heard a small cough and looked up. A man was staring at him from atop a brown-and-white painted pony, only a few yards away. He had somehow avoided the booby trap, and now looked at the scene before him with mild amusement. Something about him looked familiar. He was Mexican, with long black hair and an impressive mustache, and he wore a bolero jacket and black pants, and pointy boots with bright silver spurs.

"You look younger than I thought you would be," the man said. "And don't try it. I'm not interested in arresting you."

Xavier put the gun back in the holster.

"Want something to eat?" Xavier said, holding up the cold beans.

"No, *gracias*," said the man, grinning.

"Well, then what do you want?"

"Nothing, just saw you here. Thought I'd find out if you were really a ghost."

"So? What do you think?" Xavier said, folding his arms.

"Well, if you are, you're the smelliest ghost I've ever met." The man grinned. Xavier blushed. It was true he hadn't bathed in a while.

"So, why aren't you interested in the reward?" Xavier said, changing the subject. "Four thousand bucks is pretty good money."

"I don't need it. Besides, if I go anywhere near a sheriff's office, I'll be shot on sight. Let me introduce myself. I'm Joaquin Murieta."

"You can't be!" Xavier said, eyes wide. "Your head was in a box a week ago, being shown off at a saloon! Some bounty hunters got the reward for capturing you! They cut your head and your hands off as proof!"

"That wasn't me, *señor*."

"You sure?"

Joaquin Murieta felt his head and patted his hands. "*Sí, estoy seguro*. That wasn't me." He leaned forward in his saddle, resting his elbow on the horn. "They get tired of looking, you know, those bounty hunters. And one Mexican is as good as another. So they catch some other poor guy who stole something. You'll see. They'll probably do the same for you. If they can't find you, they'll find someone else."

Xavier's heart fell. He hadn't thought of that. He hoped some innocent person wouldn't be hung for the Ghost Rider's crimes. Joaquin lit a thin cigar and offered it to Xavier. He shook his head. The lean Mexican drew a deep breath and exhaled several smoke rings.

"So, is what they say about you true?" Xavier asked him, impressed by the rings.

"What? You mean am I crazy, out of my head? *Muy loco*?" He shrugged. "Maybe. Out here life is cheap, *mi amigo*. Those men killed my wife. She was all I had, all I ever really wanted. They took that, and for that they had to pay. Yes, I committed murder. Why not? I had nothing more to lose. But now . . ."

Joaquin gazed off into the distance and gave a slight shrug of defeat. "Anyway, now I'm free. The bounty hunters caught someone, cut off his head. I'm free to do what I want. Maybe I'll go back to Mexico. You should think about it. Pretty soon this land will be all torn up, the gold will be gone, all that will be left are the greedy, crazy, and desperate. It's time to go."

"I haven't finished what I need to do," Xavier said.

Joaquin shrugged. "Well, make sure you know when you're finished. This place grows on you. After all of this freedom, it's hard to go back." Joaquin tugged on the reins of his horse until it grunted in protest.

"I'm glad I saw you. I don't think you're a ghost. You're good, though. Almost as good as me." With that, Joaquin spurred the horse, which bolted through the brush in an explosion of hooves, its creamy tail flying behind like a banner. They were gone so fast, Xavier wondered if it was a dream, but Joaquin's cigar lay smoldering at his feet.

Two days later, after his fifth robbery, where he had left a particularly menacing message, he had his second visitor.

+ CHAPTER SIXTEEN +
BALTHAZAR

Xavier knew Black Rabbit was there because Dancer told him. Robot or not, Dancer's senses were as keen as a real horse's, so when his ears pricked up and angled toward a pine tree about twenty yards away, Xavier prepared for company. His last message, a particularly grisly one written on the chest of an old prospector—MURDER FOR A JAR OF RED RUM— was a clear invitation.

Only the day before, Black Rabbit had robbed a stagecoach. After relieving the passengers of their possessions, he'd liberated a large bottle of rum from the driver, poured it all over the coach, and set it on fire. Nobody had been hurt, though two of the horses ended up with singed tails. It seemed like a desperate move, calculated to get attention, Xavier thought, the actions of a jealous kid who was tired of somebody else being in the limelight.

After Xavier had left the message, he'd made camp in a place that was not difficult to find. If the bounty hunters discovered it, he would have to leave quickly, so he kept careful watch. That was why he noticed Dancer's interest in the tree. A posse wouldn't take so long to reveal themselves, so Xavier was pretty sure his quarry had arrived at last.

Xavier nonchalantly cooked a can of beans for supper. After enough time went by, and he figured the eavesdropper was good and bored, he ambled over to the tree and stood under it. He heard the click of the hammer of a gun being pulled back.

"Are you going to keep watching me or you gonna come down and introduce yourself?" There was a pause, then a figure dropped from the branches.

Seeing Black Rabbit again gave Xavier a squirrelly feeling in his stomach; their last meeting had ended in an embarrassing hike back to Hangtown in his long johns. Black Rabbit didn't seem to recognize him, however, and Xavier realized he, too, was blinded by the outfit, the trappings of the Ghost Rider.

"So, you're the Ghost Rider, huh?" Black Rabbit said, still leveling his gun at Xavier.

"Maybe."

"Well, you're not much of a ghost. I could shoot you, sure as I'm standing here."

"Why don't you then?" Xavier said, half hoping he would. He knew the underwear worked like a charm, having blocked no less than four bullets from heroic stagecoach passengers already. Black Rabbit ignored the challenge, shoving his gun in his holster instead. *He really isn't a killer, just a pretender,* Xavier thought. *He won't even kill a ghost.*

"You're causing quite a stir in these parts," Black Rabbit continued.

"Why don't you have a seat?" Xavier said, heading back to the fire. "It's warmer over here. You're the notorious Black Rabbit, aren't you?"

"That's right," Black Rabbit said proudly, obviously pleased that someone of the Ghost Rider's caliber had recognized him.

"Well, I sure am glad to make your acquaintance, Black Rabbit," Xavier said, offering his hand. "You're an inspiration."

Black Rabbit seemed to make up his mind about something and approached the fire. He took Xavier's hand, shook it once, and sat down.

"I was a little worried about you," he said, eyeing Xavier carefully. "These are my stomping grounds, you know. Thought maybe you were looking for a fight."

"I am sorry about that, I truly am," Xavier said. "But I've got a bone to pick with some people around here. That's all I'm gonna say. I've made my mark, though. If you want me to move on, I'll move on. Beans?"

"Uh, no," Black Rabbit said, holding up his hand as though to shield himself from the gloppy mess. "I already ate. And I don't mind your hanging around. It's nice to have some company. Gets a little lonely in these hills."

Xavier waited for the inevitable question. Finally, Black Rabbit pushed back his hat and leaned toward the dancing flames, revealing his unusual pair of eyes, one blue and one brown. He poked the fire with a stick.

"So, what exactly do those messages of yours mean?" he said.

"What do you think they mean?"

"Well, people say with that first one, 'Borrow or Rob,' you were announcing yourself as a kind of Robin Hood. Like, when you steal from the gold diggers, you're not really robbing them, because they were taking that gold from land that didn't belong to them anyway. Of course, nobody really understands why you're giving back what you stole . . ."

Xavier smiled enigmatically and shrugged. Black Rabbit waited for an explanation, but once it was clear he wasn't going to get one he continued.

"Then the second message—'Was It a Rat I Saw'—that one confused people. They thought maybe you were working with someone who was about to turn you in, and you were warning him that you knew what was up. That theory was confirmed by your third message, 'Name No One Man,' implying again that you were working with a partner."

Xavier poked the fire idly with a stick. Black Rabbit went on. He was warmed up and enjoying himself.

"All right, then the message 'No Evil I Did, I Live On' was like a plea of innocence. This was like your first message, letting folks know that you didn't consider your actions to be bad, and also that you would keep on going until you decided to leave. I like that one. It was like a direct challenge to the lawmen to try to catch you. That showed some guts. Then the last one, 'Murder for a Jar of Red Rum,' that one scared some folks. But they heard about what I did, and thought it was a comment on my deeds. I took it as a personal call. So, here I am."

"You seem to have it all figured out," Xavier said.

"Nope, I just told you what other folks have been saying in the towns, at least from what I hear. Personally I think it's a lot of hogwash."

"You do?"

Then Black Rabbit laughed. It was a silly kind of laugh, bright and whimsical, that tickled the air like soda fizz. For the first time, Xavier thought he was getting a glimpse of Balthazar, the boy underneath the costume. There was something impish about him, and he seemed lighter than air, a Peter Pan weighed down by black clothing and heavy boots.

"It's just puzzles!" Black Rabbit announced gleefully. "Palindromes! Your messages read the same frontward and backward. That's all they are! It's a doggone put-on!"

"You got it!" Xavier joined in the laughter, slapping the other boy on the back. "You mean to tell me no one else has figured it out yet?"

"Not a one," Black Rabbit chortled. "I tell you, I haven't had so much fun seeing people run around getting all excited about nothing. You're just out here having fun. That's why I wanted to meet you . . . we're like two peas in a pod, you and I. That's all I'm doing, too. Just having some fun."

"You know, I sensed that when I heard about you," Xavier

said. "I thought, here's a fellow who is just like me. We could be friends if only we could meet."

"Maybe we can pull some capers together!"

"That would suit me just fine."

"You gonna tell me how you disappear? How you make those people disappear before you write on them?"

"Well," said Xavier carefully, "that I can't do. It's kind of a magic trick, and it's a rule that a magician never tells his secrets. You never know when you'll have to use them to get out of a scrape . . ."

Black Rabbit looked disappointed, but only for a moment. "All right, that's fair," he said. Then after an awkward moment, he said, "Well, maybe I'll see you later." He gave a shrill whistle. A lean black stallion galloped from the woods and trotted to his side. In one swift motion, Black Rabbit swung himself onto the animal's back.

"Maybe," Xavier answered, touching the brim of his hat in a sort of lazy pretense of tipping it.

"By the way, you should look out for the Foggerty Brothers. There's five of 'em, work together as a posse. They've got it out for you. Their Aunt Minnie was in one of the coaches you robbed."

"I gave everything back. I always do."

"Doesn't matter. You gave her a scare, and that's enough for them. You can't miss 'em. They all got long hair, like Buffalo Bill. You know, Buffalo Bill Cody? Wild West Show?"

Xavier looked at Black Rabbit blankly. Of course he'd heard

of Buffalo Bill Cody and his Wild West Show. Cody was a fur trapper, gold miner, Pony Express driver, and Army scout, but he gained notoriety when he created his Wild West Show, an outdoor spectacle using a cast of hundreds to play the cowboys and Indians and including live bison, elk, cattle, and other animals. But the Wild West Show didn't appear until well after the Civil War. Balthazar, a product of the Victorian Age, would have heard of it, but Black Rabbit, gold country bandit, shouldn't have.

Xavier wondered if it was a slip up on Balthazar's part, or if it was a test. And if Balthazar was testing him, why was he doing it? Had Xavier done something to make Balthazar suspicious? He squinted his eyes and shook his head.

"Sorry, don't recall meeting a fellow with that name," he said. "Nor heard of a show like that. What is it, a circus?"

"Yes, a Western circus," Black Rabbit said, suddenly relaxed. He touched the brim of his hat, clucked his tongue once, turned his horse around, and quickly disappeared into the night.

After he left, Xavier unrolled his bedroll. Though the days were balmy in the Sierra foothills, at night the temperature plummeted. To keep warm, Xavier had taken to sleeping in everything except his boots and hat, and he hadn't taken his clothes off now for three, maybe four days. No wonder he smelled bad.

He took the leather diary from his saddlebag and opened it up again, drawing closer to the fire so that he could see the spidery handwriting. He knew a little French and Spanish, and had been able to figure out a phrase or word here and there, but it still made little sense. Archibald Weber switched languages midsentence; only the most accomplished linguist would have been able to decipher it. Or perhaps somebody outfitted with one of the translator devices available at the Owatannauk Library, set to understand all known languages.

Xavier wondered what information was held in these pages that demanded such careful protection. He made a mental note to get up at the silver hour, make a quick trip to the Owatannauk Library, and see if Jenny would let him borrow one of the translators.

But he didn't get a chance. Xavier was still nestled deep in his bedroll when he felt a sharp rap on his back that felt like someone had thrown a brick at him. He scrambled out of his bedroll to see Dancer with his hind leg raised, poised to kick him again.

"Thanks a lot, Dancer," he groused, rubbing his shoulder. "If you're trying to get my attention, I prefer a soft nuzzle to a kick in the back."

The horse made no sign that he cared what Xavier's preferences were, but remained tense, facing the forest, almost as though he was pointing.

He *was* pointing. Ten minutes later, Black Rabbit appeared, emerging from the forest in a direct line to Dancer's muzzle. Xavier was thankful that he hadn't been caught asleep. Black Rabbit seemed impressed that Xavier was up with a campfire already blazing.

"I brought breakfast," he said, holding up two trout. Xavier smiled. He was so sick of beans, he would almost have eaten dirt and worms. Trout looked like a meal fit for a king.

"I've got some oatmeal—the good kind, no bugs in it at all—and corn bread, too," Black Rabbit said as he laid the fish down on a flat rock and pulled out an impressively large Bowie knife from his boot. He started to scrape the scales off the fish. "Go get it out of my saddlebag. It shouldn't be too broken up."

"Where'd you get it?" Xavier asked, unfastening the bag and pulling out the sweet-smelling bread. It was still warm.

"Snatched it off a windowsill on my way over," Black Rabbit chuckled. "Somebody got up mighty early to make that bread. Next time they won't leave something like that out where any wild dog or vagrant can grab it."

"Or outlaw."

"Yeah, or outlaw," Black Rabbit laughed.

The boys gobbled up the breakfast in no time. Xavier thought it was the best meal he'd ever had.

"That sure hit the spot, Black Rabbit," he sighed, leaning back on a rock. "Those beans and beef jerky lose their appeal real quick."

"You can call me Lew," Black Rabbit said. "And I know. It's not easy living out here."

"You ever miss wherever you came from, Lew?" Xavier asked slyly. "Ever think about going back?"

"I can't go back," Black Rabbit said, his jaw set. "It's too dangerous." Xavier didn't push him further. Now was not the time.

"I know a place where we can cool off," Black Rabbit said. That sounded like as a good an idea as any, and Xavier was just grateful he hadn't suggested robbing a stagecoach. He scattered the ashes from the fire and swept the ground with a branch, then mounted Dancer and followed Black Rabbit into the forest.

"I don't believe you've told me your name, Ghost Rider," Black Rabbit said after a few minutes.

"It's Xavier," Xavier said. He couldn't see what difference it would make if Black Rabbit knew his real name or not. It was all he could do to remember to call him Lew, and not Balthazar or Balt, or even Albert or Walter, so he decided to keep his end of it simple.

"And this is Dancer," he added, patting Dancer's neck.

"I was going to say that Dancer is a mighty fine horse. I don't think I've ever seen a horse that fine that wasn't winning races."

"Yeah, he's a fine animal all right," Xavier said, fighting the temptation to show off some of his tricks. "How about your horse?"

"This here is Orion," Black Rabbit said, patting the horse's neck. "He's tough and surefooted. Gotten me out of trouble plenty of times."

As they rode up into the hills, Black Rabbit was getting more and more comfortable and chatted amiably, relating some of his past escapades, but only ones as Black Rabbit, nothing about his childhood. Finally he asked Xavier about his family.

"Not much to tell, really," Xavier said. "My family's in

Boston; I'm an only child. Don't know where my mother went. My father was pretty hard on me, so I ran away."

"Why was he hard on you?"

"He wanted me to take up the family business. Kept me busy all the time. But I had ideas of my own."

Black Rabbit nodded, but seemed lost in his own thoughts. Xavier allowed him to think without interrupting. He was sure Black Rabbit was aching to say something. It was obvious that he was lonely and missed just having a conversation with somebody. And the more he talked, the more his outlaw persona peeled away like onion skin, revealing Balthazar underneath, raw and tender.

"Here we are," Black Rabbit announced suddenly. He jumped off his horse and broke into a run.

Xavier dismounted and chased Balthazar through the trees and brush until the foliage gave way to an open vista overlooking a thirty-foot waterfall. At the bottom of the falls was a large swimming hole. The area was sheltered on all sides by the forest, though overhead the cloudless sky was a bright blue circle. A hawk passed above, drifting lazily in a figure eight.

Black Rabbit was already tearing off his clothes. "Come on, Xavier!" he cried. "Last one in is a polecat!"

Xavier hesitated, then tore off his clothes as well. Now the boys raced to the edge of the cliff. They grabbed their knees as they jumped, two cannonballs landing with an enormous splash.

They came up with whoop and holler.

"That was great!" shouted Xavier. "Let's do it again!"

They did, scrambling up the path that led to the top. This time they did swan dives, Xavier first, with Balthazar following. They played a game of follow the leader. Balthazar did a jackknife dive. Xavier did a flip. Balthazar did a twist. Xavier pretended to run in space. Balthazar flapped his hands. Xavier stretched out his arms and yelled, "I'm an airplane!"

"You're a what?" Balthazar called down from the cliff. Xavier clapped his hand over his mouth.

"I said, 'I'm in the air, playing!'" Xavier yelled back. Balthazar shrugged, yelled the same thing, and a moment later was under the water, pulling Xavier under with him.

They raced each other across the pool. Just as Balthazar was about to win, Xavier grabbed his ankles and pulled him under, then tried to swim over him, but the wiry boy shoved him aside, and they fought to be first to the waterfall. They gave up, calling it a draw, and crawled onto the rock ledge, panting from exertion. They crouched behind the sheet of water thundering from above, blinking from the mist, then dove through it. The crushing weight of water pushed them down and tossed them around so they had to fight their way back up.

As he burst through the surface of that cold pool, Xavier felt born again. Balthazar was laughing his funny laugh, and as they lay out to dry on the rocks near the pool, naked under the sun, neither one of them looked much like an outlaw.

"I don't think I've ever had so much fun," Balthazar murmured, his eyes closed.

"Me too," Xavier said, watching him out of the corner of his eye. They lay there a little longer. Xavier said nothing. He knew there was no rushing this; he had to be patient. Finally Balthazar spoke again.

"I ran away from my father, too," he said.

"Yeah?"

"Yeah."

"You said it was dangerous for you there," Xavier said.

"I think my father was trying to kill me." Balthazar turned on his side, beads of water on his wet cheek sparkling in the sun.

"You're not sure?" Xavier said, putting his hand behind his head with his elbows out to cushion it from the rock.

Again Balthazar said nothing, then he rolled over on his back again.

"Xavier, have you ever felt that you're meant for something important, and that everything is pushing you in that direction?"

Xavier let the question hang in the air a moment. "Yeah, I do," he said after a while.

"Really?"

"Yeah. So what?"

"So what if it's something you don't want to do?"

"Then don't do it."

"It's not that easy. It's like trying to run away from your destiny. Like you don't have a choice."

"What happens if you don't do it?"

"Bad things."

"What happens if you *do* do it?"

"Bad things."

"Then I guess it doesn't make much of a difference what you do." Xavier turned on his side, propping his head up with his hand over his elbow. "Does it?"

"It just depends on who the bad things happen to." Balthazar sighed and sat up. "I'm dry. Let's get dressed."

They made their way up the path to their pile of clothes. Balthazar's hair was still wet and clung in clumps to his forehead and neck, sticking up in strange curly swirls around his ears. When he was finished dressing, he was Black Rabbit again. He hopped on Orion. Xavier finished dressing only moments later and mounted Dancer.

"What are you going to do?"

"What I've been doing. Have fun as long as I can."

"This was a lot of fun," Xavier said, nodding at the swimming hole.

"Yeah." Black Rabbit turned his horse. "See you around."

Balthazar spurred Orion to move at a fast walk, but then looked back over his shoulder and spun the horse around to face Xavier. Orion protested the move with a snort.

"Don't tell anybody about it. The swimming hole, I mean."

"Who would I tell?" Xavier said with a shrug. Balthazar smiled, turned Orion back toward the forest, and left in a different direction from the way they had come.

+ CHAPTER SEVENTEEN +
INDIANS!

XAVIER HEADED BACK TO CAMP, WHERE HE WOULD change and set out for Hangtown. He couldn't wait to tell the others everything that had happened. The story was so good he wouldn't have to embellish it, but he rolled the events over in his head to make sure he didn't forget anything.

He felt sorry for the others, trudging through the past week as ordinary townsfolk. Nina was playing piano for a bunch of tired prospectors; Rowan was spending hour after hot hour digging in the dirt for a few paltry nuggets. And Xanthe . . . what was she doing? Laundry? He laughed, despite himself.

After changing into his civilian clothes, he stuffed Archibald Weber's diary into his saddlebag and headed toward Hangtown. He left Dancer in the woods a mile outside the town and walked the rest of the way.

When Xavier reached Lily's saloon, the place was in an uproar. Even as he approached he could hear men stamping their boots and shouting for the "little princess," which, from the huge poster on the outside of the building, was none other than Nina. The eight-foot-tall painting depicted her in a sea green gown with a diamond tiara on her head, her curly black ringlets spiraling down over her shoulders.

He pushed through the swinging doors. Nina was sitting at the piano, dressed just as she was in the poster, her arms folded stubbornly as the men chanted and stamped. She was clearly not about to perform.

Xavier felt a hand on his arm. It was Lily, her eyes frantic.

"Thank goodness you're here! The child refuses to play!"

"What's going on?"

"She's a big hit, that's what's going on! I've been able to charge admission for an afternoon *and* an evening show. She's well compensated! She's being unreasonable!"

"Why don't you talk to her brother? And where's Xanthe?"

"It's complicated."

One of the men stood up. "Either she plays now or I want my money back!"

"Don't worry, Earl, she'll play," Lily snapped.

"No, I won't!" shouted Nina.

"Hang on, Miss Lily, I'll fix this," Xavier said. He walked over to the stage. For a moment, Nina's eyes lit up, but then they darkened, and she pushed herself out from behind the piano. She jumped off the stage, gripping his arm.

"We need to talk," she said.

"She doesn't look like she's about to play squat doodle!" Earl shouted, lifting his chair in the air. He brought it down on the edge of the stage and it splintered into several pieces, one of which he waved in Lily's direction. "Now give us our money back!"

A few of the other men were on their feet. Big Jake had brought a shotgun out from behind the bar, and was holding it at the ready.

"Maybe you should give them their money back until we sort this out," Xavier said to Lily.

"Don't you think I would if I could? I already spent it!"

"On what?"

She rolled her eyes, then pulled herself up proudly. "Gambling debts. And no, I can't get the money back, not unless I'm willing to sell part of my establishment, and I'm not willing!"

Another chair crashed, this time on a table.

"Well, if you don't do something soon, you're not going to have an establishment," Xavier said. "Nina, what's all this about?"

"Why don't you ask her?" Nina said, glaring at Lily.

A piece of wood flew by, grazing Xavier's head, and for a moment he saw stars. He ran over and snatched the shotgun from Big Jake, pointed it at the ceiling and pulled the trigger. The shot exploded, shattering the chandelier. Glass rained down on the surprised patrons.

"OK, everybody just *chill out!*" Xavier shouted.

"My chandelier!" gasped Lily.

"Next person to break a chair gets a butt full of buckshot,"

Xavier said, leveling the gun at the crowd, which quieted to a low grumble. Xavier turned back to Nina and Lily Rose. "All right, now what's going on here? Nina? Where's Rowan?"

"He's at the mining camp. I haven't seen him for two days."

"Couldn't Xanthe get him to come back?"

"We need to talk," Nina said again. "Privately."

Xavier looked at the men, who were getting restless again. "OK, a free round of whiskey for everyone," he called out. "And keep it coming. I'll be back in a minute."

"You must be joking!" Lily shouted over the cheers of the patrons.

"I'm not laughing," Xavier said.

Nina led him up to her room and closed the door. "Where have you been?"

"What's that supposed to mean? I've been carrying out the plan. Where is everyone?"

"Listen, Xave, a lot has happened since you left. First of all, Rowan has been up at Glitter Gulch for two days, but people who've seen him say he doesn't look well. I'd have gone up there, but I don't have mobility. We needed you here."

"What about Xanthe?"

"Xanthe's been captured by Indians."

"What?!"

"The Indians—the Miwoks, to be exact—are mad at the miners for digging up the land. Three days ago somebody's campfire got out of control and started a fire that burned up half the Miwok village. So the Miwoks raided two of the biggest ranches around here and stole nearly a hundred horses. It was crazy! Horses stampeding right down Main Street, braves whooping it up, people shooting! Thankfully, nobody was killed, but Xanthe was out there yelling at people to stop shooting. I tried to get her back inside the saloon, but the next thing you know, one of the Indians just scooped her up and took off. They were going to take me, too, but Xanthe shoved me out of the way with her foot. I've got a bruise on my hip . . ."

"Keep going."

"OK. So the men of the town got together and decided to get the horses back. They put together a posse and invaded the Miwok village. When they came back, they had about half the horses, and they left Xanthe behind as part of the deal."

"Deal? What deal?"

"They split the horses and gave them Xanthe to make up for burning the village. If you had checked in, you'd have seen that things were falling apart! Didn't you see the handkerchief on the stagecoach had changed color? That was my signal!"

"Hey, I was busy!"

"We agreed that you would check in with us! That we would share information!"

"Nina, I've gotten a lot done! I met Black Rabbit, I got this really cool horse, we hung out at the swimming hole . . ." Xavier was rambling, caught off guard by Nina's anger. This wasn't how he wanted to tell the story, but it kept dribbling out under her unwavering glare. "I found Archibald Weber's private apart-

ments, I . . . met Joaquin Murieta . . . he's not dead you know, and
. . . I've been the Ghost Rider! The notorious bandit of the West!
And you're blaming me for . . . I don't even know what you're
blaming me for! Geez, do I have to do everything around here?"

Nina looked like she wanted to strangle him.

"What do you think we've been doing all this time, Xavier
Alexander? Nothing? Who do you think is responsible for
the Ghost Rider's reputation anyway? The reputation that got
Black Rabbit to reveal himself? Who do you think has been
scouring this area for information, information that could help
you if you bothered to come down and get it! Did you know
that a particularly nasty group of men calling themselves the
Foggerty Brothers have been on your tail? We've been plant-
ing all kinds of false clues for them, but there are five of them,
and they are going to skin you alive if they find you!"

"I was just following the plan I set . . ."

"You set? *You* set? We *all* made the plan, and it included
checking in and sharing information! This mission is not about
you. We're a team. We are *not* your followers. Besides, nobody
wants to follow someone who's so full of himself! Xavier
Alexander, you have a big, fat head!" She folded her arms. If her
eyes could shoot bullets, he would have been dead right then.

Xavier was speechless. He *had* thought of the others as his
followers. He *had* assumed that he was the leader of this mission, the most important person, the hero. They were only supporting players in his story.

"The reason I'm not playing the piano," Nina continued,

"the reason I'm causing so much trouble is because I'm trying to get them to go back and rescue Xanthe. You weren't here to help, and it's the only leverage I have."

At that moment, Lily clomped up the stairs and opened Nina's door. She draped herself on the arm of a chair. "OK, the free booze seems to have calmed them, but that chandelier and the drinks are going to cost you a bundle."

"Quiet!" Xavier and Nina barked at her in unison. Lily opened and closed her mouth.

"How the heck could you leave Xanthe with the Miwoks?" Xavier demanded. "She was your employee!"

"Not really," Lily said cagily. "I had to let her go."

"What?"

"I couldn't find any use for her! She can't cook, she can't wash anything without putting holes in it, and her mending . . . *Dios mío*! Her stitches looked like a mass of knots, and then she'd prick herself, bleed on the clothes, and have to wash them all over again! I swear, that girl is about as useful as two dead flies!"

Xavier would've laughed, but he was too worried.

"What do the Miwoks want with her?"

"I suspect they want her to be someone's wife."

"Oh no!" Nina moaned. Lily shrugged.

"Their numbers are considerably reduced since last winter. An illness wiped out a good portion of their tribe. They need somebody to do the women's work and to have babies. I wouldn't worry, I'm sure they are treating her well."

"Miss Lily, I don't care if they erected a totem pole in her honor. Xanthe is my sister. She's a free woman, and I intend to keep it that way. Now, if you want to continue to have a business, you have two choices. You can either give those men their money back, which it seems you are unable to do, or you can help me get Xanthe back, and Nina will perform tonight."

Lily mulled this over as a steady pounding came from the saloon below. There was a crash and more tinkling glass.

"All right! I'll come up with something," she shrieked. "Just stop them from tearing my place apart!"

"Do I have your word? I'm not playing games here," Xavier warned.

"Yes! Yes! Lily Rose's word is as tight as a bear trap!"

"OK, Nina," Xavier said, "three songs. That'll cool them off. And . . . I'm sorry. You're right. I'll change."

Nina nodded, straightened her tiara, picked up her skirts, and descended the staircase. The pounding turned to cheers. Moments later, the sound of piano tinkling could be heard as she played a selection from the opera *Carmen*. Now the men pounded the tables, but to the beat of the music. Xavier turned to Lily, who had laid herself out on the sofa with her feet raised on the ottoman, and her arm draped over her forehead, looking thoroughly beaten.

"All right, what can we do?" Xavier said.

"Give me a moment," the woman moaned. "This has not been a good day."

"Miss Lily, my patience is wearing thin," said Xavier, using the same phrase he'd heard his mother utter a million times. "I can tell Nina to stop playing, you know."

Lily sat up. "Listen," she said. "I've been living here coming up on five years now. The Miwok are not unreasonable. They just need help. It's all business with them. We need to trade something for your sister."

"Like what?"

"Well, some of them like the white man's clothing; maybe they'll take some of those Levi's. They like rifles, too. And whiskey. Let me put something together . . ."

"Yeah, you do that," Xavier said. "And round up as many men as you can. Promise them more free drinks if you have to." Lily started to protest but Xavier talked over her. "I'll pay for it! I just need to have a show of strength when I face them. You have until tomorrow morning. I'm going to find my friend Rowan."

"Hmm. Rowan. Yes, you should find him," Lily said, her expression suddenly somber. "Don't be shocked by what you see. The last time he came through here he . . . well, he was changed. I'm worried about that young man."

Xavier dashed down the stairs and out the door to the strains of the saloon patrons singing a raucous version of "Oh! Susanna." The lyrics had been changed, reflecting the times.

I came from Salem City
With my wash pan on my knee,

I'm going to California
The Gold Rush for to see.
It rained all night the day I left
The weather it was dry
The sun so hot I froze to death
Oh brothers, don't you cry.
Oh! Susanna. Oh don't you cry for me.
I'm going to California with a wash pan on my knee!

+ CHAPTER EIGHTEEN +
GOLD FEVER

Nina had struck a nerve. Why had Xavier not checked on Rowan, when even he could see there was something going on with him that was not quite right? And why hadn't he checked back in with the others? He knew why. He was having too much fun being the Ghost Rider, and he didn't think they were doing anything important. Nina was right. He was full of himself.

HOST: Well, due to poor ratings, *Great Guys* will no longer be seen at this time, replaced instead by our new hit show, *Guys with Fat Heads*, starring the one and only Xavier Alexander. Xave, say hello to the audience.

(The audience stares as the sound of crickets can be heard)

XAVIER: I'm sorry. I'm not in the mood. Good night.

When he got to Glitter Gulch he hid Dancer in the woods and found Ed, Pete, and Oliver, who were taking a coffee break, laughing uproariously as Bret Harte finished up what must have been a hilarious story. Pete looked up as Xavier approached.

"Xavier! You just missed one of the rip-roaringest stories I've ever heard. This fella's got talent!" he said, slapping Bret on the back.

"Hey, Bret," Xavier said. "I didn't know you'd be here!" He was happy to see the writer. He could use the support when he went looking for Rowan.

"Just mining for stories," Bret said, filling up his cup with more of the black brew. "I've been all over; talking to people, listening . . . I shared some of the better ones with these men."

"It may interest you to know that one of these men is one of the fellas we were looking for. Oliver Weber." Xavier gestured to Oliver, who nodded amiably. "Oliver, you've just had the pleasure of listening to one of the finest storytellers in the world . . . Bret Harte. Rowan and I shared a stagecoach with him on the way up here."

"Ah! This is a small world," Bret said, shaking Oliver's hand. "It's nice to meet you, Mr. Weber. I hope you find your fortune here."

Oliver shrugged. "I'm not sure what I'm doing here," he said. "You ever feel like you're not where you're supposed to be? I'm just drifting, you know. California is an uneasy fit for me. Sometimes I feel like a piece of a jigsaw puzzle that's been smashed into the wrong place."

"We all feel like we should be somewhere else," Pete said wistfully.

"Not me," Ed laughed. "Where would you go if you weren't here? This is where it's all happening, boys!"

"There are grave things brewing in the East and in the South," Oliver said. "A war's coming, one that's gonna decide the future of this country. I feel like I'm wasting my time here."

"You'll be whistling a different tune when you find a gold nugget as big as a country ham," Pete said. "And what about you, Xavier? We heard you had gone to Negro Hill to try your luck. Looks like it didn't pan out, huh?"

"I'm here to find Rowan," Xavier answered. The men grew silent, their eyes darting to one another.

"What's wrong?" asked Bret. "If Rowan's up here, I'd love to see him."

"No, you wouldn't," Ed said gruffly. He was silent for a few more uncomfortable seconds then sighed. "Xavier, I'm afraid your friend is . . . well, he's gone plumb loco."

"What is that supposed to mean?"

"I've seen this happen to men before," Ed said, putting a firm hand on Xavier's shoulder. "They find a little gold, and they get this look in their eye, you know, like a dreamy sort of look. They start thinking about how their lives are going to change, how they're going to live it up like kings. But you can only claim the land if you're working it. You can't leave it for more than a couple of days before it becomes open to anybody. A feeling starts growing in these men that they've got to protect their stakes, that everybody's trying to grab what's theirs. They can't trust anybody.

"Your friend thinks he's found a rich crevice somewhere back in the woods. He came out here a few times, jumpy as a bull-frog, and when a couple of men asked him what he was up to he nearly snapped their heads off. The next time he came back he looked mangy and mean, like a starved coyote. Came sniffing around for some food, but the men didn't like how they'd been treated the first time, so they refused to give him any."

"I threw him a sack of oatmeal," Pete said. "I doubt he knew what to do with it, though."

"Well, a couple of fellows tried to follow him, and he started throwing rocks."

"Big rocks," Pete added.

"He started cussing them out, threatening them . . ."

"Rowan cussing? That doesn't sound like him at all," Xavier murmured.

"It wasn't him. I'm telling you, he's changed." Ed took his hand off Xavier's shoulder. "Look for him if you want, but bring some protection."

"I'll come," Bret said, standing.

"Begging your pardon, sir, but you really aren't much protec-tion," Ed said, eyeing Bret's fancy attire. "Not unless you plan on blinding him with the shine of your nice patent leather shoes."

"Very funny," Bret said. "But never fear. Remember, I have this little beauty . . ." He reached into his vest and pulled out his small pearl-handled pistol. "It was stolen from me by that highway robber, the Ghost Rider, but a few days later I found it hidden in my hat. Very strange."

"We are not shooting Rowan," Xavier said. "No matter what he does. Now let's go. I know exactly where he is."

They had almost reached the ravine where Rowan had slid away from the bear when a low voice growled from behind a large group of boulders.

"Get out of here! This is my strike!"

"Rowan, it's me! Xave!"

There was a moment of silence, then: "What do you want?"

"I want to talk to you!"

Again a moment of silence, then a thin figure slowly peeked out from behind a boulder.

Xavier hardly recognized this version of his friend. Rowan was stooped from fatigue, his mud-caked clothes hanging off him like a scarecrow's. His hair was filthy with dirt and sticks. He had a large bruise on his cheek and his fingers were bleeding. He scratched his arm feverishly.

"Is anyone with you?" Rowan croaked.

"Yes, Rowan, I am," Bret said. Rowan's eyes immediately narrowed.

"Rowan, what happened to you?" Xavier said.

"I'm glad you're here," Rowan said, ignoring the question. "You shouldn't have brought him, though. You know what a big mouth he has. He'll tell everyone within miles. We'll have to stay up all night fighting them off."

"You already look like you've been up all night," Xavier said.

"I'm not interested in gold," Bret said. "You're sick, my friend. You need rest, and a doctor."

"Yeah, right!" Rowan spat. "You'd love that, wouldn't you? I close my eyes for a second, and then what? Somebody hits me over the head and dumps me in a ditch and steals my claim. It's mine! You keep your grubby hands away from it!"

Rowan was screaming nonsense now. Xavier had half a mind to shoot him with the tranquilizer gun.

"Maybe you should stand over there," Xavier said to Bret, pointing to a boulder several yards away. "Don't follow us. You'll only end up getting beaned by a rock. I'll be OK."

Bret shrugged and took a seat on a flat stone, flicking a few dead leaves off his jacket. Xavier took Rowan by the arm.

"Show me the claim," he said.

They slid down into the ravine. Rowan picked his way through the exposed roots and grass until they reached the little spring where Rowan had first plucked the large gold rock. Rowan's pick and shovel were there, along with a pan. Large holes now pocked the area, none of them deeper than a couple of feet due to the soil being thick with clay. It looked like a manic mole had been at work.

Xavier put his hands on his hips, surveyed the scene, then turned to Rowan, who actually did look a little like a manic mole, with his dirty hair sticking out in all directions and his eyes scanning the woods for imagined interlopers.

"Rowan, what are you doing? Did you forget what we came here for?"

"No, of course not!" Rowan snapped. "But this . . ." He swept his hand across the muddy spring. "This is important! Don't you see?"

Xavier shook his head. No, he didn't see.

"It's a blooming bonanza! I can't leave yet! If I go anywhere, even for a few minutes, somebody else will grab it! I've got to protect it!"

"You mean you've found more gold?"

"Yes! Well, not yet, but it's there all right! I can feel it! I know this is going to sound crazy, but it's almost like it's calling out to me . . . 'Rowan! Rowan! Over here!'"

"That does sound crazy." Xavier looked at his friend, his bloodshot eyes wild with dreams, his body swaying from the mere effort of standing.

"Rowan, I think this is a waste of time. I don't think there's any more gold here, and if there is, you don't know how to find it. You don't know what you're doing. You could be digging here forever!" Xavier recalled one of Ed's Gold Rush tall tales, about a man who was so desperate to find gold that he dug a hundred holes. When he finished the last hole, he was so exhausted he fell into it, breaking his neck. When his friends arrived they realized that all he'd done was dig a hundred graves. He shook the thought out of his mind.

"You don't understand," Rowan muttered. "You've always had money. You don't know what it's like to live in an apartment with paper-thin walls and bums hanging around the front door! You don't know how it feels to get a hamburger instead of a cheeseburger because you're worried about spending an extra ten cents! Or having to wear shoes that are falling apart! Or having your phone service cut off! Or getting a secondhand bike for Christmas!"

"Rowan, that's not the point . . ."

"Of course it is! Of course it is! My dad could use a million dollars! We could live in a nice apartment! We could go to the Bahamas for a family vacation! We could get a huge TV! We could . . ."

Xavier grabbed him by the shoulders and shook him.

"Rowan! Shut up! Just shut up! I get it! You want to make money! But Xanthe's been kidnapped by Indians! We've got to save her!"

Rowan stopped his rant. He wrenched away from Xavier and leaned against a rock, panting and blinking, his body drenched in sweat. "What? What did you say?"

"I said Xanthe's been kidnapped. We've got to round up a group and get her back. I can't do it alone, and nobody in Hangtown is going to help except Lily Rose, and she's not much help, I can tell you that."

Rowan stared at Xavier, his face hard, his eyes narrow. "You're lying. You're just trying to get me to leave. You want . . . you want this place for yourself! You've been talking to the guys at the camp, haven't you? Ed and the rest of them. They bribed you, didn't they? *Didn't* they?! They've been waiting for me to leave just so they can come in and scoop it out from under me. Well, let me tell you something, I'm not going anywhere with you, you filthy liar . . ."

Xavier had run out of ideas. He tackled his friend, knocking him to the ground. Rowan fought back, kicking and clawing. For someone who looked like a starved chicken, Rowan was tough to pin down. He squirmed out from under Xavier, threw dirt in his eyes, then gave him a swift kick in the back.

As Rowan scrambled to his feet, Xavier brought him back down with a leg sweep, then leaped on top of him, but in a surprise move Rowan curled his legs around Xavier's neck and flipped him backward. In an instant Rowan was on top, kneeling on Xavier's arms. Xavier's karate training was useless at this point; he couldn't move. To his horror, his friend had lifted a large rock over Xavier's head and looked as if he was about to drop it.

A shot rang out and Rowan was flung backward. Bret slid down into the ravine and jogged over to Xavier.

"Are you all right?"

"Yeah, but Rowan's been shot!"

"I know, I shot him!" Bret said, twirling his pearl-handled pistol. "You see? It did come in handy after all."

Xavier tore off a piece of his shirt. "It looks like it just grazed you," he said to his friend. Rowan tried to fight him off but was too weak and in too much pain. Finally he gave up, allowing Xavier to wrap the wound.

"So you want to kill me, too!" Rowan growled at Bret. "I should've known . . ."

"For the last time, we're not here for gold," Xavier said. "You've got to come back with us to help save Xanthe from marrying an Indian!"

"Your sister is marrying an Indian?" Bret said. "How fascinating!" He took his notebook out of his pocket and started writing.

Rowan's eyes darted back and forth between the two, then fell on an object wrapped in cloth that had been thrown from his shirt during the fight. He flung his hand out to grab it but winced from the pain. Bret closed his notebook, walked over to it, and picked it up.

"Give that back to me!" Rowan yelled, but instead Bret peeled back the cloth. It was the large chunk that Rowan had first discovered with Xavier in their escape from the bear. Bret gave a low whistle.

"That's my gold!" Rowan screamed. "You've got no right to keep it!"

"It's beautiful, quite a specimen," he said, turning it over. "It's not gold, though."

"What? What do you mean?" sputtered Rowan. "Of course it's gold, just look at it!"

"I *am* looking at it. It's shiny and brilliant. Pure gold is a dull yellow color in its natural state. What you have here, my friend, is an enormous chunk of pyrite. Fool's gold."

Bret handed the rock back to Rowan, whose face had drained of color. Small grunts and strangled sounds rose from somewhere deep in his throat, and then, with an anguished cry he collapsed, unconscious.

Rowan awoke at the camp the next morning with the help of several cold compresses and the smell of pork-and-bean soup cooking over a fire. Pete fed him, as he was too weak to feed himself. After his meal, he refused to speak to anyone, choosing to huddle in Ed and Pete's cabin under a blanket. Xavier could tell he was embarrassed.

"It's OK, Rowan," he said for the hundredth time, sitting on the cot next to his friend. "I don't hold it against you. We're still friends. You were just . . . I don't know . . . under a spell."

"I'm so sorry," Rowan finally mumbled. "I can't believe I was stupid enough to believe I could possibly discover a gold vein. I'm an idiot. Fool's gold. Figures."

"You're not the first person to make that mistake."

"Was Xanthe really kidnapped by Indians?"

"Yes."

"What about Nina?"

"She's fine."

"What can we do? We can't take on a whole tribe . . ."

"Lily Rose seems to think that Xanthe isn't in any immediate danger except that she may be married soon. We're going to show up with a big group of men, bluff them into thinking we may start an all-out war, and then, once they're good and scared, offer to trade something for her instead. If you're well enough to travel, we should go. I've also made a lot of head-way with . . . you know who. I'd like to tell you about it."

Xavier had to wait to tell Rowan about Black Rabbit, for Bret accompanied them on their way back to Hangtown. This meant leaving Dancer hidden in the woods. Xavier would come back for him later. As the friends walked, they contin-ued to plan how they would rescue Xanthe from the Miwok tribe. Rowan said very little, and Xavier could see he was still exhausted.

Once they reached the Huckleberry House Hotel, Rowan slept for several hours, during which time Xavier told Nina all that had happened. She was particularly intrigued by Archibald Weber's diary, and it was her idea to give the book to the Chinese doctor, Dr. Wu, who came to treat Rowan's fever and various cuts and bruises. The doctor took the book in his hands and ran his fingers along the binding, then opened it. He turned the pages slowly, scanning the parts that were writ-ten in Chinese, raising his eyebrows a few times and at other times nodding or furrowing his brow. Finally, he closed it and handed it back to Xavier.

"That is a very interesting book," he said. "I can't read most of it, of course."

"What did the Chinese part say?"

"It speaks of a land where there is much suffering. People are too frightened to defend themselves or take back what is theirs. Later in the book five warriors appear. 'Saviors,' I think you would call them. That's all."

"Thank you," Xavier said. "I know it's confusing, but it helps."

"I know a lot of people in this town," Dr. Wu said, adjusting his glasses. "There is a Swede who owns the bar next to my pharmacy, an Italian blacksmith, a Portuguese fellow who owns the mercantile shop. And there are others. I can get more of this book deciphered for you, if you like."

"Yes, please! That would be wonderful!" Nina said.

"Uh, wait a minute, this book is valuable. I mean, it's the only copy," Xavier said.

"Yes, but it's of no use unless we know what it says," Nina reminded him. "I think we can trust it with the doctor . . . can't we?" she said, leveling her green eyes at the man.

Something about her expression made Dr. Wu straighten up. "Yes, little sister," he said. "You can trust me. I will not let anything happen to it, you can be sure of it."

Xavier was satisfied. He handed the book to the doctor, who tucked it into his medical bag. He bowed and departed.

After the doctor left, Rowan insisted he was well enough to set out to the Miwok village. Despite Lily Rose's assurances, he had concerns about Xanthe's safety. Was she tied up someplace? Forced into hard labor? Who knew what the Indians were capable of?

When they went downstairs to the saloon, they found Lily had already assembled a trunk of items for the boys to trade. She told Big Jake to bring the horses around. Xavier was surprised when he showed up with three stallions and a mule.

"Where are the rest of them?" he asked as the large man strapped the trunk to the mule.

"The rest of what?" Lily said cagily.

"The rest of the horses! You know, for the volunteers?"

"We had a little bit of trouble finding volunteers," Lily said delicately.

"What do you mean? " Rowan jumped in.

"You didn't try hard enough!" Xavier charged.

Rowan wandered among the saloon tables. "We need help!" he pleaded. The men paid him no mind but continued playing cards. "Hey! Listen!" Rowan shouted again. He grabbed the nearest table and upended it, sending the cards and the drinks sliding to the floor.

A hush came over the bar. Heads turned to the scrappy young man with the passionate eyes. The four men at the table placed their hands on their holsters.

"There's a girl's life at stake here! We need a bunch of tough, courageous men to bring her back where she belongs! Now who's coming?" The silence was so complete you could almost hear Big Jake shift his toothpick from one side of his mouth to the other. Rowan glared at the group. "What are you, a bunch of cowards?"

The four men stood. Rowan didn't back down, putting his hands on his hips, almost daring them to do something. Xavier was impressed; Rowan really had been affected by the spirit of the Wild West . . . maybe too much. Then the men shrugged, picked up the table, collected the cards and returned to their game. One of them ordered another round of drinks.

"They're not cowards, son," Lily Rose said, gently pulling Rowan back, "they just don't think she's worth the trouble."

"Yeah, what's the big deal," one of the card players drawled. "After all, she's just a Negro."

Xavier's blood shot to his face. Something in him snapped. *Just let it roll off like water off a duck's back*, he warned himself, remembering Nana's advice, but his hands had already curled into fists.

He felt a hand on his shoulder. "Hold on, brother," a soft voice said. It was Chester Lee.

Xavier gulped and took a deep breath, clearing his head. Chester kept a grip on Xavier until he brought his anger down to a low simmer. The ex-slave's expression spoke volumes: *I know what you're thinking, brother. I'd love to see you do it, but it's not worth it.*

"I'll join you," Chester said. "Let's go. I've got my own horse."

Xavier, Rowan, Chester, and Bret set out for the Miwok village. Chester explained that he had actually returned to Hangtown to see Xanthe. He was hoping she might entertain a courtship with him. He went on talking about his dreams of settling down and starting a family, but Xavier was barely listening; he was distracted by Rowan's response to Chester's affection for Xanthe. The suspicion and irritation playing across his friend's face was priceless.

Their plan had to change. Without a large group of men they couldn't possibly bluff the Miwoks. Xavier hoped that

Lily Rose had packed something extraordinary in the trunk or they might find themselves becoming hostages as well. Every once in a while he heard rustling from the bushes and suspected that they were being watched. This was confirmed when they got to the village and were intercepted by a welcoming committee of five Miwok men, whose expressions were anything but welcoming.

"What do you want?" a stern-looking man demanded.

"You are holding this fellow's sister against her will," Bret said, taking the lead. Bret didn't quite strike the imposing tone that Xavier had hoped for. With his genteel outfit and his notebook at the ready, he looked like he might compose a sonnet, not pose a threat. But he was the oldest in their group, and Rowan pointed out that it would be highly unusual for a brown-skinned person to be acting as leader.

"We've brought some fine merchandise that might interest you," Bret continued. "Perhaps you'd like to trade."

The Miwok man turned to the others and said something that caused a good deal of laughter. Xavier wondered if that was a bad sign or a good sign.

"Wait here," the first brave said. He left the group and went back to the dwellings, which looked like bark-covered trees and were a short distance away in a field. The other Miwoks remained, their faces betraying nothing. It felt like a staring match.

"Where'd he go?" Rowan whispered nervously. "Is she here? What do you think they've done with her?"

"Shut up," Xavier muttered out of the side of his mouth. Rowan shut up.

After a good ten minutes, the first man returned with another man. This one had a careworn face, carved from years of leadership. The older man pointed at Xavier and Chester. "You come with me," he said. Xavier and Chester jumped off their horses. Rowan started to as well but was stopped by the younger Miwok man.

"No. You stay here."

"It's all right, Rowan," Xavier said. "We'll be fine."

After they walked a short distance, the older man said, "I think there is a misunderstanding. Your sister is the brown-skinned woman from the place they call Hangtown."

"Yes, she was kidnapped so that she could be made a wife. That's what I was told."

"That was our first idea, yes. But she cannot do anything a wife can do. Her baskets are filled with holes and fall apart too fast. Her cooking has caused much sickness. She gathers berries that no animal would eat. When she pounds acorns, she leaves bits of shell in the powder and gives us all toothaches."

"Then why are you keeping her here?"

"We aren't. She won't leave. She says she feels sorry for us; she says she wants to help. But please, you must take her back to your people. She is getting in the way. And she argues."

The older man led them through the village, walking past several dwellings where women were busy weaving baskets and blankets and pounding acorns on a large flat rock pocked with indentations from grinding. Children kicked a buckskin-covered ball around a field.

They walked around a semisubterranean structure with a hole in the top that looked like it might be a sort of chimney. There, sitting in front of it, was Xanthe with a Miwok woman, trying to twist grass into long coils for a basket. The Miwok woman pursed her lips as Xanthe's grass flew in all directions.

"It's not *my* fault," Xanthe whined. "There must be something wrong with the grass." The woman said something, and Xanthe shook her head. "I don't know what you're saying, but I'm saying that somebody gave me some slippery grass."

The older brave called out a name and Xanthe looked up. "Stop calling me that," she snapped. "My name is Xanthe." Then she saw Xavier and Chester and jumped to her feet, the twisted strands falling from her lap into a loose pile. The Miwok woman threw her hands in the air, got up, and walked away.

"Xave!" Xanthe cried, running over. "Chester . . . what are you guys doing here?"

"We came to save you, but it looks like maybe we're saving the Miwoks," Xavier joked. "What was that name he called you?"

"Nothing," Xanthe said. "Look, I don't think they're going to let me go. I'm engaged to the chief's favorite son, and they're short-handed. They need me here." She thrust her chin up nobly.

"Xanthe, first tell us, are you all right? Are you hurt?" Chester said. Xavier was embarrassed that he hadn't asked those things first.

"I'm fine; the Miwoks have treated me quite well . . ."

"Do you want to join the tribe?"

"Well, I'm not sure about that exactly . . ."

"I wouldn't blame you if you did. I've been tempted myself," Chester said, looking around. "At least you're treated like an equal here. You know, when I was working the plantation, we'd hear of slaves that had run off and hid with an Indian tribe. They could make themselves a good home there. Just blend right in, a full member of the community. The whites won't give you that."

"That's true, but Chester, the whites aren't going away. Their numbers are getting larger." Xanthe lowered her voice. "The time of the Indians is over. They know it. It's only a matter of time before . . ." Her voice trailed off.

Chester squinted and gazed beyond the Miwok village, taking in the grand landscape that seemed to be shrinking with every passing hour. "Yeah, this is all gonna change," he said finally. "You know what's funny? I thought gaining my freedom would make all the difference, but every day is still a struggle."

"I think one day we'll be treated the same," Xanthe said carefully. "I believe that every single person, of every single color, is connected. We'll all finally realize our similarities far outweigh our differences. It might take a while, but it's something to fight for."

"Yes, I suppose that's part of our mission," Chester said with a smile. "As Mrs. Pleasants would say." Xanthe laughed. Chester joined her. "You're a wise woman, Xanthe Alexander."

"Why, thank you."

Xavier was getting restless. This conversation was getting a little too sappy for him. He approached the older Miwok man.

"I'd like to make a trade for my sister, but I want to be fair." Xavier said loudly, a smile creeping to his lips. "How about my sister for . . ." He felt around in his pocket. "For this hanky?" He handed the older man the handkerchief, still dusty from their stagecoach ride.

"That's fine," the man said. "She's free to go. Please, take her."

"Hey!" Xanthe yelled. "I'm worth a lot more than a dirty handkerchief!"

"I think it's a fair trade," Xavier laughed.

Chester stopped Xanthe's hand in mid-swing. She raised her eyebrows, slightly shocked. "Let's go home," he said.

Rowan's face looked like it was going to explode when Chester led Xanthe by the hand into the clearing and helped her onto his horse. Xanthe only smiled at Rowan and shrugged as Chester nudged the animal with his heels and steered toward the woods. Bret tucked his notebook into his pocket and followed, with Rowan and Xavier bringing up the rear.

"Good-bye," the older Miwok man called out, using the same name for Xanthe he'd used before.

"Excuse me, what does that mean?" Xavier called back to him.

"It means, 'Bird who talks much, listens little!'"

"My name is Xanthe!" Xanthe shrieked back, amid the renewed howls of laughter.

+ CHAPTER NINETEEN +
THE FOGGERTY BROTHERS

"I TOLD YOU, ROWAN, I TURNED HIM DOWN!" XANTHE insisted after being needled for the tenth time about the private conversation she'd had with Chester on the way back to Hangtown. The time travelers were now sitting in Nina's room in the Huckleberry House Hotel. "I told him I was too young to make that sort of commitment but would consider it in a couple of years if he was still interested. That's it! No biggie!"

"You tell a guy you're interested in marrying him in a few years and that's no biggie?"

"I don't live here, remember? He's going to have a tough time finding me in the twenty-first century! Look, he's a nice guy. I didn't want to blow him off. Now can we please get back to Archibald Weber's notebook? I wish I'd seen it before you gave it away," Xanthe said, turning to Xavier.

"Don't worry about it. I didn't get to see it either," Rowan said, putting the other conversation aside for the moment.

"It's just that my French and Spanish are pretty good, better than Xave's anyway," Xanthe continued. "I might've been able to read it . . ."

"Number one, your French and Spanish are not better. Number two, you couldn't read this book by yourself in a million years. There are languages in it I didn't even recognize. Some are really ancient."

"I wonder what Archibald Weber was trying to hide?" Rowan murmured.

"I don't know. Maybe they're notes about some new invention."

"Written in a hundred languages?" Xanthe said doubtfully.

"Maybe he can't read it either," Nina said. "Maybe it was written by different people."

"I don't think we're going to be able to figure anything out without looking at the diary," Rowan said. "Let's concentrate on Balthazar."

"Well, I'm pretty sure he trusts me," Xavier said. "In a weird way, I think I'm the first friend he's ever had. But now I'm stuck. How do we get him back to the Owatannauk?"

They all mulled the problem over. After a few minutes, Rowan looked up. "You have to tell him the truth."

"But as soon as he knows we're from the Owatannauk, he'll think we're in cahoots with Aunt Gertrude, which, by the way, we are," Xanthe pointed out. "She's who he's been running from all this time!"

"We don't really know what he's running from," Rowan

said. "All we know is that he's afraid. And that he doesn't trust anyone."

"Rowan's right," Nina said. "We knew we would have to reveal who we were to Balthazar at some point. We've just got to tell him in a place where he can't run away." She thought for a moment and her eyes brightened. "I know, like a jail cell!"

"Whoa, hold on, we're moving a little fast here," Xanthe cautioned. "Nina, are you suggesting what I think you're suggesting? Turning Black Rabbit in? He'll never tell us anything after that! And he certainly won't follow us back home!"

"We have to corner him first and convince him later," Nina said. "Rowan and I can meet with the Foggerty Brothers and tell them where and when to find Black Rabbit and the Ghost Rider. Xave will be the bait, and Xanthe, you can set the alleviator closer to the swimming hole—Xavier can show you where it is."

"It's not a bad plan, Xanthe," Rowan said. "We'll force his hand. Balt will either have to go to jail with the Foggerty Brothers or escape into the alleviator with us. Either way, we have him in a small space where we can talk to him."

"I don't know, he'll think we've betrayed him," Xavier said, suddenly feeling protective. "He'll never go back to the Owatannauk. He'll only escape again, and we'll be right back where we started."

"Only it'll be worse, because he won't trust us either," Xanthe added.

"I'm beginning to think we shouldn't take him back to the

Owatannauk," Rowan said thoughtfully. "From what Xavier said, Balt isn't just some jerk who's trying to make trouble."

"No, he seemed pretty nice, actually," Xavier said. "We could be real friends . . . in another time, another universe."

"So maybe Balt isn't the problem," Rowan continued. "Maybe he has a good reason for staying away from the Owatannauk. Maybe the real problem lies in Archibald Weber."

Again, they pondered that possibility in silence, but were interrupted when Dr. Wu came up the stairs to the room where they were sitting.

"Hello. I hope you are feeling better," he said, turning to Rowan. "I've brought some tea that will improve your *chi* . . . your inner energy." He rummaged through his satchel and pulled out a small, pungent sack, which he handed to him. Then he turned to Xavier and handed him the book.

"Here. I'm sorry, but I was unable to make much more sense of it."

"What did you find out?" Xanthe said, grabbing the book from Xavier's hands. She turned the pages carefully, tilted her head, and squinted, as though that might illuminate something in the foreign words on the page.

Dr. Wu hesitated, trying to find the right words. "I think . . . maybe it's a story. A strange tale of a great battle . . . and other things. The Swede said there is something about planets. The Portuguese man says there is a description of a young man, the leader of five warriors, sacrificed in a most horrible and painful death. The Italian was certain the book was about music. I found a man from Germany who thought it had instructions of some sort, and a man from the Sandwich Islands who said it was about an upheaval . . . an earthquake of enormous proportions. But it was the minister from Virginia who could read Ancient Greek and Latin who summed it up best. He said that the book was evil, written by the devil, and I think I agree. There is something wrong with this book, and I am nervous just being in the same room with it. So now that you have it back, I suggest you destroy it."

With that, Dr. Wu gave a terse bow and hurried back down the stairs. Xanthe stopped flipping through the book, placed it gently on the floor, and pushed it away with her foot.

"Don't be so superstitious!" Xavier said, stuffing the book in his shirt. "From what I just heard, Dr. Wu could have been describing the Bible! Now where can we find the Foggerty Brothers?"

"We're really going to do this?" Xanthe said. "It could backfire big time. I don't think we'll get a second chance."

"I think Balthazar needs to know the truth," Rowan insisted. "If we're up front with him, hopefully he'll be up front with us. And if his father is the problem, if his father really wants to kill him . . . which I find hard to believe . . . well, maybe we can help him. But nobody can solve anything as long as we're all pretending to be something we're not. I think that makes sense, doesn't it?"

"I think he's right, Xave," Xanthe said, resigned. "Nothing can change unless we start telling the truth. That's what real friends would do."

"All right," Xavier sighed. "Let's do it."

"The Foggertys come in every night to hear me play," Nina said quietly. "They're downstairs in the saloon right now."

"Can you get Balt to the swimming hole tomorrow at the golden hour?" Rowan asked Xavier.

"I think so," Xavier said. "Yes, I'm sure of it. But I've got to rob a stagecoach to do it . . . Xanthe, would you mind . . . ?"

"Yeah, yeah," she said, waving him off. "There's a morning stagecoach that leaves Hangtown at about nine o'clock. Is that early enough?"

"Perfect."

"You won't have the alleviator to escape to . . ."

"I know. Just try to make sure you're the only one in the coach."

"Rowan, you have to do all the talking to the Foggerty Brothers, you know," Nina said.

Rowan looked slightly stricken, but then girded himself and rose from the sofa. "I'm ready," he said.

Xavier and Xanthe peeked down into the saloon through the slats of the banister and watched their friends approach the table where five similarly dressed men sat quietly drinking whiskey. They all had hair down to their shoulders, wore long, tan dusters, and each had a wide-brimmed hat in front of him on the table. After a word from the Popplewells the men rose, picked up their hats, and followed Rowan and Nina up the staircase. The twins ducked into Xanthe's bedroom, which adjoined Nina's, and left the door open a crack.

The Foggerty Brothers ranged from tall to extremely tall, and even through the crack in the doorway Xavier could see Rowan starting to sweat.

"So you say you saw both of 'em?" a brother with gray hair and a long scar on his cheek said, his voice low.

"That's right. Twice," Rowan answered quickly. "Both times I saw them it was right before sunset. It was at a beautiful little swimming hole, about three miles north of the stagecoach road, the one that leads to El Dorado, right where the road bends around the rockslide and that big live oak that was split by lightning . . ."

"Slow down, Rowan, slow down. You're talking too fast," Xavier murmured under his breath.

"He's nervous," whispered Xanthe. The Foggerty Brothers didn't seem bothered by Rowan's speediness, so Xavier relaxed. They'd probably dealt with all kinds of oddballs in their line of work, so maybe Rowan didn't stick out as being unusual.

"I know that place," the scarred brother said.

"Well, I was exploring up there with my sister here, when we came across the two of them getting ready to dive into that swimming hole. Black Rabbit and the Ghost Rider. I could tell it was them from the clothes they were wearing before they took 'em off. From what they were saying, they go there all the time, around sunset. I bet if you stake out that swimming hole—at sunset, mind you—you'll find them."

"Why are you telling us this?" A youthful, clean-shaven

brother asked. "Why don't you just go to the sheriff's office, tell him about it, and collect the reward yourselves?"

Beads of perspiration appeared on Rowan's forehead. The Foggerty Brothers waited as he hemmed and hawed.

"We don't think the sheriff can do the job right," Nina piped up suddenly. "I was a victim of the first Ghost Rider robbery and I want him caught for what he did, humiliating the driver that way. But the Ghost Rider's a clever man. The sheriff just doesn't have the smarts to catch him. Besides, he can't do it alone, and who would he collect for his posse? The drunks sitting in the bar downstairs? We think this is a job for professionals. And by the way, we're not giving up the reward, we want a cut. One third. Together those crooks are worth seven thousand dollars, so we'll take a cool two thousand for ourselves."

The scarred brother raised his eyebrows and started to chuckle. "Well, now! Aren't you a wild whippersnapper!"

"I'm nothing of the sort," Nina replied evenly. "That's the deal, take it or leave it."

"And you thought Lily was a hard woman," a fancily dressed brother with a musketeer-style mustache murmured to a stocky one with a full beard. "This one makes her look like a sweet little lamb!"

"What if we took your information, captured the two of them, and hightailed it out of here, leaving you with nothing? What would you say to that, little lady?" said the stocky brother.

"No, no, that's not how we do things," said the scarred one.

"We'll honor that deal, my dear. It's only fair. If it pans out, you'll get your money."

Nina offered her hand to seal the agreement. The scarred one took it and kissed it lightly, then tipped his hat. "We'll see you after we nab our quarry. That's a promise." He placed the hat on his head and swept down the stairs, his duster flapping behind him. Each brother in turn tipped his hat to Nina, nodded to Rowan, and followed, leaving the sweet smell of whiskey and cigarillo smoke in their wake.

"OK," Rowan said to the Alexanders as they emerged from the room. "Now it's up to you guys." He held out a fist, and the others made one as well. They pounded them together.

"I'm off," Xavier said. He turned to Xanthe. "I'll see you in the stagecoach."

"Yeah. See you." Xanthe stopped him before he reached the first step. "Xave, be careful." She paused. "And thanks for saving me, even though I didn't need ... well, you know."

"You're welcome," he said, giving her shoulder a squeeze. "But I couldn't have done it without the others, including Chester, and that's the truth."

As Xavier walked downstairs he pulled his hat over his eyes, hiking up the collar of his coat so the Foggerty Brothers wouldn't see his face as he passed.

Outside the night air was brisk and the wind had kicked up. Clouds covered the moon. It would be hard for him to navigate through the woods, but it also meant he would be harder to find, if anyone was looking. The air smelled of rain coming, a dank, earthy kind of smell. He hoped it wouldn't start until he reached Dancer. The horse had a poncho in its saddlebag that he could use as a tent. He also prayed that if it rained it would be over by the next day, otherwise there would be no reason for Balthazar to go to the swimming hole.

The downpour started about five minutes later. By the time, hours later, that Xavier reached Dancer, he was soaked to the skin and shivering.

"Hello, Dancer boy, did you miss me?" Xavier chattered, slapping the horse's flank. Dancer grunted and moved away slightly. Xavier searched the saddlebag for the poncho and finally found it, then tried stretching it across a couple of bushes to construct a makeshift tent. The results were disheartening. Even though the tree branches provided some cover, the ground was quickly growing muddy.

"Man, I wish I could find a cave or something," Xavier groaned. He felt a soft nibbling at his elbow. Dancer had grabbed him by the shirt and was starting to walk, tugging him gently. Xavier twisted his arm away.

"Don't worry, I get it, I'm following," he said.

Dancer led him to what looked like a small tunnel made of four boulders stacked against one another. There was just enough room in the opening to lay out his bedroll.

"You're amazing, Dancer, you know that?" The horse whinnied and shook its head. Xavier peeled off his wet things and put on a flannel shirt that had stayed dry in the saddlebag. He laid out the bedroll, snuggled deep inside, and in moments he was fast asleep.

• • •

The next morning the sun woke him. Xavier checked his
watch and saw that he still had an hour before the stagecoach
would arrive. His civilian clothes were still wet from the night
before, so he spread them out on the rock to dry and changed
into his Ghost Rider attire. Then he rode Dancer to the point
overlooking the stagecoach road.

He was a little nervous. This was the first time he was going
to attempt a robbery without the security of the alleviator
waiting for him. He would have to escape with only the help
of Dancer. He hoped Xanthe had been able to secure a coach
without any other passengers, though that was unlikely.

Then he saw it, a stagecoach with a white handkerchief fluttering from the door. He spurred Dancer down the hill and
blocked the road. As soon as he saw the coach come around the
bend he shot his gun in the air, and Dancer reared up just for
the heck of it.

The coach stopped. The nervous driver stumbled out of the
driver's seat with his hands in the air. Apparently the reputation of the Ghost Rider was enough to keep him from trying
anything. *Thank goodness for cowards*, Xavier thought.

"Look, mister, I don't want any trouble," stuttered the
driver. "You can have all the money you want, but you really
don't want to look in the coach. There's a sick colored woman
in there, she's got some kind of horrible disease. Coughing and
hacking and spitting, her eyes practically rolling out of her
head . . . by gum, not one person wanted to climb in there with

her. I'm taking her as far as Negro Hill, where I imagine she'll give up the ghost pretty quickly."

Xavier was glad he had the kerchief over his mouth, he could hardly keep from laughing at what must have been a stellar performance on Xanthe's part. "You expect me to believe that?" he growled. "Get her out of there."

"Please, sir, she's really not well . . ."

"I said get her out!"

The driver knocked on the door and quickly backed away. Xanthe gingerly stepped from the coach, squinting. She took a few wavering steps, then her knees buckled and she fell.

"Take her purse and her jewelry, and remove your own as well," Xavier said. "And put them in the saddlebag."

The driver did as he was told.

"Now you, lady. Pick up the bag and bring it over here. You stay where you are!" he cried, pointing his gun at the driver, who had moved to help her. Xanthe dragged the bag over to Xavier, tugging on it as though she were as weak as a kitten.

"Hurry up!" Xavier barked.

Xanthe scowled, then limply lifted the bag. Xavier snatched it and swung it over Dancer, then drew his gun and shot the driver in the foot. The man squealed in horror and scrambled back into the driver's seat, but before he could whip the horses into action he had slumped over, fast asleep.

"Now what?" said Xanthe. She watched curiously as her brother climbed up next to the man and pulled a quill pen from his pocket.

"Now I write a message to Black Rabbit," Xavier said, searching his pockets. "Shoot, I must've left the ink in my shirt," he mumbled. "I guess I'll have to use blood again."

Xanthe winced as Xavier cut himself with his knife and used his own blood to write on the driver's forehead, NOW DO I REPAY A PERIOD WON.

"What does that mean?" she said.

"It means whatever you want it to mean," Xavier said. "But I think Black Rabbit will get the message loud and clear, which is to meet me at the swimming hole. Come on, I'll show you where it is, then take you to where Gertrude put the alleviator. When it's the golden hour, you've got to change it to the coordinates of the swimming hole and set it down there before the hour is up."

"It'll be there," Xanthe said. "By the way, this horse is pretty cool. You really lucked out. I admit it, I'm jealous."

"Want to go for a little ride?" Xavier said, hoisting himself up. Xanthe grinned as he pulled her up behind him. In an instant they were flying down the road, as Dancer's hooves and Xanthe's squeals echoed through the canyon.

Xavier made sure not to go to the swimming hole until the golden hour. If the Foggerty Brothers showed up early, he didn't want them to chase him first and tip off Balthazar. He waited until he could see the alleviator shimmer into sight at the far end of the pool, visible only to those carrying the special keys. At the same time, he noticed some movement around the perimeter. The Foggerty Brothers were already there.

He slid quietly off Dancer. "Don't let anyone capture you," he whispered to the horse. The stallion fluttered his eyelids, which Xavier took to mean "OK." As the horse disappeared into the woods, Xavier started to undress, removing his hat, his duster, his boots, his shirt and pants, but keeping on the bulletproof underwear, just in case.

He was sitting on the rock when a shadow fell over him. He whirled around and saw Balthazar standing behind him.

"Hey, Lew, I thought we could go for a swim . . ."

Balthazar slowly drew his gun, pulling the hammer back until it clicked.

"What . . . what's the joke?" Xavier said nervously.

" 'Now do I repay a period won,' " Balthazar said. "Is that another one of your meaningless palindromes or have you come to confess?"

Before he could respond, Balthazar tossed something at Xavier, which rolled along the ground and stopped at his feet.

"That yours?"

Xavier looked down. It was the bottle of red ink that he had been looking for.

"Ye-esss . . ." His mind raced to remember where he had left it. Then he recalled his civilian clothes, his shirt and pants, drying on the rock back at his camp. Balthazar pulled another object from his shirt.

"But this isn't yours, is it." It was a statement, not a question. Black Rabbit held out the leather diary, the one that belonged to his father, Archibald Weber.

Xavier's eyes darted from the book to Balthazar's face, which held a mixture of hurt, hatred, and rage. At that moment, Xavier knew his connection to Balthazar had evaporated.

Xavier hoped his silver tongue could salvage what was left of their friendship, but Balthazar didn't give him a chance. His arm shot out and Xavier flew back, blood gushing from his nose.

"I should've recognized you," Balthazar said. "You're the guy I robbed in the forest with his friend. The ones who were woefully ignorant about bears. You look different when you're dressed up, but now in your long johns, it's as plain as day."

Balthazar kicked Xavier's ribs, and Xavier howled, curling into a ball. He covered his head with his hands as Balthazar kicked again and again. Each time Xavier felt the boot hit his skull with a dull thud, and his field of vision was filled with blinking lights.

Balthazar squatted next to him. *Good,* Xavier thought. *Move closer, just a little closer . . .*

"You tell them I'm not coming back," Balthazar hissed. "I'm never coming back."

That was all the time Xavier needed. He twisted his body, whipping his leg around, catching Balthazar's ankle, and sweeping him off his feet. Balthazar fell hard, but was up again, eyes blazing.

"We're here to help you!" Xavier said, catching his breath. His body was sore all over. "We need to talk . . ."

But clearly the last thing Balthazar wanted to do was talk.

He charged Xavier like a bull. Xavier jumped, flipping over him, and gave him a sharp jab with his elbow, which sent him skidding into a rock. Balthazar was up in an instant, blinking and spitting dust from his mouth. Then a smile crept across his face. He settled into a martial arts stance, feet apart, arms wide, hands open. He beckoned to Xavier. Bring it on.

Xavier settled into the same stance, and they circled each other for a minute. Then Balthazar flew at him with a flurry of jabs and kicks. Xavier could tell he was outmatched. Balthazar's feet seemed to be everywhere: on Xavier's chest, on his face, on the back of his head, his back, his ankles . . . and he had yet to land a good kick or punch himself.

"I need to take more lessons," he gasped aloud to himself.

"You'll need more than that, my friend," Balthazar said sarcastically. "I learned Shaolin kung fu in the northern mountains of China from Master Chueh Yuan himself, the man who revised the eighteen fists of Lo Han into the seventy-two fists, and developed the hundred and seventy movements. Then I learned the five animal styles from Master Zhue Yuen."

Xavier was impressed. He had gotten his martial arts training in a strip mall next to a Laundromat and a doughnut shop.

Now Balthazar was spinning over him like a top. It was an astonishing move, turning Balthazar into a sort of human torpedo. Xavier rolled out of his way, grabbing a large branch that had broken off a tree. As Balthazar hit the ground, Xavier rammed him. Finally, a solid hit! Poles had always been Xavier's specialty, and now he spun this branch like a propeller, whacking Balthazar several times until the superior fighter finally grabbed it and, with a deft move, flipped Xavier on his back, wresting the branch from his hands at the same time. Balthazar held the stick like a spear over Xavier's throat.

"You're not a killer, Balthazar," Xavier said, hoping that this wasn't the point in time when he'd become one. Balthazar startled slightly at the mention of his name.

"No. I'm not." He launched the branch into the woods. Then he picked up Archibald Weber's diary, which had fallen on the ground, and hurled it into the swimming hole.

"Hey! What are you doing? Do you know what that is?!" Xavier shouted.

"Yes. Do you?"

Xavier ran to the edge of the swimming hole, searching the water for any sign of the book. It had disappeared.

"'Scuse us, ladies, we don't mean to interrupt," drawled a low, gravelly voice. Out from the trees trotted five white horses, each carrying a Foggerty Brother. The scarred one was first, followed by the musketeer, the stocky one, the clean-shaven one, and the fancy one bringing up the rear. In the thick of the kung fu brawl, Xavier had forgotten all about them.

"This has been very entertaining, but we're getting hungry," said the stocky one.

"You fellas fight like Chinamen," the fancy one remarked.

"But it's not gonna do much good against a Winchester," added the clean-shaven brother.

"That's for sure," added the musketeer brother. "Now, why

don't you gentlemen come along real quiet, and we won't have to mess up your clothes with bullets and blood."

Xavier spoke under his breath. "We can escape, Balt. I've got two alleviator keys . . ."

"Huh. Alleviators. So that's how you disappeared after your robberies. Figures."

"We don't have to go back to the Owatannauk, but we do have to get out of here!"

"I'm not going anywhere with you. You lied to me. Everyone there lies to me. It's all one big trick, you know. Nothing is what it seems. They just want to use me . . ."

Xavier wasn't sure what Balthazar was talking about, but time was growing short. The Foggerty Brothers were getting restless, and the golden hour was almost over.

"Let's go, boys," the scarred one said, walking his horse toward them. His brothers followed. "We can do this the easy way or the hard way."

Xavier put his hands up, as did Balthazar. Then Xavier gave a low whistle, and waited.

A crash in the bushes behind the brothers startled them and they turned just in time to see Dancer leaping over their heads, spooking the white stallions. The robot horse landed in front of Xavier, who swung himself onto its back.

"Let's do it the hard way!" Xavier yelled.

The brothers had recovered their bearings and were now shooting. Xavier could feel the impact of the bullets thumping against his back, unable to pierce the body-armor underwear.

He kept his head low, for he hadn't had time to grab his hat. He turned Dancer toward the group and charged straight for them, reaching out for Balthazar.

"Balt!" he cried. "Grab hold, I'll swing you up!"

He overshot him and wheeled Dancer around to make another pass.

"I don't think so," Balt said with a bitter laugh. "I'll take my chances with them."

Much to the surprise of the musketeer brother, Balthazar held his arms up in surrender. The brother jumped from his horse and quickly slapped a pair of handcuffs around the young man's wrists. Xavier made one last pass, grabbing his hat off the ground and shoving it onto his head, just in time to feel three bullets pop against the back of the brim.

He hadn't expected to be caught by the Foggertys at the top of the falls. The plan was that he and Balthazar would be down in the swimming hole and could simply run to the alleviator. He was thirty feet above the pool and there was only one thing to do: jump. Xavier closed his eyes, jabbed his heels into Dancer's flanks, and hung on for dear life.

When the horse's hooves left the ground, everything seemed to move in slow motion. It was as though Dancer had sprouted wings and they were flying right over the swimming hole. The wind held them up, whooshing into Xavier's face. His eyes started to water. But then horse and rider were falling, tilting into a nosedive like a glider that's lost its momentum, tipped so far that for a moment Xavier was afraid Dancer would flip on his back, and then they were underwater and Xavier was still desperately trying to hold on with his knees, but the bracing cold caused him to gasp and he swallowed and choked, and then they were up again, and Dancer was swimming, then climbing onto the shore, his hooves sinking only slightly in the mud.

Out of the corner of his eye, Xavier spotted something caught among the rocks . . . the diary! It had landed on the edge of the shore. He snatched it as Dancer rose out of the water, galloping toward the alleviator, which shimmered brightly in front of them.

Xavier could see Xanthe, Rowan, and Nina hiding inside the machine, urging him on, then flattening themselves against the walls as Dancer charged inside. The door closed, and they disappeared in a burst of light.

+ CHAPTER TWENTY +
HOME AGAIN

As soon as the foursome landed at the Owatannauk, they were met by the aunts, who whisked them down into the subterranean parking garage, leaving Dancer in the lobby. They all piled into Gertrude's pickup truck—a tight fit, especially for Nina, who was wedged between the large bones of one aunt and the ample flesh of the other—but no one complained.

"We were listening from Gertrude's station," Agatha said. "We heard the fight." She shifted around in her seat to look at Xavier. "You're going to need a lot of ice packs, young man. You've taken quite a beating." Xavier had no idea what he looked like, but he couldn't help but notice the blood staining his long johns.

"Nobody told me he was a kung fu master. If I'd known, I would've tried something else . . ."

"We didn't know," Agatha said. "It doesn't matter. From what we heard, all of you have accomplished quite a bit. You are to be commended."

"But we failed," protested Nina. "We don't have Balthazar with us, and as a matter of fact, he's in terrible danger!"

"True, but we have more information than we've ever had before, and we do know where he is, as long as he doesn't escape from the Froggity Brothers."

"Foggerty Brothers," the foursome corrected in unison, giggles and snorts following.

"Yes, that's right. Foggerty Brothers."

During the drive to the aunts' house each of the junior detectives described their part in what had transpired over the past week. It was a useful exercise, for none of them had a sense of the entire picture until they had all finished speaking. Xanthe was able to explain why she had wanted to spend time with the Miwoks; apparently they were no strangers to the famed Black Rabbit. He had befriended them early in his criminal career, giving them much of the gold he had stolen so that they could trade with the townspeople in a more meaningful fashion. In response, they taught him how to hunt more efficiently, how to make his way through the woods without being detected, and at times they had hidden him from bounty hunters. The name they had given him was a strange one, which translated to "Laughing Storm."

Nina related more information about the "Froggity Brothers," as they were now teasingly known among the group. They were regulars at the saloon. The leader, the gray-haired, scarred one, was a favorite of Lily's, and visited often.

"It's a good thing you escaped," Nina said to Xavier. "After they left, Lily Rose told me that their plans for the Ghost Rider were not the same as for Black Rabbit. Black Rabbit was going to trial, but in their minds they had already convicted the Ghost Rider and sentenced him to death. Xave, you wouldn't have gotten much farther than the Hangtown oak tree."

Rowan also had useful information to contribute, despite his gold-mining detour. After spending more time with Oliver, he found that the man's mind was always on the woman he'd left in Bloomington, Adelaide Clemens, and that what lured him to gold country wasn't the promise of riches, but rather the promise of adventure. Yet even with this thrill-seeking streak, he seemed anchored by his optimism, his sincere belief that through hard work and diligence anything could be within your grasp.

By the time they rolled up to the aunts' place, the sun had set. They piled out of the truck and were greeted by the familiar scents of the old house. Each time traveler took a welcome hot shower, then dressed for bed, even though it was only just after sunset. The comfort of soft pajamas and slippers was what they all wanted right then.

Aunt Agatha treated Xavier's wounds, which were numerous. Most of them were only surface scratches or bruises, but one injury was permanent. During their fight, Balthazar had knocked out one of Xavier's teeth, an incisor.

"Well, that'll be a nice souvenir," he said wryly, inspecting the gap with a hand mirror. "I can get myself a gold tooth now. You know, in honor of the Gold Rush."

"Ooh, Mom and Dad will love that," said Xanthe. "After a

thousand dollars' worth of braces, I'm sure they always hoped you would end up looking like an old prospector."

They sat down for a late dinner of thick beef-and-barley soup with salad and French bread. Xavier was overjoyed when he saw the spread, so tired was he of pork and beans, burned coffee, and having to pick crawly things out of his food. Normally he wasn't much of a fan of vegetables, but when he bit down on the salad and heard a loud crunch, and tasted the clean, sweet juiciness of the lettuce mixed with the tartness of the tomato, tears came to his eyes. Everyone had two helpings of everything.

After dinner, they gathered in the living room with hot apple cider and a plate of Gertrude's homemade peach scones. Now that they were clean and fed, it was clear that the aunts wanted to get down to business.

"Again, I want to stress just how pleased we are with the headway you've made," Agatha said, taking the lead. "But as we all know, it's not over. I'm going to assume that the Froggity . . . *Foggerty* Brothers succeeded in transporting Balthazar to the Hangtown jail. He will be tried, and no doubt found guilty. I'm not sure what the punishment will be, but my guess, from the name of the town, is that they will be inclined toward hanging. Therefore it is imperative that we spring him from jail, ideally before the trial."

Xanthe raised her hand and Agatha acknowledged her with a nod.

"But then what? Xave says Balthazar isn't any more interested in coming back here than he was before we found him."

"We may have to force him back," Gertrude said quietly. "For his own good."

"Excuse me, Aunt Gertrude," Xavier said hesitantly. "I'm pretty sure that's not going to work. He said he'd rather die than come back."

"Really?" She looked crestfallen.

"Well, he said it didn't make a difference, he was going to die either way. And now that I think of it, he said his father, Archibald Weber, wanted . . . well, I know this can't be right . . . but that he wanted to kill him."

"Why, that's absurd!" Agatha interjected. "Archie loves Balthazar, more than anything!"

"I'm only repeating what he said," Xavier answered.

"Why would he say something like that, I wonder?" Gertrude murmured, drumming her long fingers on a side table.

"Exaggeration?" Nina suggested. "I know that when I get really mad I say a lot of things I don't mean."

"He's not mad," Xavier said. "He's depressed. And the way he said it . . . he sounded heartbroken. He feels like he's been betrayed."

The aunts frowned. Xavier suddenly remembered the book he had rescued. He'd forgotten to mention it to the aunts.

"What book, Xavier?" Agatha said, picking up his thoughts. "The item that Balthazar threw away, was it a book?"

"Yes . . ."

Gertrude turned, suddenly interested. "You asked him if he knew what it was, and he said he did. What was it?"

"I . . . honestly, I don't know," Xavier said. "Just a book I found. He threw it into the waterfall though. It's gone."

Something kept him from telling them the truth. He tried to clear his mind so that Agatha wouldn't figure out that the book was sitting on the bed in the guest room upstairs, and shot a look at Xanthe and Popplewells. The other junior detectives seemed to pick up on his meaning; nobody contradicted his story, and they all had strangely blank expressions on their faces. Gertrude seemed to have moved on, but Xavier thought he detected a flicker of suspicion in Agatha. He tried to slam his mind like a door, thinking instead of something ridiculous: a cow wearing a dress doing slow cartwheels along a telephone wire. Agatha shook her head, trying to clear it of nonsense. She frowned at Xavier, who smiled pleasantly back.

He didn't want to tell the aunts about the book. First of all, he didn't want them to know where he had gotten it. Secondly, he knew they would take it away. They'd think it was dangerous. Or evil. And they would never give it back to him.

Agatha and Gertrude had moved on to discussing a plan that he knew wouldn't work. Gertrude was going to place an alleviator outside the jail cell, for the cell itself was too small. When Balthazar was taken out for his trial, she would snatch him, taking him back to the Owatannauk. But what would happen to Balthazar once he was there? Whatever they needed him for, it was doubtful he would comply. And the first chance he could get to steal an alleviator key and escape, he would take it. In fact, the only way to keep him here would be under lock and key . . .

With a jolt Xavier knew what he had to do. But he was afraid. For the first time in a long time, he was afraid to do something. He spent the rest of the meeting trying to ignore his fluttering stomach.

When it was time for bed, the aunts once again thanked the foursome for all they had done. They had found Balthazar, and gotten him into a position where he was confined and could be easily captured. The aunts toasted their success with their teacups of cider, but their meaning was clear: Thank you very much, but we can take it from here.

Once the foursome were upstairs, the Popplewells came into the twins' bedroom and plunked themselves on the beds.

"Well, that's it," Rowan said. "We did it. I guess."

"Somehow it doesn't feel very satisfying," Xanthe said with a shrug.

"No, not at all," agreed Nina. "In fact, I feel horrible. There's something not right. I don't know why, but I feel bad for Balt."

"I know what you mean," agreed Rowan. "He seems like a pawn in all of this. Pushed around. I kind of wish it wasn't over. There must be something we can do."

"It doesn't have to be over," Xavier said. They all looked at him. He had taken the diary out from under his pillow. "There is someone who is in the middle of this whole mess who has not been consulted. We need to talk to Archibald Weber."

"Xave, you can't be serious," Xanthe said, sitting up straight.

"Nobody's seen him for years . . . at least that's what Gertrude says . . ." Rowan added.

"I think I can find him," Xavier said. "But . . . I need you guys with me. I can't do it alone."

"Of course you won't have to. I'm in," Nina said, almost immediately.

"Me too," Xanthe said.

"Is this going to involve almost getting killed?" Rowan said, with his usual hesitance. "I'm really not interested in almost getting killed."

"Better that than *actually* getting killed," Xanthe joked.

"Thanks for reminding me," Rowan answered, adding a playful shove.

"I don't know what we're getting into. I just know that the aunts . . . well, I think they're wrong. If the whole point of this venture was to capture Balthazar and bring him back, they will probably be able to do that much. But if the point was to bring him back to address these 'dark forces at work,'" Xavier said, using Gertrude's own words from the beginning of their mission, "I don't think they have any way of getting him to do that. We just don't have enough information about what's really going on, and the only person who can shed light on this is the author of this book, Archibald Weber. I think we should pay him a visit at the silver hour."

It was with no small amount of trepidation that the foursome quietly tiptoed down the staircase that spiraled around the outside of the aunts' house, and made their way to the resort hotel. The moon was full that night, and the chill in the air carried with it the dampness of the ocean, but Xavier knew his shivering was not from the cold. They had all worn their regular clothes, sweatshirts, jeans, and sneakers. Xavier didn't bring the book. He was fearful of what might happen if it was reunited with its true owner.

They turned on their flashlights as soon as they entered the musty building, shining the bright circles of light around the expansive lobby. They made their way to the secret hallway, then walked slowly past the doors of the rooms that they had explored what felt like ages ago, until they reached door number twenty-one.

"Fibonacci numbers," they all said together, and then they laughed nervously.

"Here's where I went in," Xavier said, pointing at the rubble on the floor in front of the hole in the wall. He shined his flashlight inside the hole, but it did little to illuminate the room. "Well, here goes nothing." He took a deep breath and ducked inside.

The others followed, and once they were through, they shone their flashlights around the sitting room. Xavier allowed them to explore for a few minutes before he led them down the hallway to the laboratory. When they got there, Xavier found the door wouldn't open. He twisted the knob, shaking the door a few times.

"This wasn't locked the last time I was here . . ."

"Weird," Xanthe said, shining her flashlight around. "It doesn't seem as dusty in here as it is in the rest of the hotel."

"Maybe because it's been sealed for so long," Rowan suggested. "No air currents to push around the dust . . ."

"You guys," Nina whispered hoarsely. "It's coming. The silver hour. I can feel it."

Xavier could, too. His heartbeat raced as he felt the familiar tingling of every molecule in his body vibrating. The light was too dim to really see much of the transformation, but as Xavier sensed the prickling rush of heat and ice course down his body, the lamps that lay behind the beautiful wall sconces suddenly shone brightly, and the hallway was bathed in a golden light.

For the first time they saw the interior of the apartment clearly. They were standing on a Persian carpet that stretched the length of the hallway. Large wooden beams framed the doorways. A grandfather clock in the hall started to tick, its pendulum swinging in measured regularity, its hands now pointing at the correct time. The door to the laboratory, however, remained locked, and with a sudden feeling of dread, Xavier remembered that the hole they had come through was probably sealed. They were now captives in the chambers with whoever was imprisoned there.

He heard a noise, the creak of footsteps, and whirled around. It was Otto.

"Good morning," he said. "We've been expecting you."

+ CHAPTER TWENTY-ONE +
THE BOOK

"IF YOU WILL PLEASE COME WITH ME TO THE PARLOR," Otto said, gesturing back down the hall.

The foursome turned and followed him in silence, but when they turned the corner to the living room, they couldn't help but gasp. The room, which they had only partly seen with their flashlights, was aglow from the fire blazing in an ornate fireplace. The Tiffany lamps, now lit, acted as prisms, throwing geometric splashes of color on the surrounding surfaces.

What truly caught their attention was the vast collection of clocks: cuckoo clocks, alarm clocks, a huge train station clock, hourglasses, sundials, and intricately balanced mechanical inventions with visible gears and pendulums and balls rolling down ramps, all marking time with the same precision.

"Take a seat by the fireplace. Please make yourselves comfortable," Otto said.

Xavier had no idea if they were in trouble or not. Otto's

range of emotion ran from slight irritation to amiable pleasantries; he was not a creature of extremes.

"Otto, is Archibald Weber here?" Xavier asked.

"Yes. He'll be with you in a moment. He's asked me to see if you require any refreshments. Water? Tea? Banana milk shakes?"

"Banana milk shakes?" Nina giggled.

"Mr. Weber's favorite beverage is banana milk shakes with whipped cream and chocolate sprinkles. They are always available at the hotel," Otto said. "Any time of day."

"I'll have one of those!" Nina said enthusiastically, ignoring the exasperated looks from everyone else.

"Oh, I guess I'll have one, too," Xanthe said, giving in to temptation.

Rowan asked for a glass of cranberry juice and Xavier for a hot cocoa. As soon as Otto left the room, a voice came over a sound system. It was a familiar voice, for they had heard Gertrude's scratchy recording of it, but now it was clear as a bell.

"Xavier and Xanthe Alexander, Rowan and Nina Popplewell, welcome," Archibald Weber said.

They glanced around the room, half expecting to see him walk through the wall, or pop out of the footstool like a jack-in-the-box. Anything seemed possible.

"There is no point in looking for me; I'm not in the room with you," he continued. "This is for your safety. I'll explain in due time, but let me assure you, you are in no danger. None at all! You can relax."

These words did nothing to relax any of them. They continued to glance warily around the room, as classical music suddenly filled the air. Nina smiled.

"Beethoven. Piano Sonata number fourteen, C-sharp Minor, opus twenty-seven, number two. *The Moonlight Sonata*," she said.

"Yes. It's my favorite piece," Archibald Weber said. "Lovely, isn't it?"

"I don't recognize the recording."

"That's because I'm playing it myself."

Nina's entire body seemed to float with pleasure. "You . . . you play piano?" she asked in a tiny voice.

"For close to a hundred years now. I've had lessons from the best: Beethoven, Mozart, Bach, Brahms, Chopin . . ."

"So what are you, some sort of Phantom of the Opera?" Rowan said loudly. "Because we're not here for a concert. We have some questions. And we're tired of the games!"

Xavier was impressed. It was remarkable how bold Rowan became when his sister's safety was at stake. He had gotten to his feet and was addressing the ceiling.

The music stopped. "I was merely waiting for Otto to return with your drinks. Ah, here he is now."

On cue, Otto appeared around the corner with a tray of drinks. Once they were served, he motioned for them to be seated, then he positioned himself in front of the entrance to the hallway.

"I know why you're here," Archibald Weber began after

everyone had settled back into their seats. "And as Otto already said, I have been expecting you. Actually, this is a meeting I've been looking forward to having for some time. I wasn't sure when the opportunity would arise, but as soon as my notebook disappeared I knew that one . . . or all of you . . . had breached my prison."

"Prison? Why prison?" Xanthe said. "What have you done to be locked up?"

"Before I answer that, allow me to propose a little game, if you'll excuse me, Rowan. Old habits die hard. I, too, have questions. I've heard so much about you, but there is so much more I want to know! Unfortunately, our time together is short, so we'll forgo the social niceties and get to know each other this way. We'll each take turns asking questions back and forth. You must answer with complete candor. As long as we are truthful, the game can continue, but if somebody lies, or doesn't want to answer, then the game ends."

"Who wins and who loses?" Rowan said warily.

"Either we all win or we all lose," Archibald answered.

"Well then, what's the point?" Xavier said.

"Is that one of your questions?" Archibald asked.

"No, we're still establishing the parameters of the contest," Xavier snapped.

"Fair enough. There's a prize, of course. Winners live, losers die. Those are the stakes."

"Kind of serious for a game," Rowan mumbled.

"All games are serious. Now let's begin. I'll go first. Rowan, your life is horrible. Why don't you just pack it in and give up?"

Rowan's face turned a rosy pink as he choked violently on his juice, some of it coming out of his nose. Nina jumped up and pounded him on the back.

"Excuse me, Mr. Weber," Rowan finally said with contained anger. "But I don't know what you mean. My life is not horrible!"

"Oh dear, is the game over already?" Archibald Weber sighed. "Of course your life is horrible. It's been extraordinarily unfair to you! You lost your mother, your father is too busy for you. You're poor. Your sister outshines you in all respects. You will always be unremarkable. Average. Overlooked. I don't see how you get up in the morning."

Rowan wrestled with something inside himself, tensing every muscle in his face. "I'm sorry you have such a low opinion of me," he said tightly. "As for my life, I would much prefer to be my humble self than an offensive, mean-spirited genius."

"I'm sorry, but that's really not an answer."

"Because it's not a real question!" Rowan snapped. "Why don't I give up? Because I'm only fourteen, for Pete's sake! I've got my whole life ahead of me! And I don't accept your assessment of me. You don't have to be a star or be famous to do great things, you know. I have faith that nothing is in vain. If you try to do something and it doesn't work, that doesn't mean it wasn't worth doing. Nothing's wasted. Nothing."

A light laughter filled the room. "Very good," Archibald

Weber said. "That was a wonderful answer. And I'm sorry to be offensive, but these questions are not meant to be easy."

"OK, it's our turn," Rowan said. He thought for a moment. "Why are you imprisoned?"

"Rowan, you should've asked about Balthazar!" Xavier hissed.

"I want to know who we're dealing with here," Rowan whispered back. "There's a reason he's locked up. Is this guy a killer or just insane?"

"I'm neither," Archibald Weber said. "I won't count that as a question since it wasn't directed at me. And you needn't bother whispering, I can hear everything. To answer your question, I am sequestered behind this wall because I have an illness, which so far has been incurable. I've sealed myself up here in quarantine to protect others. It's why I can't see you in person, or attend board meetings."

The foursome stared at each other, crestfallen. Archibald Weber was sick. The man they'd all fantasized about, the brilliant, eccentric puzzler, was dying.

"My turn," Archibald continued. "Xanthe. Of the four of you, who is the most expendable?"

Xanthe's eyes flashed. Xavier clapped his hands to his ears, hoping she wouldn't unleash the full force of her temper, but he needn't have worried. Xanthe bit her tongue, frowned and fumed, looking from one person to another. Finally she threw up her hands.

"I know you're not going to like this answer," she said with controlled politeness. "But none of us is expendable."

"You're not thinking hard enough," Archibald said gently. "You and your brother are clearly the most valuable. Your minds are quick and precise, your bodies strong and capable, you're both courageous and thoughtful, both expert strategists. You've even developed a keen sense of silent communication between you. But Rowan is not any of those things; he's just lucky to have you as friends. And Nina is only eleven, just tagging along . . ."

"Excuse me, but you can stop picking on Rowan. Rowan is far from weak," Xanthe snapped. "His strength is his heart, his moral rectitude, which you would never understand, but it's just as important as brains and brawn, maybe more so. As for Nina, she is the least expendable of us all. And I think you know that. You're completely focused on her."

Xanthe looked slightly surprised at her own pronouncement, but as soon as she said it, everyone knew it was true.

A light chuckle filled the room. "Touché, my dear. Touché. Proceed."

"All right," Xanthe said, gaining confidence. "Why did Balthazar run away from you?"

"Why indeed. Hmm." There was a long pause, and then Archibald spoke again. "He was angry with me for . . . my priorities. He thinks I was too hard on him. You must understand, Balthazar is a special boy with special talents. When somebody has a talent so strong, so exceptional, should he be allowed to fritter it away? Or is it his duty to develop it, hone it to perfection, and use it to improve life on this earth? Would we have had Mozart if his father had not pushed him? It's not an easy question to answer. Sometimes people don't want to do what their skills are leading them to do. They suppress them, let them lie fallow. They spend a lifetime trying to escape their own destiny. I consider this an enormous tragedy. A waste."

"I don't see anything wrong with people who just want to enjoy life . . ." Xanthe began.

"No? I suppose that depends on why you think you were put here, what the point of your life, and all human life, is. Do we have a calling? A purpose? Or are we all just here to use up resources until the cosmic party is over? But I digress.

"Parents are not always expert at encouraging the best out of their children, and I admit I was probably the worst at it. As soon as I realized what Balthazar's place in the world could be . . . had to be . . . I decided to prepare him for it. The same way a father who recognizes musical talent in his child gets her the finest instrument, the best teacher, and pushes her when her spirits flag, refusing to allow her to quit, so I did with Balthazar. His destiny was . . . is . . . to be a great leader. With the alleviators I took him all over the world, all over time, and his mentors were the most powerful men in history, both famous and infamous: Augustus Caesar, Winston Churchill, Napoleon Bonaparte, Kublai Khan, and others. And he did learn invaluable lessons of leadership, but there was something he was missing, I could tell. He was not happy. He was not embracing his role in life. Then I thought of someone who might be able to get through to him, my personal hero, the man I admire most.

Someone who I hoped would fill in that gap . . . But when I took Balthazar to Illinois he disappeared."

"He said you were trying to kill him," Xanthe said. "Is that true?"

"Ah-ah-ah! No follow-up questions!" Archibald laughed. "It's my turn. Nina, if you listen very carefully, what are all the things you can hear at this moment?"

Nina hesitated. "What do you mean?"

"I think you know exactly what I mean. Listen carefully, and tell me everything you can hear."

Nina closed her eyes. "OK, I can hear Rowan scuffling his feet, Xavier jingling something in his pocket, Xanthe's chair creaking. The grandfather clock in the hallway ticking. Down the hall, maybe where you are, some kind of electronic equipment humming, like a generator or something. Outside, birds tweeting, tennis balls bouncing, people . . . phantoms, laughing, talking. Plane flying overhead. Tree branches. Ocean waves . . ."

"You can hear all that?" Xanthe interrupted.

"Please, let her continue," Archibald said sharply. "What about the music?" Nina was silent for a moment. Her eyes darted to the others.

"Are you still there?" Archibald said.

"Yes, of course," Nina said quietly. "There's always the music."

"What does it sound like?"

She sighed. "It's off-key. Way off-key. Honestly, it sounds

like a mediocre high school band playing with oven mitts on their hands. It's why I play the piano the way I do, you know, why I'm driven to play. It's like . . . if I can play perfectly, then I can correct it . . . make the music in my head beautiful. I need to make it sound right!" She stopped, aware that her voice had become urgent.

"Thank you."

"What are you talking about?" Rowan whispered to his sister. "What do you mean 'there's always the music'? What music?"

"Is that a question for me?" Archibald Weber said. "I'd be happy to answer it . . ."

"No!" Nina shouted. "It's my turn to ask." She took a deep breath. "The book that Xavier took from your study . . . what is it?"

"Ah, yes. The book. That's what started this whole thing, you know. It's been destroyed, has it not?"

"Answer my question first," Nina said evenly.

"That book is a diary of events I've witnessed personally," Archibald began. "It's my journal, one of many, but it's the last one I was working on before I became . . . afflicted. I wrote it in many languages so that it could not be read by any one person."

"You wrote it all yourself? You can speak all those languages? That's not a separate question, it's a point of clarification," Xanthe added quickly.

"I've done a lot of traveling over a long period of time, my dear. I've had plenty of opportunities to pick up knowledge. As I said, my journal is not meant to be read by anyone except myself. The only other person with the kind of linguistic training necessary to read it is Balthazar, and against my better judgment I allowed him to read it, and it upset him, which was of course understandable. You see, that book holds information about the future . . . his future."

"Wait, you said it contained descriptions of events you witnessed personally . . ."

"Yes."

"Are you saying you traveled into the future?"

"Yes, I am."

"How?" Nina squealed.

"That's a new question, not a clarification of the old one," Archibald said. "So it's my turn. Xavier. At this moment, are you prepared to die?"

Xavier fell into a cold sweat. What could he possibly mean by that question? "Uh, no, I'm not. In fact, I am completely unprepared. I don't have a will, I haven't picked out a cemetery plot, I've got a lot of free movie coupons I haven't used yet, and right now I'm wearing underwear with holes in it. So I'll pass on the dying right now, thank you."

"You haven't found anything in life you would die for . . . ? Clarification," Archibald challenged. Xavier was quiet.

"Well . . . I don't know," he said finally. "What do you mean?"

"A new mother could tell you who she would die for in an instant," Archibald replied. "A husband could tell you, a soldier could tell you."

"I see," Xavier said. He thought for a moment, but his heart provided the answer. "I suppose . . . well, I would die for my sister, for Xanthe. And Rowan and Nina." He was looking down at his feet, but now he raised his eyes and saw his sister and friends smiling back at him. It was clear they would do the same for him.

"Do you have a question?"

"How did you travel to the future?"

"I didn't plan it. I don't have the technology to do it myself; I went by invitation. It happened when Balthazar was about twelve years old. I was tinkering with something in the laboratory, I don't really remember what, when suddenly a young woman—she couldn't have been more than seventeen or eighteen years old—appeared by my side. This was before the laboratory was sealed, but still, it was unusual for anyone to enter my private quarters.

"Because I am always carrying an alleviator key, I could see that she had used one of my alleviators to enter the room . . . that's how she got past the locks and the guard. I asked her what she wanted . . . actually, I demanded it of her quite loudly because she startled me so. She told me her name, and said she was from my future. She said she was desperate, she needed my help. I followed her into the alleviator, and we jumped into the future, or rather, to *her* present. I could do this, you see, because I was using an alleviator from the future, not one from *my* present.

"What I saw while I was there was a world you wouldn't recognize. I had to record it somehow . . . the scientist in me demanded it. But I knew this information could be dangerous in the wrong hands; it had to be cloaked in some way. That is why I recorded it in the fashion which you perceived. When I returned, I showed my notes to Balthazar, hoping it would spur him to embrace his destiny, but it did exactly the opposite.

"Too late, I realized that no person should know their future. One is either lulled into complacency, or worse, consumed by desolation. This is what happened with Balthazar, you see. And now he's trying to do whatever he can to avoid that destiny. But this was not the intention of the girl. She told me she was showing me these events so that I might prepare Balthazar for what lay ahead. He alone can change the course of the future . . ."

"Let me guess . . . in doing so, he'd have to die," Xavier said.

"That is correct."

"We're the four warriors, aren't we?" Rowan said. "The ones you mention in the book. The four of us and Balthazar . . . that's a point of clarification."

"I believe so."

"And we're the ones fighting the dark forces?"

"Yes."

"Are we successful?"

There was a long pause.

"I'm afraid the game is over," Archibald answered.

The depression that settled over the room was palpable. But within that depression Xavier could feel his anger boiling to the surface.

"You know, we came here to get some ideas for how to convince Balthazar to come back, but you haven't given us anything useful! Are we seriously supposed to believe that some girl from the future has the one and only answer to saving us from so-called dark forces, and that is for Balthazar to sacrifice himself?"

"It may help you to know that the girl who visited me from the future is Nina."

They all became quiet again.

"It's not an easy thing for me to ask of him. He is, after all, my son. My only child. I love him with all my heart. But make no mistake, there is a war going on. An invisible, secret war. And in times of war, there are casualties. You have to weigh the worth of one against the worth of many."

"Why not one of us?" Xavier said finally. "Why can't we do whatever it is Balthazar is supposed to do?"

"Balthazar was helping me to develop an invention that allows you to identify other time travelers. You see, that's where the threat is coming from. Someone in the future has infiltrated the past and is changing the course of human events. I need Balthazar to finish this invention so that we can find this person and stop him before . . . well, before the future gets any worse."

"I don't think we can be of any help there," Xanthe said. "Balthazar doesn't trust any of us, and who can blame him for not wanting to come back? It's kind of hopeless."

"Ah, but that's just it! That's the one thing that will make him change his mind! You must do everything in your power to give . . ." As Archibald spoke, his voice seemed to fade and the pitch rose higher and higher until it sounded like the faint buzz of a mosquito. They all strained to hear him, but the end of the silver hour was upon them. The lights turned off, the fire extinguished, and soon they found themselves back in the creaky old hotel suite with a hole in the wall.

Xanthe rose from her seat, dusting off her pants.

"I didn't catch what he said," she coughed. "What in the world are we supposed to give Balthazar to get him to come back?"

"Beats me," Xavier said.

"I didn't hear it, either," Rowan said, picking off the cobwebs that had settled on his arms.

"I heard him." They all turned to Nina. She had a grim sort of smile on her face. "He said we should give him hope."

+ CHAPTER TWENTY-TWO +
VIGILANTE JUSTICE

THE CHILDREN SNUCK BACK INTO THE AUNTS' HOUSE
without detection, but they were not about to go to bed.
Instead, Rowan put a kettle on the stove and made a pot of
strong tea, and they settled around the kitchen table to talk
about what exactly they could do to give a doomed person
hope. The discussion went around in circles. Balthazar could
be a great leader, a hero, but at the cost of his life. Is it worth
it? In times of war, what makes someone willing to make the
ultimate sacrifice?

"Somehow I feel like we're missing something," Xanthe
sighed, blowing the steam off her teacup.

"Yes, I know what you mean," agreed Rowan, who had gotten up from the table and started pacing. "You know what's
strange? Those questions Archibald Weber asked us. None of
his questions made any sense. They were all over the place."

"He likes spirals," Xavier mused. "He even talks in spirals."

"Which means, if we circle around long enough we'll get to the point," Xanthe said thoughtfully. "What's wrong, Nina?"

"I can't believe this is all my fault," moaned Nina. "Why did I ever come back from the future . . . ?"

"Hey, you thought you were helping," said Rowan. "Don't beat yourself up, let's just solve it."

"Well, all of the questions were kind of personal," Nina said, after a moment. "They sure weren't easy to answer."

"What was he really asking though?" Xavier said. "If there is one thing I've learned in this whole adventure, it's that nothing is what it appears to be. Stories that are supposed to be true are really half fiction. Even the Wanted posters had wrong information because the eyewitnesses weren't accurate. They described me as having a hump on my back!"

Xanthe snickered. "Maybe you shouldn't slouch so much."

"You think that Archibald Weber's questions have another meaning?" Rowan said, intervening before the twins started bickering.

"Yes," Xavier said, "and if we know anything about him, we know he loves puzzles, so now I'm sure of it. The question he asked me, for instance, is an easy one because he clarified it. He asked whether I was ready to die, but I think what he was really asking was, what is something that I . . . or anyone . . . would be willing to die for?"

"And your answer was friends and family," Rowan recalled.

"Yes. And Xanthe, he asked you who was most expendable, and your answer was no one. But what was he really getting at?"

"Who knows? But I wasn't about to give him a name, even if one did pop into my head! I'd never sell out a friend, I'd rather di—" She stopped herself. "He was testing my loyalty. Our loyalty. That's what it was about."

"And my question, about how I manage to keep going, that was about faith!" Rowan said brightly. "Faith that things will get better. And Nina's question . . . what was that about anyway? All that stuff about music?"

Nina heaved a big sigh. "This may or may not sound crazy to you, but ever since I can remember, I've heard music in my head. Sometimes it's really loud, drowning everything else out, sometimes it's like background elevator music."

"Like Joan of Arc and her voices from heaven," Xanthe murmured.

"Well, I don't know about that, but it's there, and it doesn't sound good. I hear mistakes, clinkers. Sometimes it sounds like the instruments need to be tuned. But it's gotten worse over the years. What I said about it being my reason for playing piano is true. It's almost an obsession, I'm afraid. I keep playing and playing, trying to change the music in my head. It doesn't work, though. And I really don't see how it relates to anyone else's questions."

"It's not about obsession, it's about passion!" Xavier concluded. "My question was about what you would die for, and your question was about what you live for. What motivates you, what pushes you forward!"

They all meditated on this for a moment. Their thoughts

whirled in their heads like windblown leaves, settling into a new arrangement.

"So we have faith, loyalty, passion, and . . . selflessness, I guess. What does that give us?" Rowan mused.

"It's a recipe," Nina said quietly. "It's a recipe for hope. These are the things we must give Balthazar if we're going to bring him back." As soon as she said it, they all knew she was right.

"It's also four things that Balthazar never had," Rowan said. "He feels betrayed, lonely, and used, and that there is no point in doing anything since his future has already been written. He has no faith in anyone, no motivation, nothing to live or die for, no one who has been loyal to him in any way."

"How can we convince him otherwise?" Xanthe said. "We're even part of the problem. Just when he thought he found a friend, that person turned out to be a spy . . . No offense, Xave, but that's how he sees it, I'm sure."

"You know what? You're right," Xavier said. "He doesn't trust us. He has no reason to. But the least we can do is show him that we are loyal to him, that we still consider him a friend. We've got to save him. Not Agatha and Gertrude, but us. After all, according to that book, he's going to be our leader."

"OK, maybe," Xanthe said. "But I don't know if I trust that book. You hung out with him for a while, but I barely know the guy. I don't consider him *my* leader. In a pinch, I don't think I'd put myself on the line for him. Just being honest."

Rowan and Nina nodded; clearly they felt the same way.

"But I *do* know him," Xavier said. "And I have a really good feeling about him. There's got to be some way for us to get through . . . Oh my gosh, I've got it! Something Chester said reminded me of it! Remember, Xanthe? When we were with the Miwoks he said something about our mission . . ."

"Xave, he meant our mission as brown-skinned people, you know, fighting for equality," Xanthe said.

"I know. But don't you see? *It's all the same mission.* You said it yourself. One day people will realize that we're all connected. Our mission is to make Balthazar feel that connection."

"Wow, that's amazing," Xanthe said, obviously pleased.

"I know, it took me a while to realize it, too . . ."

"No, I mean you actually listened to something I said."

Xavier grinned. "Well, once in a while you get lucky and actually say something worth listening to."

"That's nice in theory, Xave, but how are we going to 'connect' with him when he hates our guts?" Rowan said.

"We can't do it, but there is one person who can!" Xavier exclaimed. "Someone I think Balthazar will listen to. He kind of started this whole thing, so he's the perfect person to end it."

"You don't mean Archibald Weber, do you?" Rowan said. "Because that's probably the last person Balthazar wants to see."

"No, not Archibald Weber. But Archibald Weber did tell us who it was. Boy, have we been dopes! Remember during the question game? He said he took his son to Illinois to see the man he most admired, his personal hero, so that Balthazar would get to know him and learn from him. *That's* who we need! That's the man who can get through to him!"

"We're going to take Balthazar to have a chat with Abe Lincoln?" Xanthe asked.

"No. Think, you guys! Archibald Weber's personal hero. A man he admired so much he multiplied him ten . . . twenty . . . maybe a hundred times over. *We see him all over the hotel!*"

Xanthe, Rowan, and Nina looked perplexed, then one by one, as the realization flowed over them, they started to laugh.

"Archie's father," Rowan said. "We'll take him to Oliver Weber."

When Gertrude came down to make breakfast, the children were ready with their arguments.

"Aunt Gertrude," Rowan said as she began to crack eggs into an iron skillet. "We've been talking, and we would like to have another chance to bring Balthazar back. We're afraid that if you just snatch him and try to hold him against his will it's going to backfire."

Agatha entered, wrapped in a silk kimono. It was a beautiful robe, but she had made the unfortunate choice of pairing it with slipper socks that looked like tiger's feet. Little white felt claws stuck out where her toes should be.

"What's that? You want to go back?"

Xavier nodded. "I developed a pretty good relationship with him . . . I mean, before he figured out who I really was. We'd like to give it another shot."

"I suppose it couldn't hurt," Agatha said after mulling it over for a moment. "Gertrude, what do you think?"

"Well, there are two things to consider," Gertrude said, moving a whisk around the pan. "First, Balthazar has to be saved. Second, we have to grab him unawares or he may fight, in which case all four of you may end up getting caught, and would have to suffer the consequences, and I think we all have a pretty good idea of what those consequences might be."

"One of you can help us with that," Xanthe pointed out. "The four of us plus Balthazar only makes five people disturbing the balance of matter and antimatter. Six is the limit, so there's still room for you to come."

"You really think you can convince him to come back on his own?" Agatha said. "I thought you said he didn't trust you anymore."

"I know someone who can get through to him," Xavier said, choosing not to elaborate. It didn't matter though, for Agatha had already read his mind.

"Oooh . . . yes, I can see how that might work. I never thought of that!"

"Thought of what, Sister?" Gertrude said, adding chopped green onions to the eggs.

"I think we should let them try. They've got an interesting plan. We can talk about it over breakfast. Now, who wants fresh orange juice?"

The four friends spent the rest of their day on Main Street looking through stores and eating pie at Hilda's coffee shop. By late afternoon they were back at the library to dress in their

Western attire and do some last-minute research. After that they set out for the Owatannauk with Agatha and Gertrude, who were both wearing the severe black clothing of the Christian Temperance League.

Gertrude gazed at the alleviator globe through the hand-held microscope, setting the coordinates for the Hangtown jail. Suddenly she leaned forward, adjusting the eyepiece. "Oh dear . . ." she murmured.

"What is it?" Xavier asked.

"We've got to hurry," Gertrude said, tapping the coordinates into the keypad.

Xavier peered into the eyepiece and saw tiny figures gathered around the jail. A smaller handcuffed figure dressed in black was led into the crowd. A taller man tied a rope around the hands of the small figure and attached the other end to the saddle of a horse, then rode up and down the street, dragging the figure behind him.

"Oh man! They're gonna hang Balt right now!"

Xanthe, Rowan, and Nina crowded around the microscope to see what was going on.

"I'm setting the alleviator here at the end of Main Street," Gertrude said. "Xavier, be careful, they may recognize you as the Ghost Rider. Come on!"

"Good luck!" Agatha sang out as she stepped out of the alleviator. "I'll see you there!"

"Yes, good luck!" Nina said, following her out.

"Wait, aren't you coming with us?" Rowan asked.

"Nina has something else to do," Agatha said. Before they could hear the explanation, Gertrude pushed the button. The doors slid shut, the humming increased, and the next moment they had disappeared from the twenty-first century.

As soon as the doors to the alleviator slid open, the three older children sprung into action. Gertrude was already halfway down the block, her long legs carrying her with the speed of an ostrich.

The musketeer Foggerty brother had stopped dragging Balthazar around and had placed him on a horse beneath the hanging tree. Balthazar's eyes were dull and listless; he wasn't putting up any kind of fight at all. The other four Foggertys circled through the crowd on their horses.

"Lew Rabbet, also known as Black Rabbit, you have been found guilty of stagecoach robbery and harboring a criminal—the infamous Ghost Rider—and for that you have been sentenced to hang by the end of a rope until the time that you are determined to be dead," barked the scarred Foggerty. "You have any last words?"

The crowd was still, waiting to hear what this young man was going to say in the last moments of his life. A man with a badge on his shirt pushed his way forward.

"Now, Johnny Foggerty," the sheriff started, "you know perfectly well the judge said Lew Rabbet wasn't supposed to be hung until next Tuesday so he could have time to give us information about the whereabouts of the Ghost Rider."

"This way's faster," snarled Johnny, the scarred Foggerty. "If he's got something say, he should say it quick, afore his windpipe is crushed."

Balthazar remained silent.

"You see? He's got nothing. No point in putting off to tomorrow what you can do today. Go ahead, Lee, give him the necklace."

The musketeer Foggerty rode up beside Balthazar and slipped a noose over his head, tossing the other end over a tree branch. He flipped it around the branch a few more times, then tied the rest around the trunk of the oak tree.

Just as Lee Foggerty raised his hand to slap Balthazar's horse on the rump, a small arrow embedded itself in the flank of Lee's horse, which startled and bucked, sending Lee tumbling off its back to land unconscious in the dirt. Xavier turned to see Xanthe holding a child's toy bow and arrow, which she'd snatched from a bucket outside the mercantile store.

"See? I did learn something from the Miwoks!" Xanthe said proudly.

Just then Gertrude pulled a rifle from under her skirt. Balthazar turned and saw her, his eyes narrowing with recognition just as she aimed both barrels at him.

Blam! The bullets hit the rope, splitting it a foot above his head. The noose fell limply around his neck. He was free.

"Who did that?" Johnny Foggerty roared. The crowd parted. Gertrude had disappeared, leaving Rowan holding the gun.

"Hey, it's that informant!" the stout Foggerty shouted.

Rowan dropped the gun and ran.

In that split second of confusion, Xavier raced up to Balthazar and vaulted onto the horse, which spun around, kicking and bucking.

Cries went up in the crowd. "It's the Ghost Rider! He's making off with Black Rabbit!"

People scattered in all directions, and soon the only ones left were the Foggerty Brothers, Xanthe, Rowan, and . . . where was Gertrude? Xavier couldn't see her, due in no small part to the twisting of the wild creature beneath him.

Xavier gripped the horse's mane until his knuckles ached. He could barely stay on, and keeping Balthazar balanced in front of him was nearly impossible. Out of the corner of his eye he saw Rowan race into Lily Rose's place, with two of the Foggertys pursuing him on horseback. He smiled, knowing just how much Lily would hate the mess they would make. But he had his own problems to worry about.

"What do you think you're doing?" Balthazar snarled. "I told you I'm not going back!"

"We're not taking you back!" Xavier shouted.

Now Rowan had run into the Chinese pharmacy, the Foggertys right behind him. There was a loud crash, a tinkling of glass, then both horses exploded through the picture window without their riders and took off down the street at a full gallop. Seconds later the stout Foggerty and the youngest Foggerty stumbled out of the pharmacy rubbing their eyes and roaring with pain, apparently blinded by some chemicals.

Xavier had just about gotten the horse under control.

Balthazar was another matter. He head-butted Xavier in the nose and blood splattered all over the place.

"Stop trying to break my nose!"

"I don't want to be saved!"

"Shut up! We're doing it anyway!" Xavier was starting to think maybe hanging him wasn't such a bad idea.

Xanthe had managed to reach the alleviator, and sent one arrow after another at the Foggerty Brothers, hitting one in the back of the neck and another in the cheek. The men weren't seriously hurt by the little arrows, but the surprise of the attack was enough to dislodge them from their saddles, and they were forced to chase Xavier on foot.

Meanwhile, Rowan had managed to elude the blinded brothers and had also ducked into the alleviator. As Xavier urged the horse forward, he could feel the sharp thump of bullets hitting his back and was thankful again for the bulletproof underwear.

They were galloping at top speed toward the alleviator. But then something dashed in front of them, blocking their way. It was Johnny, the scarred Foggerty, gun drawn.

"Not so fast, Ghost Rider," he said evenly. "You've got a few things to answer for yourself." He shot the horse. It buckled and fell beneath them. Xavier and Balthazar tumbled onto the road. Xavier stood up slowly, hands raised. The gun was aimed right at his forehead. He couldn't hide behind his underwear anymore. Johnny Foggerty smiled, stroking the trigger.

"Ghost Rider, I find you guilty of robbery, mayhem, and extreme arrogance, and I sentence you to death."

Suddenly a lasso slipped over Johnny Foggerty's head and shoulders, and with a snap his arms were cinched to his side. His gun went off and he shrieked. He'd shot himself in the foot.

Xavier looked up. There was Gertrude sitting in an oak tree, holding the other end of the rope. She jumped down from the branch and, with a tremendous howl, Johnny Foggerty was yanked upward, swinging and twisting like a grotesque piñata. As the old woman deftly tied the rope around the trunk, she shouted, "Run, boys! Run!"

Xavier ran, and he saw Balthazar was running, too, despite his earlier ambivalence. The last Foggerty was gaining ground, but Gertrude was much faster. She snatched the boys up like footballs, one in each arm, and charged the final twenty yards, leaping gracefully into the glimmering box. Rowan pounded the button, and as they disappeared into the great white light, they saw the Foggertys, two rolling in the dirt rubbing their eyes, one passed out on the ground, one desperately searching the street for the most wily criminals to ever hit Hangtown, and one swinging from the tree, roaring at the others to cut him down, as blood slowly dripped from his boot.

+ CHAPTER TWENTY-THREE +
DESTINY

THE DOORS OPENED TO ROLLING HILLS. ALL WAS STILL except for the sound of birds in the magnificent oaks and the warm breeze whistling through the grass. Sunset had not yet begun, but the purpling sky in the east alerted Xavier to the time; they had spent perhaps half an hour rescuing Balthazar, and so they had roughly only half an hour left.

"Where are we?" Balthazar said, glancing around warily.

"We're just outside Glitter Gulch," Rowan answered.

Balthazar turned to Gertrude. "You can't hold me, you know. I'm just going to run away again. Whatever little mission my father has put you up to in his megalomaniacal plotting . . ."

"Your father is doing nothing of the sort," Gertrude interrupted. "He's dying."

Balthazar blanched. "He is?"

Gertrude said nothing, but her silence spoke volumes.

"Hey! Over here!" called Nina. They turned and saw her waving from across a hillside. "This way!"

The group started toward her. As they drew closer, Balthazar blinked in surprise.

"You're the eight-year-old child star, the piano player at the saloon!"

"I'm no more an eight-year-old child star than you are an outlaw," Nina retorted.

"You still haven't told me why I'm here."

"We want you to talk to somebody," Rowan said. "That's all."

"Who's that, my father?" Balthazar sneered. "Well, you're wasting your time. I've got nothing to say to him, and couldn't care less about what he has to say to me."

"Not your father," Nina said, waving to a man who was seated under a towering oak near a second alleviator, sparkling several yards away. "Your grandfather."

Oliver Weber jogged down the hill and up to Balthazar. "Hello, Walter. It's been a long time," he said pleasantly. "Ah, but it's Balthazar . . . Balt, isn't it? Forgive me, I'm still trying to catch up. I should've known we were related. The eyes, you know."

Balthazar nodded, not sure what to make of this turn of events. Oliver clapped his hand on Balthazar's shoulder.

"This is amazing, isn't it? The future! Time travel! I would never have thought it could be done in a million years! And I've been told that a son of mine is responsible for the astounding invention that has made this all possible. Your father! That's always been my dream, to have a family, someone to carry my name forward, with each generation hanging their accomplishments on the family tree . . ."

"What are you doing here?" Balthazar interrupted. "Who brought you?"

"That woman, over there," Oliver answered, gesturing to Agatha, who was now standing in the distance with Gertrude. Together they looked like a tall pine and a tumbleweed. Agatha waved, then stepped into the alleviator and in a blink of an eye she was gone. Xavier knew she had to leave so as not to disturb the balance created by having too many people in the past at once.

"Oh. Right. So now they've got you working for them, too?" Balthazar muttered.

"I think you know me better than that, Balt. I came of my own free will, because I wanted to see you. We were having such a good time on the ship, remember? Making plans, talking of adventure, of exploration, our hopes and dreams . . . you told me you couldn't wait to see your first Indian! It made those long dreary days on that smelly boat bearable.

"But then you left. I was shocked . . . hurt even. I thought you were my friend, a kindred spirit, a partner. You said you were being chased by a tall, scary woman, but even then I knew you were really running from some other, darker demon.

"I see now that I was right. The woman who brought me here told me an incredible story about a young man so disillusioned that he wanted to destroy his own life. He fixed it so that his father would never be born. He led his grandfather on a path far different from the one he intended to pursue. It sounded like science fiction! I wouldn't have believed it, except that it rang true. You see, in my heart I know I belong with Adelaide, that I should never have left her."

Balthazar scuffed his foot in the grass, lowering his gaze.

"I wrote my Addie a month ago and got word back from her yesterday. Seems like the first note I received from her was a cruel prank. I understand you may have had something to do with it. It's the lowest kind of person who snatches away a man's freedom to make his own decisions about his life. Whether by trickery or force, it makes no difference."

"Sorry about that," Balthazar mumbled.

"I accept your apology. I'm glad you're taking responsibility for your own actions. Freedom is something I feel very strongly about . . . it's a sad paradox that this country was founded on freedom and yet it is being denied to so many." He turned to Xavier and Xanthe. "I'm sure you appreciate what I'm talking about."

The twins nodded.

"That's the other reason I'm going back. I suspect a war is coming, and I'm going to fight. I've been wasting my time here. I met a former slave who came up to Hangtown from Negro Hill . . . in fact, I believe he knew you two," he said, turning again to Xanthe and Xavier.

"You mean Chester?" Xanthe said, surprised.

"We shared a stage with him from San Francisco," Xavier said.

"A real gentleman," Oliver continued. "Anyway, we got to talking, he told me his story, and I told him mine. I was impressed by his determination to fight for what he believed in. His willingness to put himself on the line so that others wouldn't have to suffer what he suffered. It was inspirational. I thought to myself, what am I doing out here when a much bigger, much more important adventure awaits me back home? That's when I knew I had to go back."

Balthazar folded his arms. "What if I were to tell you that I know your fate? That I know for a fact there will be a war, that you will enlist, and that you'll die fighting? That you'll never see your wife and child again? That your destiny ends violently, in pain and sorrow?"

"I would call you a liar."

"But I'm from the future. I *do* know your fate. You should thank me for convincing you to head out west. I saved your life."

"Listen, Balthazar, you may think you know my fate . . . or your own fate for that matter, but do you? Do you really?"

"Yes . . ."

"My dear boy, fate is nothing but an illusion! You determine your own fate. You make your own destiny. You say I'll die in the coming war, and yet I am perfectly free to shoot myself in the heart right now and prove you wrong. Are you saying I'm invincible? That nothing can kill me until I go to war? That's insanity!"

Balthazar frowned, opened his mouth to say something and

then closed it, shaking his head. He looked down at his feet for a moment, and when he raised his head there were tears in his eyes.

"I read a book. It's the worst book I've ever read. It's about fighting and pain and sacrifice. I'm the hero of that book. I'm also the victim. I don't want to go back if that's what's in store for me! I don't want to die!"

"Son, you're dying *here*. It's not a violent death, but it's slow and painful, nevertheless. Life moves forward, not backward. You can't live in the past. So please, start living. And don't worry about the future. I don't know what's going to happen, but I'm certain it will be a surprise."

"That's what Bret Harte said . . ." Xavier murmured.

"Who?" said Balthazar, rubbing his eyes with the heels of his hands.

"He's a writer," Xavier explained. "A funny fellow we met while we were out here. I can tell you what he'd say about all this. If you don't like the ending of that book you read, write a better one! And give it a surprise ending. The best stories have surprise endings."

"That is excellent advice," Oliver said.

Gertrude approached. "I'm afraid we've run out of time," she said.

"If you excuse me, I've got a wedding to plan," Oliver said with a grin. He offered his hand to the four friends and shook theirs heartily.

"It's been a pleasure meeting all of you," he said. "I'm going to have a dickens of a time keeping this to myself, but I suppose

I'd better or I'll be labeled a raving lunatic. The future! I hope this isn't just a whiskey dream. Now, if you'll excuse us, I'd like to say something to Balt in private."

Gertrude led the others up the slope, to the alleviator that Nina and Agatha had taken. When they looked back, Balthazar and Oliver were in a tight embrace. After a few seconds, they broke apart and Balthazar trotted after them. His expression was curiously calm.

"Let's go home," he said.

When they arrived at the hotel, it was just beginning to revert back to its deteriorated state. As soon as they left the alleviators and the doors closed behind them, the machines became dull and dingy, their glitter gone, the magic over. Balthazar walked slowly down the hallway and into the lobby. He drew his finger along the dust on the grand piano and crumpled one of the dried flowers that had fallen off an ancient bouquet.

"This is the Owatannauk? What happened to it?"

"The last time you saw the hotel was close to ninety years ago," Gertrude explained. "It's been through a lot since then. It was closed down, boarded up, and abandoned."

"But . . . why?"

"It's a long story," Gertrude sighed.

"But the phantoms . . . ?"

"The phantoms are still here, only visible at the golden and silver hours, of course."

"Then I just missed him," Balthazar said, disappointed. "I wanted to see him . . . to say something to him . . . my father, I mean."

"I'm afraid you'll have to wait until the silver hour, my dear," Gertrude said, resting her hand on the young Weber's shoulder. "But I have to warn you, the hotel isn't the only thing that's changed in your absence. Your father is quite ill. I can't allow you to get too close to him, or you may get sick as well . . ."

Balthazar's face clouded over, his eyes glittering with a boldness the foursome would never have dreamed of directing at Gertrude. "Miss Pembroke, I am going to see my father. If it makes me sick, it is still a far better future than I thought I had. I appreciate your concern, but you're not my guardian, and I'm not asking your permission. This is my home."

With that, he bolted up the stairs.

The junior detectives all knew where he was going and followed on his heels, up to the second floor, and down the hall. Gertrude shouted for them to stop, but something kept them going; it was as though Balthazar's courage had freed them all from her grip. They raced through door number four and the labyrinthine passageway to get to the secret hallway. When they reached door number twenty-one, Balthazar stopped, surprised by the hole in the wall.

"What's this?"

"Yes, what *is* this?" Gertrude cried, rushing up to them, appalled at the mess. "This area was sealed! It's quarantined, for the safety of others . . . Balthazar, wait!"

Balthazar was already squeezing through the hole. Gertrude stopped the junior detectives before they could follow.

"Who did this?" she demanded.

"I did," Xavier admitted.

"You went inside?!" Gertrude said sharply. "You broke into Archibald Weber's private apartments?! I . . . I'm stunned!"

"Nobody said it was off limits . . ."

"Believe it or not, Mr. Alexander, obtaining frequent-flier status does not give you free rein to knock holes in the walls of the hotel!"

"We're sorry, Aunt Gertrude, but it all turned out for the best," said Xanthe. "It wasn't until we talked to Mr. Weber that we figured out what we had to do . . ."

"You spoke with Archibald Weber? Without consulting me?"

The foursome shuffled their feet guiltily, speechless under Gertrude's stern glare.

"Um, can we go inside?" Nina said meekly after a minute. "Balt is in there alone . . . he seemed kind of upset . . . maybe we should, you know . . ."

"Oh, go ahead," Gertrude said abruptly. "I . . . don't know what to think!" The friends scampered through the hole, leaving the old woman in the hallway to decide how angry she should be.

They found Balthazar wandering around the dim room, picking up items and putting them back down. "It doesn't look the same," he said finally. "Where did all of these clocks come from? When I left, my father didn't have nearly this many . . ."

"The clocks!" Nina gasped. "Look at them! They're working!"

As if on cue, the clocks suddenly went off in a cacophony of chimes, bells, and gongs. Mechanical birds poked their heads in and out of tiny doors, miniature wooden people danced and played instruments, a metal monkey did flips, a carved bear in a hat and jacket rode a unicycle in a tight circle.

And then the lights came on.

"Why is everyone standing around in the dark?" chuckled a familiar voice.

There, leaning against the doorway, was a man they all knew, yet none of them had ever seen before . . . except one.

"Dad."

"Balt."

They stood awkwardly for a moment, until Archibald Weber stretched his arms wide.

"Come here, son."

Balthazar hesitated only a moment, then launched himself into his father's arms. Archibald wrapped himself around his son like a cocoon, as Balthazar sobbed in great, anguished groans. The Popplewells and the Alexanders shifted uncomfortably.

"Maybe we should go," Xanthe murmured to the others, edging toward the hole in the wall. "I think they need a moment."

They slipped out and stood in the hallway, where Gertrude

was waiting. Before she could say anything, Rowan nodded toward the room.

"They're back together!" he said.

"Who's back together?"

"Archibald Weber and Balthazar. They're hugging each other."

"But that can't be," Gertrude said, checking her watch. She frowned and scratched her head, now too confused to be angry.

Nina put her ear to the opening in the wall.

"Give them some privacy!" Rowan hissed.

"I just want to know what's going on!" she hissed back. "I'm getting bored!"

"Well, I'm getting hungry, but I'm not complaining about it!"

"You just did!"

"Quiet, you guys. You're starting to sound like me and Xave," Xanthe whispered.

"Hey, I found some lemon drops in my pocket!" Xavier said, passing them around. After ten minutes, Archibald Weber's voice rang out.

"Excuse me! Are you still there? Please, do come back in. I would like to talk to all of you together."

The foursome crawled back through the hole and were greeted by a much happier father and son. Their conversation had obviously done them both good.

"First, I want to thank you. You have no idea what an important thing this is that you've accomplished. You four have surpassed my greatest expectations. My gratitude knows no bounds. I'd give you all huge, shiny medals, but for now I hope you'll accept my humble but hearty handshake."

"Excuse me . . . a little help?" Gertrude called out.

They all turned to see the statuesque woman waving from the hole. She had managed to fit just her head and one arm through the opening.

"Gertrude! Dear Gertrude!" Archibald Weber cried, rushing to her aid. "It has been a long time, too long, since I've seen you."

"Yes . . . yes, it has . . . But Archie, how is it that you're here? Now? I . . . I don't understand . . ."

"All will be made clear, dear friend," Archie interrupted. "But first we must get you through. You are in a decidedly undignified position."

"I'll say. She looks like Winnie-the-Pooh stuck in Rabbit's hole," Xanthe whispered to Xavier.

He barked a laugh, attracting much more attention than he wanted. "Sorry. Something caught in my throat," he explained, giving Xanthe a subtle shove.

"How is Agatha?" Archie asked Gertrude, pulling on the wood around the opening of the hole.

"Worried. As am I."

"Don't be," Archibald said gently. "Now that Balt is back, I'm back, too."

They all tore away at the wood and brick, and in no time Gertrude was standing with them in the living room, brushing the dust from her clothes with Archie's help.

Xavier couldn't take his eyes off Archibald Weber. His face looked familiar, of course, the midpoint between Oliver and Balt, and he, too, had the unusually colored eyes. He was taller than Oliver, and lean, with thick black hair and a mustache that curled up, accentuating his broad smile. He looked good . . . too good.

"Excuse me, Mr. Weber . . ." Xavier began

"Call me Archie, please."

"Um, Archie . . . aren't you supposed to be sick? Are we in danger of catching this disease of yours?"

"Eww, I forgot about that," Xanthe murmured, not so subtly wiping her hand on her skirt. Rowan and Nina looked worried.

"Yes, Archie, I was wondering the same thing," Gertrude said.

"You are not in danger of catching my disease," Archibald said with a slight smile. "You see, my disease is called depression. I first experienced it when my wife died after a trip we'd taken back in time to medieval England. Frances always complained that I kept my work from her, that I wouldn't let her use the alleviators. I was just protecting her from the rigors of time travel . . . she had always been delicate . . . sickly, you see. Ultimately, when she insisted, I relented, and let her come with me. I couldn't deny it to her . . . I couldn't deny her anything. I loved her too much. Sure enough, she caught a virus and died a week after we returned. Now I see it wasn't the travel so much as the attention she wanted . . . she wanted to share my life and saw the time machines as being my mistress of sorts.

"At any rate, she was gone, and I folded into myself, leaving Balt in the cold. The second time I fell into depression was after I went to the future and saw those things I recorded in the notebook. I admit, those images frightened me, but after I thought about it I realized that great men are forged in difficult circumstances, and that Balt, perhaps, would be a great man. My mistake was in sharing this information with him. As I've already told you, it is a horrible thing to know your future. Balt tells me that the future is unknowable, and indeed I have been a fool to think that there is only one future ahead of us! My goodness, after all my experience, you would think I'd know that there are countless futures, an infinite number of possibilities, and that lovely visitor—my dear Nina—only showed me one of them.

"But it was too late—the damage was done and Balt left me. Again, I was overwhelmed by grief and despair; I fell into a dark state. Life didn't mean much to me anymore. I knew I'd made a terrible mistake and nothing would cure me except Balt's return. I decided to remove myself from society altogether. I had the door sealed. I have a passageway that allows me to reach the alleviators, but I rarely used it. I pulled away from everyone who cared about me. I didn't know it, but I was dying, and yet because of the strange properties of this hotel, I never actually passed away. Can you imagine? An eternity of dying. It was torture."

"Agatha and I thought it was something we had done," Gertrude said.

"I am sorry, dear Gertrude. You have my deepest apologies. After Balt, you and Agatha are the ones I have treated the worst. All my dear teacher wanted to do was guide my son with love and joy, to show him the bounty of this magnificent world, and I replaced that generous spirit with isolation, responsibility, and horror. I kept you both in the dark because I couldn't risk anyone finding out that I traveled to the future. I was afraid . . . afraid you would think me, well, evil. That you might disapprove of what I was doing."

"We did disapprove."

"Well, obviously I should've sought your counsel instead of avoiding it. But it all changed last year. You and Agatha presented four young people for frequent-flier status. These four," he said, turning to the junior detectives. "The four of you reminded me of the four warriors, the four knights of the future, and I recognized Nina as soon as I saw her. For the first time, I had hope that I might see Balt again. Then, when Gertrude told me you had figured out who Walter Ebb really was and that he had gone to California with my father, Oliver Weber, I knew in my heart you would be successful. I've been planning this homecoming ever since."

"What about our last meeting," Rowan said. "Why didn't you tell us all of this then?"

"Well, I do like games. And I was afraid to tell you too much. Information can be dangerous. That was what started all this to begin with. You were right, though—I took Balt to the Republican Convention to meet my father, not Abraham

Lincoln." Archibald turned to Balthazar, who was grinning from an overstuffed chair.

"I hoped you would hit it off with my father, and would learn from his example, but I had no idea you would run away with him. That was what you call a happy accident. You spent months on that ship with him, and I can see he rubbed off on you, despite yourself."

"It's true," Balthazar admitted. "I liked Oliver right away. I wanted to be just like him. I also wanted to hurt you, so running away did both things. I could be with my grandfather and you would become a phantom, a victim of your own invention. I'm truly sorry, though. I overreacted, I guess. But now it's back as it should be. Oliver went back to Bloomington and you're no longer stuck in the phantom world."

"Yes, everything is as it should be," Archibald said, putting his hand on his son's shoulder. "However, I never became a phantom."

The teens exchanged confused glances. "Of course you've been a phantom," Rowan said. "You had to be. We were right here in this room when the transformation occurred . . ."

"For youngsters who are experts in solving puzzles, I'm surprised you don't see how illogical that is," chuckled Archibald. "All right, let me tickle your brains. If I was a phantom, if I had never been born, then who built the hotel? Who built the alleviators?"

The groan from the foursome was so loud it drowned out the ticking of the clocks.

"We've been such idiots!" Xanthe exclaimed, slapping her forehead.

"Do you mean to say you've been living in the hotel all this time? For ninety years, sealed up behind this wall? Without anyone knowing the truth?" Gertrude said, disbelievingly.

"Yes. That is exactly what I'm saying. When Balt left, it was easy enough to convince everyone that he had changed history and that I was a phantom. At the time, if you remember the history of this hotel, the police were investigating me. It was convenient for me to disappear. I said I had a contagious disease as an excuse for sealing the door, but it was just a cover."

"But where were you when I broke in?" Xavier asked. "And when we came to visit you? How did you make it seem like the room was transforming? Your voice even strained just as it was changing!"

"The room has been left untouched for decades, my dear boy, save for a few new clocks I've added here and there. I spent all of my time in my bedroom and library, sometimes venturing into the laboratory if the mood struck me. That's where I was when you broke in, Xavier. I was in my bedroom when I heard you hammering away. You quite surprised me."

"I saw some bedrooms," Xavier said. "But I guess I didn't find yours."

"No, you didn't," Archie said with a mysterious little smile. "And you never will. Anyway, I let the clocks run down so they only work during the golden and silver hours, when they also show the correct time. But today I wound them all up and tidied up the room in anticipation of your arrival. And as for my voice cutting out during the transformation? When I first installed the sound system it was state-of-the-art, brand-new technology. But over the years it has run down along with the rest of the hotel. Now it only works during the golden and silver hours."

"So that's why this room wasn't as dusty as the rest of the hotel!" Xanthe exclaimed. "There was someone living here!"

"But I don't understand," Balt said. "Why *weren't* you a phantom? I mean, Oliver ultimately did go back east, but for a while he was there in the Gold Rush . . ."

"Yes, that's the interesting thing about this whole escapade . . . my father *did* go to California before he went to the Civil War. Balthazar, you may have thought you were changing history when you convinced him to go to gold country, but you weren't."

Balthazar's jaw dropped, and he sputtered before finding his voice. "That's not fair!" he blurted finally. "So it made no difference at all? I didn't change anything?"

"You changed a lot," Archibald said. "Starting with me. I don't have to hide behind this wall anymore, for one thing."

"Now that your secret is out, are you still going to live here?" Nina asked.

"Hmm. Good question. I rather like the mystery of being a phantom," Archibald said, stroking his mustache. "I'm not sure I want to give it up. Of course, I'll have to ask Balthazar how he feels about it." Archibald turned to Balthazar, who was looking out the window at the empty swan pond.

"Son? It's up to you. Would you rather live in a normal house, on a normal street, and have a normal life? Leave all this behind? Forget it's even here?"

"C'mon, Dad, you know you can't do that; you created this place! You poured everything you are into it. It would kill you to leave it . . . literally. You'd start getting older."

"That's true. The Owatannauk does exist in a sort of timeless limbo of its own. My aging has been suspended as long as I've lived here or traveled through time. But I'd do it for you, son, if that's what you wanted. I'd move somewhere else. Wherever you like."

"What would you do for a living?"

"My boy, I am independently wealthy. But if you prefer a middle-class lifestyle, I could be a . . ." Archibald looked around the room, searching for ideas. "A clockmaker. Yes, that's it. I think I could be quite satisfied living a normal lifestyle, making clocks."

"You couldn't be normal for an hour! You'd go crazy with boredom!"

Archibald looked hurt, but couldn't help laughing himself. "It can't be too hard. Everyone else does it!"

"I can imagine your first clock," Balthazar continued. "It would be a stopwatch that would stop time altogether!"

Now Rowan and Nina were giggling, and Xanthe and Xavier joined in.

"How about a watch that when set ahead allows you to see what will happen several hours in the future?" added Xavier.

"Or maybe a cuckoo clock with an entire zoo inside of it?" Xanthe suggested. "Only instead of carved animals, they're real animals that have been shrunk?"

"A grandfather clock that also gives grandfatherly advice, and delivers hot cocoa . . . or banana milk shakes . . . on demand?" giggled Nina.

"I could use a clock with sixteen hours instead of twelve, so that it adds eight more hours to the day!" Rowan said over the others.

"Wait, these are all good ideas!" Archibald said. "I need to write them down!"

That sent them all laughing again, until tears ran down their cheeks and their ribs hurt.

"My mind is already made up," Balthazar finally said. "I want to live here, in the hotel. It's always been my home, and it always will be. And now that I have friends who I can talk to, it won't be so lonely."

"We don't live in Owatannauk, but you can visit us when we're not here," Xanthe said. "It's actually better that way. No one will see us coming and going from the hotel during the 'off' hours."

"Speaking of which, we should go," Rowan said. "We need to tell all of this to Aunt Agatha. Besides, if I'm not mistaken, it's dinnertime. I don't need these clocks," he bragged, waving carelessly at the wall. "My stomach clock just went off and it keeps perfect time!"

"Agatha. Miss Drake. I only saw her for a second, but then she left," Balt said wistfully. "I really miss her."

"Then she shall be our first real guest," Archie said grandly. "You, too, Gertrude. So if you would be so kind as to extend the invitation to Miss Drake, the presence of your company is requested tomorrow, at the silver hour, for an early breakfast in . . . I don't know, how about Paris, eighteen eighty-nine? We can go to the World's Fair and make a day of it. The Eiffel Tower will be brand new."

"Dad . . . can't we stay here for a little while?" Balt said gently. "I think I'd like to see the town of Owatannauk, if it's all the same with you."

"Oh. Of course. I'm embarrassed to say I don't really know my way around Owatannauk anymore . . ." Archie shrugged helplessly.

"Why don't we pick you up here," Gertrude suggested. "We can eat at Hilda's coffee shop. It's the next best thing to eating in Paris; that's where she gets all of her recipes."

Archibald smiled. "Yes, I know. That sounds perfect." He put his arm around Balt's shoulders. "Now, if you'll excuse us, we have a lot of catching up to do."

Gertrude drove the four junior detectives to Nana's house to pick her up, then headed to the aunts' house, where Agatha was waiting for them. The four friends spoke nonstop through dinner, and when one left off to take a bite of food, another would pick up the story.

Agatha was speechless, though every once in a while Nana interrupted with exclamations of "Get out of here with that mess!" and "Lord have mercy!" followed by "Well come on, now, spit it out, what's the rest of it?" When they finished, there were hugs all around, compliments and congratulations, and chocolate custard with sprinkles to top it off.

The four friends decided to spend the night at Nana's instead of with the aunts for a change. It was their last night in the town of Owatannauk. The next morning they would be on their way home, back to their regular lives, which more and more seemed to take a backseat to their new roles as Time Detectives. They all vowed to come up again in the middle of the summer. They felt a responsibility to check in on Balt, for in a strange way he had become one of them. They knew that his presence would change everything.

As Xavier lay in bed, he again found himself unable to sleep. This was becoming a bad habit, but he couldn't help thinking about what lay ahead . . . or behind, in the past. Time couldn't move fast enough for him. He wanted it now.

He swung his legs over the side of the bed and eased himself to the floor, being careful not to make a sound. Nana had ears like a wolf, and he didn't want her to catch him in the middle of what he was about to do. He lifted up the mattress, pulled out the slightly damp, slightly bent leather notebook, and opened it.

He didn't feel guilty about keeping the book. After all, Agatha kept souvenirs from her travels. In fact, Rowan had given her his chunk of pyrite, not wanting to keep it himself, and he knew that by now it was already sitting in a glass-covered case, next to hundreds of other mineral samples for sale in the curio shop. Nina had kept her tiara, and the gold nuggets she had earned from her performances as the "Princess of Glitter Gulch" would no doubt pay off some of her father's debts. Even Xanthe had kept a Miwok necklace. His souvenir wasn't from the Gold Rush exactly, but it was the item from this adventure that excited him most.

The pages smelled of mildew, the way old, water-damaged books tend to smell, and the paper was more fragile than before. The ink on many of the pages had been smeared. But much of it was still readable, if you could decipher it.

He removed the scraps of paper that had been carefully folded and placed in the diary by the Chinese doctor. They contained the many translations collected from all the different people who had seen it, written down in English by Dr. Wu in a fine, thin script. Xavier arranged the scraps in different orders, like a verbal jigsaw puzzle. Most of his arrangements didn't make much sense, but then he landed on one that did.

There were four knights, two dark and two light. They were secret agents, waging a secret battle in a secret war, led by a visionary with wild eyes. One of the dark knights was a spy, an expert at blending in. The spy was charming. The spy was powerful. The spy was the leader's trusted confidant, and when the leader disappeared, the spy became the leader.

Maybe it was wrong, this book. Maybe it was merely the fantastic scribblings of a man who had glimpsed a branch of existence that was only one out of a million possibilities. Maybe it was just a grandiose ghost story, about phantoms in another universe fighting a good fight. Maybe Xavier's arrangement of the scraps of paper was pure nonsense, its apparent meaning only fashioned from his heart's desire.

Or maybe not.

A HISTORICAL NOTE
TO THE READER

The Hour of the Outlaw is the third book in the *Golden Hour* series. Like *The Golden Hour* and *The Hour of the Cobra*, it is a work of fiction. Tales of the Old West and the Gold Rush abound, and they are often filled with exaggerations and embellishments that romanticize what it was like to live in that era. I must say that as a fan of that time period, I found it difficult to restrain myself from this inclination as well. Though living in the "untamed West" was difficult, uncomfortable, and dangerous, it symbolized the hopes and dreams of a growing nation. The West represented rugged individualism, pioneer values of hard work and fair play, wild adventure, and, most of all, freedom. All of the hardships thus became part of the Western mythology, part of what we call the American spirit, and it is this image of ourselves that we hold most dear. It has endured to this day, even though the West itself has changed dramatically.

Researching the West was like discovering a gold mine.

There are so many fascinating stories that are true, I didn't have to make many up. Here are a few true stories that I included in the book:

Abraham Lincoln's "lost speech" and the events surrounding the first Illinois Republican Convention are true. Lincoln did have the reputation of being a jokester of sorts, and he did in fact deliver a speech that was unscheduled, at the end of the last day of the convention. The speech was so powerful and mesmerizing it was simply not recorded, even by the newspapermen. William Herndon, Lincoln's law partner, tried to take notes, but then "threw pen and paper away and lived only in the inspiration of the hour." He continues his recollection, stating that "His [Lincoln's] speech was full of fire, and energy, and force. It was logic; it was pathos; it was enthusiasm; it was justice, equity, truth and right set ablaze by the divine fires of a soul maddened by the wrong; it was hard, heavy, knotty, gnarly, backed with wrath." When I discovered this tidbit of history I was, frankly, fascinated. Most of us picture Lincoln in his iconic form—seated in the Lincoln Memorial, serious, sad, and weighed down by the events of his day—yet apparently he was capable of great energy and passion!

The story of Chester Lee, the ex-slave, is true. In real life his name was Archy Lee; I changed it to "Chester" to avoid confusion with Archibald Weber. Mary Ellen "Mammy" Pleasants was also a real person, and she was married to the cook on the *Orizaba*, the boat that was going to smuggle Archy away to Panama. The cook tipped off the members of the Athenaeum

Institute, who did indeed rescue Archy and help him through his court battles until he became a free man. I took some license with Archy's life when I sent him to the goldfields. In reality he, like so many other blacks who were fed up with racism, left for British Columbia, Canada, where he lived for several years. He returned to Sacramento, where he spent the rest of his life. According to the *Sacramento Daily Union* in November 1873, "Archy Lee was found buried in the sand with only his head exposed, in the marshlands of Sacramento. He was ill and claimed to have buried himself thus to keep warm. He was taken to the hospital where he died." (You see? You can't make this stuff up!)

The tale of Joaquin Murieta is somewhat true, though his story has many versions. He was a Mexican bandit, though there is some debate as to whether his violent crime spree was in the cause of social justice (as I've suggested in this book) or simply due to greed. Like Billy the Kid and Jesse James, the preponderance of Murieta stories have elevated him to a myth. Many of the tales written about him at the time were mainly conjecture, and so it is difficult to sift through this information for the truth. It is a fact that Harry Love and his Rangers tracked down and killed a man whom Love claimed was the bandit, and cut off his head as proof of their success. The head did make the rounds in the mining communities as a stern lesson in the wages of crime, but robberies and violence attributed to Murieta were still occurring *after* his supposed death. This lent an aura of uncertainty to his execution, and many people claimed the head in the jar didn't really look like the famed bandit after all. This is an idea I introduced in the book; you can do your own research and decide for yourself the fate of that legendary outlaw.

I took the most license with Francis Bret Harte. He is one of my favorite writers of that day, and I thought it might be fun to bring him along for the ride. Though he is not widely read today, Bret Harte was very popular during his time for his colorful stories about the Gold Rush, and his stories made California famous. Harte was sensitive to the plight of minorities and disgusted with how white men were influencing the West and changing it. These themes are reflected in his work. He was also a friend of Mark Twain, and for a brief period he was Twain's editor when Twain wrote for the *Alta Californian*. Bret Harte's style is similar to Twain's; both employ common vernacular, humor, and irony. Mark Twain's mining experience is described in his autobiographical book, *Roughing It*; however he didn't travel to the West until 1861, when he went with his brother to Virginia City, in Nevada, and tried his hand in the silver mines. It wasn't until 1865 that Mark Twain arrived in California gold country, seven years after my story takes place, so I chose not to include him.

ACKNOWLEDGMENTS

I AM FORTUNATE TO LIVE WITHIN SEVERAL HOURS OF Gold Rush country, and so many of the towns I've included in this book I have visited personally. They still have much of the flavor of the Gold Rush days; you can see the original buildings and equipment, visit the Miwok village, and even try your hand at panning for gold. Seeing these things firsthand really gives you a feeling for what it must've been like to live there in the eighteen hundreds. To help guide my way, I used *Traveling California's Gold Rush Country*, by Leslie A. Kelly. It provides maps of the various towns and points out items of interest that gold country tourists shouldn't miss.

I used several secondary sources in my research. *The World Rushed In*, by J. S. Holliday, is a collection of diary entries belonging to gold seeker William Swain, as well as letters he received from his wife and brother. This is augmented by eyewitness accounts of over five hundred other gold seekers, following the entire Gold Rush saga from the trip out west to the mining camps to the return trip through the Isthmus of Panama. It was an invaluable resource. *The Forty-Niners*, published by Time-Life Books with text by William Weber Johnson, and *The Age of Gold*, by H. W. Brands, provided solid historical background about the period. *Travel Guide to California Gold Country*, by Stuart A. Kallen, described what it might be like for the average person making his or her way out west. *Roughing It*, by Mark Twain, is an autobiographical account of traveling out west, experiencing stagecoach travel, mining, and life in Western towns. It is a hilarious book at times, filled with Western phrases and dialect, as well as enjoyable descriptions of Gold Rush characters and scenery.

Finally, I would like to thank my book agent, Laura Williams, and my editor at Amulet, Susan Van Metre, both of whom have supported my writing with their skill and enthusiasm. A big thanks to friends and family who have encouraged me, particularly my husband and children, who put up with my taking hours away from family time when I'm trying to meet a deadline. But most of all I'd like to thank the children and adults who've read my books and approached me or written to me with their opinions. It is you who make the writing most gratifying. And if you're reading the acknowledgments, you are truly a fan, so you know I'm referring to you!

ABOUT THE AUTHOR

Maiya Williams was born in Corvallis, Oregon, and grew up in New Haven, Connecticut, and Berkeley, California. She attended Harvard University, where she was an editor and vice president of the *Harvard Lampoon*. She is currently a writer and producer of television shows and recently worked on the long-running hit Fox show *MADtv*. Maiya lives with her husband, three children, a Labrador retriever, a Schnorkie, two guinea pigs, two mice, and a variety of fish in Pacific Palisades, California. This is a sequel to her critically acclaimed novels *The Golden Hour* and *The Hour of the Cobra*.

The text of this book is set in Kaatskill, designed in 1929 by Frederic W. Goudy. It was made specifically for use in an edition of *Rip Van Winkle* for the Limited Edition Club. Of particular interest is that the type was designed, cut, and set in the immediate vicinity of Washington Irving's story—in the foothills of Rip's own Kaatskill Mountains, at Marlborough-on-the-Hudson. Display type and chapter titles are set in Dalliance Roman, designed in 2000 by Frank Heine for Émigré. The inspiration for Dalliance Script comes from early-nineteenth-century hand-lettering specimens.

The text of this book is set in Kaatskill, designed in 1929 by Frederic W. Goudy. It was made specifically for use in an edition of *Rip Van Winkle* for the Limited Edition Club. Of particular interest is that the type was designed, cut, and set in the immediate vicinity of Washington Irving's story—in the foothills of Rip's own Kaatskill Mountains, at Marlborough-on-the-Hudson. Display type and chapter titles are set in Dalliance Roman, designed in 2000 by Frank Heine for Émigré. The inspiration for Dalliance Script comes from early-nineteenth-century hand-lettering specimens.